Also by Cathryn Grant

NOVELS

Buried by Debt ◆ *The Suburban Abyss* ◆ *The Hallelujah Horror Show*
Getting Ahead ◆ *Faceless* ◆ *An Affair With God* ◆ *The Good Neighbor*
The Good Mother (previously The Demise of The Soccer Moms)
The Guest

THE ALEXANDRA MALLORY PSYCHOLOGICAL SUSPENSE
SERIES
The Woman In the Mirror ◆ *The Woman In the Water*
The Woman In the Painting ◆ *The Woman In the Window*
The Woman In the Bar ◆ *The Woman In the Bedroom*
The Woman In the Dark ◆ *The Woman In the Cellar*
The Woman In the Photograph ◆ *The Woman In the Storm*

THE HAUNTED SHIP TRILOGY
Alone On the Beach ◆ *Slipping Away From the Beach*
Haunting the Beach

NOVELLAS
Madison Keith Ghost Story Series ◆ *Chances Are*

SHORT FICTION
Reduction in Force ◆ *Maternal Instinct*
Flash Fiction For the Cocktail Hour
The 12 Days of Xmas

NONFICTION
Writing Is Murder: Motive, Means, and Opportunity

Cathryn Grant

THE WOMAN
IN THE TAXI

An Alexandra Mallory Novel

D2C Perspectives

1

New York City

Four million dollars.

The number floated through my mind, drowning out the pounding notes of Chopin that filled my ears while I ran. The number woke me every morning. It skittered across my computer screen in ghost letters when I was at work. It had hugged my brain during most of the fourteen-hour flight home from visiting Tess in Australia.

I'd never put a number around my desire to have a life of freedom, a life that wasn't handicapped by thoughts of what I could and could not afford. I'd never constructed a budget around the vague image forming in my mind of the beautiful home I wanted to own someday. Someday.

How could I? So far, I had no idea where this marvelous home that would satisfy me for decades might be located. I loved Sydney with its laid back culture and semi-tropical atmosphere. I was growing quite connected to the energy of New York City, and I couldn't forget the nearly constant mild weather of Southern California or the fog and funkiness of San Francisco. But there's also a rather large world with thousands of cities I hadn't even visited.

Occasionally, I wondered whether a solid location was what I truly wanted. Maybe I liked moving around, experiencing different people and a variety of scenery. Maybe I didn't really want to own a house or an apartment or a secluded piece of property. Maybe I didn't want responsibility. Or maybe, I was still figuring it out.

I liked my current job more than any I'd had before. It was fun taking photographs. I was thrilled by the challenge of capturing people when they weren't posing. I liked hearing Diana's analysis of their micro-expressions, and I liked listening to Trystan sell our clients on a better version of themselves.

But I did not like going into an office. I did not like meetings unless they involved fantastic food, and I did not like sitting behind a computer.

So what did I want?

And what was the number? Four million dollars was a lot of money. Was it enough to do everything I wanted? I thought it might be. But eight million would make me feel even more comfortable. Would ten million mean I never had to think about money again? Or was more required? The next time I flew to visit Tess, did I want to feel like a rabbit stuffed inside a magician's hat, or did I want to spread out my limbs in a first-class seat that turned into a real bed?

It used to be said that a woman could never be too thin or too rich.

Obviously, a woman can absolutely be too thin. It's a horrifying ideal—pushing women to decline dessert and eat un-dressed greens while men savor herbs and spices softened by oil, taste chocolate and whipped cream and a hundred other sweet and savory flavors. That kind of thinking has pushed too many women beyond the effort of restricting themselves to an apple and yogurt, into degrading, punishing habits. The drive to be too thin actually distorts the chemistry of some women's brains until they look at a mirror and see a woman with too much flesh, when everyone else sees nothing but tendons and bones, forcing them to turn away from the horror of it.

But too rich? I don't think so.

Four million dollars was the amount of money coming to Eileen Cook from the estate of her former fiancé and tormenter—Jim Kohn.

Eileen was still shocked by the acknowledgment in his will and equally excited and uncertain about how she was going to revise her life based on an amount of money she'd never dreamed of possessing.

I wasn't jealous. Jealousy isn't in my DNA. I'm focused on getting what I want, not fixated on what other people have. I don't possess many common feelings—jealousy, sentimentality, self-doubt.

And the last possible way I ever wanted to acquire money was by having a man give it to me.

Eileen had no idea why the money had come to her, but she wasn't going to let it stop her from enjoying what it offered. She and I agreed it was some kind of expiation for what he'd done to her psyche with his humiliating photographs. But if he had enough respect to regret it later, why had he done it to begin with? Why hadn't he begged forgiveness from her while he was alive? What made him break off their engagement and then hand over a large check from beyond the grave without explanation?

The answers to those questions died with him.

I didn't want money the way she'd gotten money—a handout from a guilty man. I had no desire to share in her good fortune. But there was no doubt in my mind, I wanted money, and if that was going to happen, I needed to give it more focused attention than just a dreamy desire for some undefined pathway to my future.

Killing people who deserve to die had taken precedence in my life. To a large extent, it dictated who I associated with and where I lived. In some ways, it had taken over my life entirely.

I wasn't sure I was happy with that. At the same time, I was fairly confident it wouldn't stop. Not as long as I had a strong, healthy body capable of getting the upper hand, and a steady mind that wouldn't let go of trying to bring a bit of balance into the world, evening the score for women I hardly knew.

2

Like throwing a bone to a dog, Trystan had expanded Stephanie's responsibilities. He'd only done it after she complained that Alex had unfairly usurped the photographer position.

She wasn't sure how that cliché had come to apply to grudging favors because dogs loved their bones. They were thrilled to have the scent and taste of meat, something to gnaw on. She supposed the point was that the dog wanted the entire steak, and all he got was the stripped clean bone.

This was more like letting a few crumbs fall off the table and expecting them to provide the same satisfaction as a gourmet meal. Alex sat at the metaphorical table eating premium steak and crusty, buttered bread, while Stephanie crawled around the legs of her chair, picking up the fallen bits.

Of course her thoughts were over-dramatized. Stephanie knew she had tendencies in that direction. For whatever reason, she often had a hard time keeping her imagination tied to reality. Besides, it was the truth. That was exactly how she felt. And she imagined that Alex reveled in her job in the same way she would tear into a medium-rare steak, blood staining her lips, pooling on her tongue.

Once she'd collected and entered the background material for a new client into their system, Stephanie was now tasked with facilitating a meeting for the four of them to review what the client had provided. It was her job to present an overview of the highlights before everyone retreated to their offices to study the finer points of a client's psyche.

She'd prepared ten slides for today's meeting. The opening slide displayed the professional headshot of their newest client. Beside the photograph was a bare-bones bio that included her age, education, and awards.

Arlinda Caruso was forty-three years old. She owned a highly-regarded advertising agency that was known for developing campaigns that skyrocketed fresh or re-invented brands to success. She was respected for her agency's ability to still get the most out of print advertising campaigns in the digital age, while also overseeing a team that understood all the bits and bytes of online advertising.

On the following slides, Stephanie had provided key insights from Arlinda's self-exploratory responses to the hundreds of questions, as well as the profile that had emerged from the standardized personality and aptitude tests she'd taken.

Stephanie wished she could present the information to Trystan in a one-on-one meeting rather than running the gauntlet of Diana and Alexandra. They would pester her with questions. They were sure to challenge her insights, doing everything they could to make her feel inadequate—someone trying to add more value to prove her worth while adding no value at all. It wasn't deliberate. The firing squad of questions wasn't intended to trip up Stephanie, at least not on Diana's part, but it would end up feeling that way.

Alexandra would say she could have read all the material and drawn conclusions more easily on her own. Diana would say she preferred to read the material before any discussions took place because she wanted unbiased information about the person they were poised to help. Trystan would tolerate their critical comments because he wanted everyone to speak their minds. Stephanie would be left wondering whether her role truly was a crumb that had fallen off the table and would have been better vacuumed up, whisked away forever.

Her hands shook as she plugged the projection machine into her laptop.

The door to the conference room opened, and Diana and Alex entered together. Diana gave her a warm smile and asked how she was. Alex simply nodded, took her seat, and turned expectantly toward the blank screen. The room was silent while they waited for Trystan.

They endured three long minutes of dead air before he finally walked through the doorway.

Stephanie began by reviewing Arlinda's desire to breathe fresh air into her career and her life. After two decades in advertising, she felt stale. She wasn't learning anything new. Developing multi-million dollar campaigns didn't give her the creative energy and satisfaction it had in the past. Everything felt routine, something she'd done a hundred times before. Handling even the most demanding clients was effortless. They seemed easy to please. There was no challenge, no adrenaline, no edgy excitement.

Arlinda wanted Trystan and his team to help her figure out where she should take her career next. She wanted to feel alive again. Her responses to the required questions, along with her personality and aptitude test results, revealed that a primary element of her makeup was that she loved taking risks. She craved it. She thrived when she didn't know what might happen from one minute to the next. She experienced sharp dissatisfaction with anything that felt safe or routine or predictable, even if it came dressed in the disguise of something new.

Contrary to what Stephanie had expected, no one interrupted while she talked and clicked through all ten slides. When she was finished, she clicked back to Arlinda's profile and sat down. The other three were arranged in a cluster at the opposite end of the table. Still, no one spoke.

Why weren't they saying anything? Had her presentation bored them? Trystan always had a comment or two right upfront. What was the matter with them?

"Anything more?" Diana asked.

"Of course there's more. These are the highlights, which is what Trystan asked for. I think her desire for risk is the most telling, so I focused on that."

Alex leaned forward, resting her arms on the table. "Why?"

"What do you mean?" Stephanie asked.

"Why is it telling?"

"Because she's successful and even though she's achieved what she wanted, there's no more risk in her career so she's dissatisfied."

"I think that's obvious. You implied there was a hidden layer to it."

Stephanie stared at Alex, gazing into those eyes that never gave a sliver of information about what the woman was thinking. Sometimes Stephanie thought the sole emotion coming out of Alex's eyes was a desire to disarm everyone around her. And she'd succeeded. Again. Always. She grabbed the upper hand and held on tight. Stephanie had no idea how to respond to the accusation that her insight was obvious. She felt a twitch of anger that swelled quickly while the room sank back into its earlier silence. The air changed, taking on a thick, oppressive quality.

"Thanks for putting this together," Trystan said.

Diana nodded. She gave Stephanie a warm smile, but her lack of comments implied she thought either the material was superficial or that she simply wanted to dig into all the questions and test answers herself, discarding Stephanie's effort.

"She's very excited to work with us," Stephanie said.

Diana laughed. "With what she's paying, I wouldn't expect anything else."

Trystan lifted his eyebrows slightly but said nothing. After a moment, he gave Diana a forgiving smile then turned to Stephanie. "Can you tell us a bit more about her expectations?"

Stephanie looked down at her hands. She should have anticipated this question. It was one of the first things he focused upon. But she'd been so excited about putting together her first profile overview that she hadn't thought much about how the discussion would unfold. "I think she…"

"Maybe she mistakes us for another kind of service," Alex said. "If all she wants is to introduce risk into her life, the solution is fairly simple. Change careers to one where she doesn't feel comfortable. Or find it outside of work—mountain climbing, learning a new sport, camping."

"She wants to explore her career and her life purpose," Stephanie said. "She wants to find deeper insight into herself, not go hiking."

Alex pushed her chair away from the table and stretched out her legs. She looked down, studying her shoes or something on the floor that Stephanie couldn't see.

"Do you have anything else to add?" Trystan asked. "Any thoughts that weren't captured on the slides?"

Stephanie shook her head. "There's a lot more, obviously. But to me, that was the key takeaway."

Trystan stood. "We all have work to do, digging more deeply into her profile. But thanks for getting us started, Stephanie."

Stephanie nodded. Her face felt soft and incapable of forming any kind of useful expression. Her skin and the multitude of small muscles around her lips and jaw had turned to pudding.

A moment later, the others stood and left the room. She felt alone and considerably lacking in value.

3

Trystan went out and picked up pastrami sandwiches and potato salad from a deli—a quick dinner for the two of us before he introduced me to Arlinda. He and I ate in the conference room, reviewing our own notes on her profile material before our scheduled seven-thirty meeting at her home. She'd asked to meet at her home because she couldn't guarantee there wouldn't be any interruptions at her office.

I wondered what her ad agency was like if there were interruptions in the evening. Did the entire staff work into the evening, needing her input for critical decisions? Either that, or she didn't want anyone to know she was meeting with us. It seemed the more truthful explanation for not wanting us to come to her office. It was the only way to guarantee privacy. It struck me as ironic that she was determined to avoid that risk.

Trystan gave the cab driver the building number for her apartment on Fifth Avenue. As the driver navigated traffic and pedestrians, Trystan read email on his phone, and I looked out the window, neither of us saying anything during the first few blocks of our drive.

Then Trystan spoke. "How are you enjoying the job?"

"It's good," I said.

"Just good?"

I nodded. I didn't turn to look at him, assuming he was making small talk.

"You've seemed distracted the past few weeks, and before our holiday break."

"Not really."

"I might interpret it as boredom."

I turned. "I'm not bored."

"Reviewing Arlinda's psychological profile, it struck me that you have some similar traits."

I knew where he was headed, but I waited for him to say it.

"You thrive on taking risks."

"So do you." I had no idea if this was technically true, but I figured a guy who had the guts to start a boutique coaching service and upgrade it into something much more lucrative, selling his elite clients on our in-depth life and career transformation, had some affinity for risk. The promises he made were considerable, and I wasn't sure we would always deliver on them. With clients like ours, dissatisfaction could develop easily, spreading far and fast.

"We're not talking about me," he said.

"Why not?"

"I'm checking on whether you're happy working with our team and our clients. I value enthusiasm."

"I think I've been enthusiastic."

"Recently, not as much."

The cab veered too sharply around a corner and shoved me against the door. The driver checked the rearview mirror. I caught his eye, but he didn't apologize. Instead, he pressed harder on the gas and bolted past a yellow traffic light.

I resettled myself. "I was distracted for a while, but it's all taken care of." I suppose I should have considered the two men I'd killed more than a distraction, but now that some time had passed, it was a fairly truthful statement.

"It occurred to me that I don't know much about your personal life," he said.

"Does that matter?"

"The better we know each other, the more effective our working relationship will be. Within limits, of course."

"Are you sure?" I smiled carefully. "How did that work out —getting to know each other at Stephanie's tragic Thanksgiving dinner?"

He gave a short laugh that he tried to hide. "I understand her better now."

"I'm sure."

"Back to you," he said.

The cab slowed and pulled to the curb in front of a sixteen-story tower.

"Too late." I settled the straps of my messenger bag and the camera case on my shoulder and opened the door.

"It's a conversation that's easily continued," he said.

The disruption to his probe of my personal life didn't rattle him, and I wondered when he would pick up the thread again.

A doorman greeted us and asked who we were there to see. A woman in a navy blue suit pressed the elevator button for us after asking what floor we required. The process provided several layers of security, trying to hide under the film of welcoming politeness.

As the elevator doors closed, I briefly considered assuring

Trystan of my enthusiasm and telling him that knowing my personal life wouldn't change anything. That would end the conversation quickly in the forced time constraints. Instead, I simply stared at the doors and wondered what he really wanted to know.

We rode to the top floor in silence.

A woman with blond hair combed close to her scalp, dramatically shaded eyes, and pale lip gloss opened the door. She wore white slacks and a white T-shirt. Around her neck was a collection of red beads, looped multiple times, resting on her breastbone.

She didn't ask our names and was obviously ready for us. She ushered us into a foyer with a black tile floor. Four doors opened off the foyer. All of them were closed. The walls between the doors were decorated with abstract art, primarily done in black and white, each with a streak of vibrant color.

Still not speaking, she opened the first door to our left. The room had a single tall window looking out on the street below. There were two small sofas and a round table in the center. The walls were painted the color of a creamy latte, and there wasn't any artwork whatsoever.

The woman left, closing the door behind her. We sat down and waited.

4

It was quarter to eight before the door opened again. A woman came in carrying a tray with a carafe of ice water, three glasses, and a plate with dark red cherries. She placed it on the table and left. I studied the firm, luscious fruit, wondering where they'd found such plump, rich looking cherries in January. Before I could think further, the door opened, and a small woman with blond and bronze-streaked hair entered. A woman who looked younger than the profile photograph I'd seen, possibly because her face was alive with energy.

"Hi, Trystan. So good to see you." She extended her hand before he could get to his feet. "And you're Alexandra." She shook hands with both of us in turn. Her grip was firm and warm.

She sat on the sofa across from us, lifted the carafe, and filled the glasses with water. She placed a cherry in her mouth, chewed, and used the tips of her fingers to ease the pit out between her lips. She placed it on one of the three small bowls arranged around the edge of the plate and licked her fingertips.

Her hair was cut in layers and wild with waves that looked natural, falling well past her shoulders. She'd used a bit of mascara and lip gloss, but otherwise, her face seemed to be free of even a brushstroke of blush. She wore a man's white shirt, black leggings, and black high-heeled sandals.

"I'm looking forward to your revelations." She laughed and ate another cherry.

Trystan smiled. "That will come. As I explained, we're going to start with some photographs."

She looked at me. "Maybe I should show you my headshots."

"This is more than a headshot," Trystan said.

She winked. "I know. You explained it all. I'm just skeptical."

"Why are you skeptical?" I asked.

"I'll be surprised if you find anything in my photographs that you can't see right here, looking at me."

"And I think you'll be surprised," Trystan said. "Let's start with you telling Alexandra a bit about yourself, so she can hear it in your own words and get a sense of who you are."

"The twenty-thousand questions I already answered weren't sufficient?" She smiled to take the sting out of the words. "Let's see…I'm forty-three."

That alone surprised me. Most women over forty seem to want to keep the exact number in the background, as if it's shameful, as if you can't guess anyway. I wondered, not for the first time if I would be the same when I reached that age. I couldn't imagine it, but it's difficult to foresee what you'll be like in a future form. All you know is where you are now and what's gone before. What I saw in myself now was nothing that I'd come close to imagining when I was a teenager, even less when I was small. When you look back, you realize you couldn't have predicted some of the pathways you ended up following.

After hesitating for a moment, she continued. "I went to school at NYU and got my MBA from Colombia Business School."

"Try to stay off the biographical stuff," Trystan said. "Let her see who you are beyond your credentials."

She laughed. "Maybe I am my credentials."

It was a curious comment. There was something about the arrangement of her features that suggested she partially believed this. She seemed both proud of her insight and terrified that she was nothing but a fleshed-out resume.

"Tell us more about that," Trystan said. "I want Alex to get insight into how that statement makes you feel. Is it a joke? A witty comment that means nothing? Or is it something you've considered?"

Her expression remained the same, so maybe I'd misread her.

"I've worked hard to get where I am. I made the most of the opportunities I was given, and I created quite a few of my own. I think when you work hard and love your work, you naturally acquire a considerable list of awards and degrees and recognition. So yes, I am those things. My career has been the center of my life, my whole life, really."

I leaned forward slightly to catch her eye. "Do you like it that way?"

Trystan's head jerked toward me. Normally in our initial photography sessions, I didn't ask questions. In most of our client meetings I said almost nothing. It was his job to sell what we offered, his job to build rapport with our clients. It was his role to ask the questions and direct the conversation where he chose.

He'd told me he thought it worked well that I was somewhat anonymous—a face and a camera. That way, the clients weren't responding to me as a person they knew. He thought it made the images less complicated—cleaner, whatever that meant.

I thought his view was fanciful. It didn't matter whether I spoke or not, our clients still reacted to me as a person. They still formed impressions of me. And of course some of them, Jim Kohn came to mind, fixated on me in a rather unprofessional way.

To his credit, Trystan didn't try to bury my question with one of his own. He waited for Arlinda to speak.

"I like working." She spoke slowly. "I've never felt there was much missing from my life. I never wanted children. I have my staff, that's enough care-taking for my taste." She smiled. "My relationship has lasted for over fifteen years, more than a lot of marriages, and I'm satisfied with it." She turned her head as if she'd heard a sound behind her. A moment later, she looked back at us. "I think work is what makes people interesting."

The room was silent, then Trystan spoke. "But you're bored."

"I don't know if that's the right word, but close."

"When did you start to notice the change in your feelings about your life?"

"About a year ago." Her expression shifted.

I wished I had my camera out. I wished I'd captured what I'd seen already. I could imagine Diana deciphering the expressions that were so subtle, but clearly reflecting something going on inside her head that she wasn't going to talk about. It was possible she couldn't articulate it even to herself.

There was something so centered and self-possessed about her. I thought I could easily spend hours photographing her. I pushed away the sudden, insistent thought that capturing her in every room of her glorious apartment would be an interesting approach. The only reason the idea had come to me was because I wanted a tour of the rooms, I wanted to see every detail. Obviously, she was an artist in the way she arranged and decorated the space around her.

I brought my thoughts back to the conversation, while a tiny wheel in the back of my mind tried to think of a way to justify my desire to Trystan. Normally he wanted our clients photographed in their work environments, interacting with their clients or employees, and in business-related social settings.

But she'd invited us to her home for this first meeting. Didn't that say something about the overlap between her home and work life?

Again I tried to return my concentration to what she was saying.

"I can't point to any event that caused the change. I can't even tell you whether it was something I tried to put out of my mind for a while. I just know it started quietly, and over this past year, it's grown into something I can't stop thinking about. And that's why I contacted you. So...you know more about me than anyone in my company, and you have all kinds of ways to dig into my psyche. I'm excited to get started."

I reached for my camera bag, and Trystan stood.

"I'll wait in your foyer and catch up on email while Alex

takes some photographs."

Arlinda winked. "Or you can watch."

Trystan didn't miss a beat. "Our photography process is one-on-one." He left the room.

I removed the lens cap. Immediately, Arlinda crossed her legs and clasped her hands around her knees, tilting her head and offering a knowing smile.

"Just relax," I said.

"Of course." She maintained the pose.

5

The photography session went well once I got Arlinda talking about her proudest moments in launching and growing her agency. She forgot about her Instagram-contrived poses, and her artful smiles. She let her back sink into the couch cushions, her arms spread along the upper edge like the wings of a graceful bird.

I moved around the room, taking closeups, profile pictures, and even full-body shots—far more than I needed, but enjoying the ambiance of the room and Arlinda's melodic voice telling the stories of her career.

It turned out her two proudest moments had been the hiring of her first employee and passing the one million dollar mark for her agency's revenue. Caruso Creative generated far more money now, of course, but that first million had made her feel like…well, a million dollars. She'd laughed for a long time after saying that, her laugh descending into a giggle.

"Is this part of what you do?" she asked.

"What do you mean?"

"I feel more excited already. The numbness is gone. I'm

seeing myself with new eyes, I think. At least right now, while I'm telling you about starting out, when everything was new."

"It's fun to remember the best parts."

She'd agreed, and while that exchange took place, I captured ten different expressions on her face.

When I said I was finished and began packing up the camera, she looked disappointed.

I rejoined Trystan in her foyer. Arlinda said her PA would contact me to provide a date when she had a client meeting that I'd be able to photograph.

The elevator ride to the ground floor was silent. We still didn't speak while we waited for an unoccupied cab. When one pulled over, I shoved my camera into the backseat and slid in after it. Trystan followed, slamming the door closed and giving the address for the office even though it meant I would have to get out of the warm cab to take the subway home.

I said nothing. No one at work knew where I lived, and I wanted to keep it that way. I'd thought it quite bold of Stephanie when she invited us all to her place for Thanksgiving. Something about letting people know your address, not to mention inviting them into your living room, watching them poke around in your kitchen, offering them use of your bathroom, was horrifying to me.

No matter how hard you try to be tidy, your body is constantly shedding skin cells, hairs, and spreading an imperceptible film of oil across every surface you touch. It's what makes your fingerprints stick. Trust me. I know this because I've spent a fair amount of time watching out for my body's exfoliation in the homes and hotel rooms where I've ushered people out of this world.

I don't want these small pieces of other people in my living space. If the shedding comes from a roommate whose presence I enjoy, it's easy to overlook. In that case, I'm happy to wipe, sweep, vacuum it away. Obviously, when I'm sharing my bed with a man who thrills me, I put up with all kinds of shedding. But other than that, I like my life clean. In more ways than one.

"You seem deep in thought," Trystan said.

Trystan's voice jarred me. I'd almost forgotten he was there as the cab wheels hummed over the pavement, keeping their own erratic rhythm. I shrugged.

"What's on your mind?"

"Cleaning."

He laughed. "If you don't want to say, that's fine."

"I don't mind saying. I was thinking about cleaning."

He nodded, a grin still spread across his face until his cheeks were squeezed into hard knobs. "I don't believe you."

"That's your choice."

The grin relaxed somewhat. "How was the photography session?"

"Good."

"Can you elaborate?"

"It took a while for her to relax. But once I got her talking about her proudest moments, she forgot about what I was doing."

"Good. Good. You're very good at this."

"Thank you."

"Anything interesting come out of that?"

"I took more shots than usual. She's very photogenic, and I guess I relaxed a bit too."

"I'm not surprised she's photogenic. She works in a visual

field. She has a heightened awareness of what creates a pleasing image. Besides, she's comfortable with who she is. People like that usually do well in front of a camera."

"Makes sense." I'd never given any thought to that, but it did make sense. He really did have some insight into people. It wasn't surprising he was doing well helping them accelerate their goals—blast out of their comfort zones, as the cliché goes. Although I thought he was wrong about one thing in Arlinda's case. She knew what created a nice image, but she was not entirely relaxed in her own skin. She posed too much.

"What I meant about whether anything interesting came out of it was referring to the conversation. What did she say were her proudest moments?"

"Hiring her first employee and seeing the agency hit a million dollars in revenue."

"Not that surprising. I think her profile showed she gets a thrill from creating something out of nothing. She no longer feels like she's doing that."

The cab took a corner too fast, and then we were racing up Seventh Avenue.

"It's good to hear it went well," he said. "Now, back to our earlier conversation."

"Was there an earlier conversation?"

"Why are you so determined to put up a wall around yourself?"

"Work is work. Play is play. I don't like to blur the lines."

"That's not entirely true. Somehow, I think you blur quite a lot of lines."

I laughed. He was right, of course. "Why would you think that?"

"You give off a vibe."

"Not very scientific. Wouldn't you need personality tests to come to that conclusion?"

He laughed. "You know that's not always necessary. I'm good at reading people. Why else would I have built this business?"

"Maybe you just *think* you're good at it."

"I've never been proven wrong."

I moved my camera bag onto my lap, ready to leave the cab the moment the driver pulled to the curb.

"Anxious to get going?"

"It's late," I said.

"Not that late. Nine-twenty."

With any other man, I would expect that comment to be followed by an invitation to get a drink.

"I'm not trying to overstep professional boundaries, Alexandra. I just think it helps the work environment, the synergy of what we're doing, the vibe the company gives off, if we know each other as human beings, not simply as job functions."

"Everyone knows me as a human being."

"Do they? What made you move to Australia?"

"Work."

"And you returned for the same reason, clearly."

"That's right."

"Do you plan to stay in New York long term?"

"I don't know."

"Where else have you lived?"

"I told you about my background when you interviewed me."

He sighed. "It creates negative energy when you're too closed off."

"I don't think I'm closed off."

He was quiet for several minutes. Only a minute or two left until we arrived at the office building. "You're very outgoing. You share your ideas about our clients, our process, but there's something missing. Life is more meaningful when you have strong relationships at work as well as in your private life."

I smiled. The cab slowed. What he didn't realize was that I didn't have strong relationships in my private life either. I'm happy inside my own head. People entertain me and challenge me. That's all. Of course I crave human interaction, but I don't need to be close, whatever that even means. Sure, I like some people better than others. And I like spending time with all kinds of people, but I was not looking to be friends with my co-workers.

Diana and I would get to know each other better, I could feel that coming. And possibly Trystan, but he was making a questionnaire out of his desire to know more about me. He shouldn't have done that. It lowered my opinion of him. Only a fraction, but it was lower. He wasn't showing his usual finesse. He was pushing like he had some right to get inside my head. I didn't like it.

He should have normal conversations over drinks and lunches and around the conference table and get to know me that way. Instead, I felt like he wanted me to consult with him, like he wanted to prowl around inside my psyche.

6

I sat beside my living room window and looked out at the street below. Streetlights cast bright circles on the dry pavement. Dead leaves, stiff with ice crystals, glittered in their bright centers. I considered opening the window and breaking the building rules with a slow, contemplative cigarette, but the thought of that icy cold air gushing into my living room, filling the kitchen, and snaking into the bedroom was enough for me to keep the window sealed tight.

At least as tight as the old building could manage.

There was clearly deterioration in the wood frame because moisture clung to the edges of the glass, and there were even a few ice crystals glistening on the ancient frame, repainted so many times it seemed as if the thing were made of thick, crisp layers of paint rather than wood. Maybe it was. Over the years, maybe the wood had decayed to nothing, and all that held the glass in place was the paint, currently a dull beige with a tinge of yellow.

I stood and went into the kitchen. A few minutes later, I was seated by the window again, holding a martini glass, gazing at the three fat olives speared with a clear plastic spike.

After the luxury of Arlinda's penthouse, the charm of my small, relatively ancient apartment had faded somewhat. The air seemed to have taken on a stale, damp smell. The window was oozing, and the furniture and the few pieces of art on my walls appeared dingy and slightly pathetic.

I wanted a nice apartment. I wanted space, I wanted comfort and beauty, I wanted the soft thick wool coat I'd seen in a department store window before my trip to Australia. I wanted to eat in upscale restaurants whenever I chose, and I wanted to feel warm. The thrill of living in New York City hadn't faded, but the cold inside my apartment was unpleasant. Even when the radiator pumped out too much warm air, filling my nostrils and lungs with dry heat, there was an underlying chill.

In Arlinda's tranquil, luxurious rooms, the temperature had been a non-entity, as if the air adapted to my presence. I'd been comfortable, my skin felt soft, and my clothes didn't scrape cold fibers against my flesh one minute and stifle me with too much heat the next.

I wanted money. I always had, and it seemed that enjoying my day-to-day life had gotten in the way of figuring out how I was going to get where I wanted to go, to get where I knew I belonged. I still had no desire for a sprinkling of gold from a dead fairy god-father, or whatever you wanted to call that post-mortem gift to Eileen.

But so far, all my work had been tasks performed for other people. My jobs had been fun, occasionally challenging, entertaining at times, and I'd moved on when I was bored. But they weren't even close to the kind of jobs that created enough wealth to last a lifetime.

The people who gathered that kind of money seemed to

be those with extraordinary talent or a focused drive that was strong enough to propel them to the heights of a corporation where the company shared its profits with you in large chunks of change. Or they found it creating their own companies, a talent of its own. A lot of people found it by investing. Real estate. The stock market.

An image of Rafe and Victoria's enormous computer screens, pulsing with charts, flashed across my mind. For months, they'd been pressuring me to learn their day-trading techniques. They wanted me to invest with them, to test whether their methods worked as well as they claimed. But there was something off about both of them—individually and as a couple—that kept me at arm's length.

Rafe flirted with me in the most overt way I'd ever experienced from a guy who was in a relationship. He gave me flowers and came close to putting his hands all over me, unconcerned about Victoria's reaction. And for good reason. She appeared unconcerned. She was almost giddy that he'd given me flowers, casually telling me it had been her suggestion.

They claimed to be raking in money every day, the crumbs that fell off others' investments sucked up on an hourly basis. She'd shown me photographs of a very expensive brownstone house on the upper east side that they planned to move into...*soon.* Yet, here they sat in an equally dreary apartment, maybe even drabber than mine. At least my front window faced the street.

But maybe that's what risk-takers are like. Slightly different from other people. They don't follow the rules, and they're not afraid of consequences.

I sipped my drink and let the vodka ease its way into my

mouth, filling it with a different kind of warmth, a warmth the radiator could never hope to supply. The kind of warm feeling in your blood that comes with sex. A little alcohol does that. Too much and your body turns icy cold, but one drink, maybe two, can be comforting.

Maybe I'd misread Victoria and Rafe.

No guts no glory, that's what they say.

Perhaps their aggressive behavior revealed guts. They were drawn to me, and they weren't going to take no for an answer. And they sensed my desire for more and knew they had a way to get there. Possibly I was confusing to them, letting them see my craving but refusing to do anything about it.

I'd taken their weird behavior as some sort of suggestion they might be trying to scam me. But in what way? It didn't seem possible. All they'd offered was a chance to learn how they did what they did. Where was the opportunity for a scam? I don't believe that people do a lot of things just to help other people. There's almost always an agenda of some kind.

I took another sip of my drink. I shifted the glass to my other hand and ate two of the olives, an indulgence, but the craving inside me at that moment was hard to satisfy.

Maybe I *was* too closed off. Maybe letting people see a bit more of me wouldn't be a terrible thing. No matter what is revealed, there are vast spaces that no one can ever access inside any human being, especially me.

Or…I could hire myself out as a killer. I certainly had the skills and experience.

7

Once the idea was in my head, I wasted no time in trying to connect with Victoria. All it took was lingering on the landing when I came home from work. While I waited, I stared down into the stairwell, imagining what it would be like to fall through that center space, past all those railings, unable to grasp a single one, a jolt of incredible pain and the sudden loss of consciousness as your body smacked the tile floor.

Fortunately, Victoria interrupted my gruesome thoughts.

As she did several times a day, she eventually came out to see if there was anyone around. Lurking outside your apartment was surely a side-effect of sitting in front of a computer for hours at a time.

She wore Ugg boots, leggings, and a long sweater with sleeves that covered her knuckles. Under that was a thick turtleneck shirt. Her head was wrapped in a wide pink band that covered her ears.

I smiled. "Keeping warm?"

"No. I'm freezing."

"The radiators aren't always consistent."

"I'm cold all the time." She licked her lips. "My skin feels like old paper."

I nodded. "I have a good lip balm. I just bought two new tubes, you can have one. I didn't open it yet." As I spoke the words, I had to stifle a shiver, thinking of sharing an already opened tube with her, with anyone.

"Really? That's so nice of you."

"No problem."

"How much is it?"

I needed to back-pedal the absolute refusal I'd given when she and Rafe tried to explain day trading to me, tried to interest me in how easy it was, proclaimed how good I'd be at it. "Consider it a gift."

She folded her arms across her ribs. "You seem different."

"Different, how?"

"Nicer."

I shrugged. "I'm the same as always."

"Half the time, I feel like you don't even like me."

I slid my hands into my pockets. I held her gaze while I tried to think about what I wanted to say—a response that would move things in the direction I wanted. "Maybe you misread me."

She stared back. I was impressed with her ability to continue looking me in the eye. She was bolder than I'd realized. At the same moment, I understood that I'd never truly looked into her eyes before.

Finally, she said, "I don't think I did."

She was right, of course, so I changed the subject. "Anything interesting happen around here while I was in Australia?"

"Nope."

"What's the timeline for moving into your new place? The brownstone."

Even that question didn't divert her. She continued looking at me, hardly blinking. "Soon."

"That's what you said two months ago."

"Did I?" She continued to stare. "I know there's something different—"

"Maybe I'm just relaxed from the warm weather and the break from work."

She grinned. "That's it. Absolutely. Your job isn't as exciting as you make it out to be. I think what seems different about you is the feeling of freedom because you didn't have to answer to a boss for two weeks."

"Could be. Or, I'm exactly the same as always."

She laughed, clearly believing her own analysis over my assurance. "We should get together," she said.

"Absolutely. That Chinese meal you made last time was amazing. I could bring wine."

Inviting myself to dinner, suggesting what she should cook, didn't appear to bother her. If it did, she didn't allow it to ripple the surface of her skin. "Tomorrow?"

"Perfect. Will Rafe be there?"

"I think so. Unless you don't want him to be."

She was easier on her own, but the friendly, welcoming self I was projecting didn't want to be difficult or perceived as anti-social in any way. "Why would I not want him there?"

She narrowed her eyes. "Because it seems as if you like him even less than you like me."

"Not at all."

She looked at her feet. She shuffled slightly, aligning her Ugg boots so the curve in the sole of one fit with the other.

She looked up at me. "I'm not stupid. You've barely tolerated us some of the time. Why the sudden change? It's fine, but I'm curious. And surprised."

"You're imagining things."

"Like I said, I'm not stupid."

"Do you want to get together for dinner or not?"

"Of course I do."

"Then it'll be great to hang out with you and Rafe."

"If you say so."

"I do." I gave her a warm, friendly, completely open smile.

She returned the smile, perhaps deciding in that moment she'd take me at my word, even though her gut said something else entirely.

"I'll bring wine and stuff to make martinis."

"Sounds good."

We said good-bye, and I went into my apartment.

I unlocked my tablet and did some research on day trading. I needed to be prepared in case they gave me uninformed or overtly misleading information. If I was going to think about putting cash into something intangible, I needed to know all I could. As I scoured the web, I thought for a brief moment about talking to one of our previous clients. Pete Torkenson was a high-powered financial advisor, and I was sure he'd have more than the average amount of information and gallons more insight than I was going to find on the web. Just as quickly, I pushed the idea to the side.

There was a limit to my tentative steps toward revealing more of myself. Even if I asked Pete a few simple questions to get his opinion of the practice, which I imagined was low, he would immediately want to know about my financial life.

I didn't have to answer, but even having the conversation

was too much.

With only a few minutes of effort, I learned that day traders did indeed make money. I also learned that ninety-five percent of the people who attempted it ended up with a net loss. This brought up too many questions that pulled me away from my searching and into the kitchen, where I mixed a martini.

Were Victoria and Rafe really so sharp that *both* of them fell into that five percent? Maybe one of them was supplementing the other. If that was the case, my money was on Victoria. She claimed she'd learned everything from Rafe, acted as though he was the expert, but I thought she was the more likely success story. Rafe struck me as the type I'd read about who looked for ways to make fast, big profits. He didn't have the painstaking patience to work in tiny increments.

My research also made me wonder how the person writing the information knew the success rate. It wasn't as if day traders reported their income to some guild or that it was tracked by a government agency. They worked in the shadows. Obviously, the majority of them paid taxes, but the IRS doesn't go around giving public information on the success rate of any given money-making endeavor.

I sipped my martini and thought about the odds. They were not in my favor.

8

Portland, Oregon

On my sixteenth birthday, I knew I wanted a car. When I mentioned this to my father on our way home from taking the test for my driver's license, he didn't respond. I said it a second time.

"Attention on the road," he said.

"It is."

"Not if you're talking."

"*You* talk when you drive."

"Don't argue. You shouldn't let your emotions come into play when you're driving. They don't teach you that in school, and they don't test for it, but it's one of the most important things to learn."

"I don't get emotional."

"All women get emotional, that's why they have more accidents."

I wondered if this was true. My skin grew hot, my body clamoring to correct all of his absurd assumptions. At the same time, I wanted that car. Picking a fight would send me in the opposite direction from what I wanted. "Okay, but I—"

"Arguing is emotional."

"I'm not arguing, and I'm not emotional. I'm just asking about getting a car. All the boys got one."

"That was different. Every child is different."

I pressed my foot on the brake, a fraction too hard.

"Careful."

"I am."

"That's why you shouldn't be talking."

"Everyone talks when they drive."

"You're still learning."

"I passed my test."

"And you can lose your license just as quickly as you got it."

"I'm not going to get into an accident."

The light turned green. I pressed on the gas ever-so-carefully, easing the car into the intersection the way he liked, holding back to be sure no cross-traffic delinquent was going to race through their own red light and T-bone us. The car behind me honked.

"Ignore that. You're doing fine."

I stuck my tongue between my front teeth and bit gently, trying to keep myself from talking. He'd told me these same things every time I got in the car for a driving lesson. He'd said them on the way to the exam, and now he acted as if I still hadn't passed. If the state of Oregon thought I was a good driver — and I was good, I'd passed with ninety-four percent — then he should stop telling me everything I was doing wrong. And making up rules as he went along.

"I need a car for—"

"No one *needs* a car. The only thing we need is the Spirit of

God dwelling inside us."

"Eric got Uncle Hank's car two weeks after he turned sixteen."

"How do you remember that? You were a child. I hope you're not keeping score. Your mother and I have told you that more than once. Score-keeping and comparing are not healthy, and that behavior isn't pleasing in the eyes of God."

I tapped the turn signal and rounded the corner onto our street.

"Slow down."

"I'm going fifteen."

"Children are playing in the street all the time."

"I'm going fifteen!"

"Don't raise your voice."

I eased my foot off the gas. Now the car was barely rolling forward. I thought we were more likely to cause an accident gliding down the street so slowly someone might come around the corner and rear-end us. I pulled into the driveway.

Inside the house, I handed the keys to my father.

"Congratulations on passing your test," he said.

"Thank you."

"We knew you would. I think your mother's planning cupcakes for dessert. A small celebration."

I smiled. "You seem awfully excited that I have my license."

"It's a milestone," he said.

"But what's the point if I can't drive anywhere?"

"You'll drive lots of places. You can run errands for your mother. You'll be able to drive yourself to youth group meetings."

I sighed.

"Don't take that tone. And don't spoil your victory with a bad attitude."

"I don't have a bad attitude."

He dropped the keys into the basket on the bookcase near the door to the family room. The keys were always in the basket to prevent loss. My father hated wasted time. Time belonged to god, and it was our responsibility to use it carefully, as carefully as we used money, as frugally as we used any resource we'd been given. Squandering things was a sin. And that applied to food, clothing, water, even the words we spoke.

When one of us couldn't find a homework assignment or had misplaced a library book, he dogged us while we hunted for it, chastising us for wasting his time, our time, and god's time.

I followed him into the family room. He picked up a magazine and settled into his armchair.

"It's not fair that Eric got a car right away, and I have no idea when I'll get one."

"When the time is right."

"That's not a time."

"What did I say about your attitude?"

I smiled. Often, a warm, subservient smile helped my father overlook my so-called attitude. "I just want to understand. Did he and Jake and Tom get cars right away because they're boys?"

"They didn't get cars right away. Tom was nearly seventeen. And Jake only got it because Eric left for college."

"So, it's because I'm a girl?"

"No. I didn't say that."

"Well, why then? Why did they get one and I don't?"

"As I explained, it varies. Tom was nearly seventeen."

That wasn't the way I remembered it at all. I remembered all three of them with cars very close to their birthdays, right after passing their driving tests.

"Then why can't it vary back to me? Since Eric was sixteen and two weeks?"

"Don't be a smart-aleck. You have your driver's license. It's a privilege."

"A privilege to run errands for Mom?"

He closed the magazine and rolled it into a tube. He whacked it against the palm of his other hand. "I don't like your tone of voice. And as I've pointed out more times than I can begin to count, neither does your Heavenly Father. You need to appreciate what you have, think about how you can be helpful to your mother, and stop begging. It's not attractive."

"I'm not begging."

He unfurled the magazine, opened it, and raised it slightly to obscure most of his face, directing his attention to the page.

I retreated to my bedroom. I reached into my purse and took out the half sheet of paper telling me I had a license to drive. I studied it, wondering whether it meant anything at all, wondering if I'd ever be free.

9

Stephanie unlocked her apartment door and stepped inside. Something about the energy level of the four rooms told her that Eileen was already home. It was unusual. Most of the time, Stephanie came home to an empty space, a place that felt as if all the air had gone out of it. On those occasions, the apartment seemed like too much with its extra bedroom for her adult daughter, its four chairs around the table.

More often than not, Stephanie sat alone at the tiny kitchen table. The sole occasion when Eileen conformed to her mother's desire for shared meals was on Sundays, and Stephanie had the distinct feeling it was done out of politeness, not a desire for togetherness.

She carried her purse to the bedroom and hung it on the hook attached to the back of the door, dropping her keys inside. She tugged off her coat and tossed it on the bed. She stepped out of her shoes and stripped off her pantyhose. It felt good to be free of the elastic around her waist, constantly rolling down over the nylon fabric, pinching her all day long.

If she did something about the few extra pounds that had settled around the middle of her body, it wouldn't be so uncomfortable.

Still, why couldn't someone design leg coverings for women that didn't feel like sausage casings? For that matter, why couldn't she feel dressed for work wearing pants and socks and shoes like every man in the city? It wasn't fair.

Her mother had always said life wasn't fair. Stephanie knew she'd said the same to Eileen over the years, a mantra she was compelled to repeat as if it had been seared into her brain, formed of her own thoughts.

Life *wasn't* fair, but that didn't stop her from longing for some kind of equality in how things worked out for people. Those who repeated that truism, herself included, seemed so defeated. It sounded as if that unfairness meant you shouldn't even try.

She changed into jeans and a fluffy sweater. She put on wool socks, hung up her clothing, and tossed the rank nylons into the laundry bag. She stepped into the hallway and knocked on Eileen's door.

The door opened. Another surprise. She was used to Eileen calling out that she was busy, following up with the insistence that she wasn't hungry.

"I wasn't sure when you'd be home, so I didn't start dinner yet," Eileen said. "I bought some trout and broccoli. I'll get it ready. Why don't you relax?" Eileen stepped into the hallway. She left the door ajar and moved around Stephanie, headed toward the kitchen.

This was so unlike her recent behavior. But instead of feeling pleasure that her daughter seemed to want to contribute to their shared living, that she'd finally pulled herself out of the funk that had followed her breakup and then the death of that awful man, this change in Eileen was a sharp piece of glass pressing against her skull from the inside.

The change had come about since Eileen had started spending time with Alexandra Mallory. It was infuriating. Stephanie hated Alexandra even more for it, and she felt faint stirrings of something like hatred toward her own beloved daughter.

Their friendship was a horrible betrayal. Alexandra had stolen Stephanie's job, sidelined her career, and spent her time trying to lure Trystan and Diana into her circle, doing all she could to make Stephanie look foolish and unnecessary. Of course, Eileen didn't know any of this, but it still felt like a betrayal that she'd made friends with Alexandra. She refused to consider Stephanie's warning that Alexandra was dangerous, not to be trusted, a user.

The situation made her doubt her daughter's maturity, her failure to recognize predatory human beings. First, that man Jim, and now this. Eileen lacked discernment. If she showed up at church for more than the holiday festivities, if she spent time reading the Word of God, she would see these kind of people for who they were. Instead, she was sucked in by money and the superficially attractive.

While Eileen cooked, Stephanie sat in the living room and brooded. A book lay face down on her lap. Her head was back, her eyes closed. She couldn't mention her concern about Alex again. She'd said it too many times already. And now, with Eileen being so warm, so engaging and social, she didn't want to spoil things by giving her daughter a lecture about her poor choice in friends.

But why would Eileen be suddenly more social and in a

better mood, engaging more with life just because Alex had started inviting her out for meals and drinks, and God knew what else? Eileen hadn't adopted any of Alex's negative traits, but she'd definitely changed. Quite suddenly and significantly.

Stephanie sighed and rested her hand on the spine of the book. Dealing with adult children was hard. It would be different, she supposed, if Eileen lived on her own. But she liked having her here, liked that she had a few extra years of closeness that other mothers didn't get.

The trout smelled heavenly. It was baking in a drizzle of olive oil, seasoned with nothing but salt and pepper. The olive oil was another new thing in Eileen's life. Although she still watched what she ate, she no longer seemed to be starving herself. She no longer obsessed over a diet that forbids even a teaspoon of excess fat, living on rice crackers and tea and boiled eggs and plain tofu. She was enjoying her food again. She'd stopped fretting over how a quarter of a pound here or there would *destroy her chances* at the modeling career she still pursued with unfettered passion.

While they ate, Eileen chattered about her photoshoot that day.

The food was incredible. The simple, light seasoning gave the fish and the broccoli a heavenly flavor. It made Stephanie feel she'd always over-dressed the food she prepared. Fresh and minimalist was so much better, it made her feel more alive. It made her feel like everything was good between her and Eileen. The friendship she'd longed for since Eileen entered adulthood was so close she could touch it with the tip of her finger.

"This makes me feel so refreshed." She took a breath and placed her fork on the plate, the tines resting upside down on a piece of trout skin. She would test the water and see if Eileen might be open to an actual adult conversation, to hearing about pieces of her mother's life. "Things have been difficult at work," she said.

"That's too bad," Eileen said. "Alex seems pretty happy there."

A chill ran across the back of Stephanie's neck. It was the worst thing Eileen could have said. The reference to Alexandra made Stephanie fear that Eileen would repeat everything she said. Worse, it brought her nemesis into full view of her mind's eye. "Well, she has a different role." Her voice was snappish, but she couldn't restrain herself.

Eileen nodded. Sympathetically? It was hard to tell.

"I feel stalled in my career." She spoke softly, immediately regretting her tone. She sounded weak, not like the confident forty-something woman she should be. And that was the crux of it—the woman she *should* be. Not the woman she was.

10

The best that can be said about the dinner with Victoria and Rafe was that the food was incredible. The woman really knew how to wrap up and pan fry a dumpling. The chicken salad was the perfect blend of sweet and spicy, with chicken so delicate it melted in my mouth.

When I asked where she'd learned to cook such incredible Chinese food, she smiled and said she'd picked it up over the years. She was looking me right in the eye and claiming her expertise with a wok and spices was casually gleaned from no one and nowhere in particular. It was such an obvious lie, I didn't understand why the source of her cooking ability was worth hiding. It seemed pointless.

Other than that, they talked about day trading, at my conversational guidance, while I sucked up the details. The more they talked, the more I understood that my guess had been correct. It was clear that despite the effort Victoria had put into making me think Rafe was the master and her mentor, she was the one who knew and understood the details. He was mostly full of visions for the *potential*.

I did make one mistake in my effort to reveal more of

myself. The mistake came in a martini glass.

When I first arrived, Vic suggested I make a round of drinks. I gladly complied. We drank them faster than we should have, and dinner was still twenty minutes away when we were all ready for a second drink. I mixed another round, and we sipped our way through those.

I was feeling relaxed and energized at the same time. I was thrilled to see where the evening might lead, how much they might say with their defenses down, while I tried to keep mine in place. The alcohol had made me hungry, and I couldn't stop dragging those incredible pork dumplings through white vinegar and chili oil, popping the whole slick package into my mouth in two bites.

We drank two bottles of Pinot Gris with the food and it went down like water, complementing the spicy food and comforting noodles.

Although it was an odd match with the Chinese feast, Vic served a cheese platter for dessert. It seemed the perfect occasion for a third martini. And so, I mixed three more, gleefully breaking my rule of two. They were healthy-sized drinks, and feeling extravagant, I stabbed four large olives onto each stick. Still, the olives and all the food I'd consumed until that point couldn't stand up to the alcohol flooding my body.

The mess on the dining table and thoughts of the stiffening food in the kitchen ate at the back of my mind while we talked and laughed and kidded around about nothing much. We were all too far gone to say much more about the ins and outs of day trading, although I had enough presence of mind to ask a few more questions, repeatedly, such as—*How much, really, do you make?*

Clearly, they had retained some presence of mind as well, because they avoided giving me a straight answer. They murmured about their brownstone and money socked away in various money market accounts and other relatively secure places.

I suggested to Victoria she should put the food away, that the three of us should clean up, but she insisted guests shouldn't be tasked with cleaning. I was torn. Much as I enjoy cleaning, I was liking the feeling of being tipsy and sprawling on the couch. At the same time, I couldn't stop thinking about the mess, I hated seeing the plates covered with dried sauces and bits of food stuck like glue to the flatware. I wanted it cleaned up, and if she didn't want my help, she could at least clear away what was on the table.

Still, we talked on, and the mess eventually faded to the back of my mind.

When I yawned and stood to go, Victoria scurried off to the kitchen as if that was her cue. The water began running full force and the sound of the fridge opening and closing, cabinet doors, and plates knocking into each other filled the small apartment.

I was slightly giddy, and my muscles felt as if they were filled with pudding when I finally started toward the front door. It was after one in the morning. I was ready to crash into bed and into oblivion. At the back of my mind was a burr reminding me it wasn't a weekend. I wondered how my neighbors would be when the markets opened, and they were foggy, less sharp, and unable to make quick, confident moves with their buying and selling.

Rafe handed my bag to me, and I felt inside for my cigarettes. Despite the early morning racing toward me, I wanted to settle myself with a smoke. I returned to my apartment for a coat and hat. When I stepped out the door again, Rafe was still there.

"Going for a smoke?"

I shrugged.

"I'll join you."

It wasn't what I'd had in mind, but I didn't want to end a rather pleasant evening with an argument. And he would absolutely argue if I told him I preferred to be alone.

We settled into the chairs on the roof deck, tugging our coats tightly around us, which didn't do much to keep out the frigid air. At least there was no breeze. I lit my cigarette and handed the pack and lighter to him, shoving my other hand into my pocket.

For once, he didn't feel compelled to fill the air with his voice and his thoughts. We smoked in silence, the street below having fallen into the post-midnight quiet of a dream.

We finished and stood. I headed toward the door to the stairwell, wobbling slightly. I'd thought the cold air would sober me up. Instead, the alcohol had settled more firmly in my blood, as alcohol does, pumping into my brain, causing it to float on a gentle sea where I thought about nothing but the movements and sensations of my body.

A moment later, Rafe was behind me. He put his hand on my cheek and turned my head toward him. He began to kiss me, long and slow. My mind was filled with a loud hum, and the kiss was…pleasant. I failed to object to his mouth upon mine, thanks to an awful lot of wine and three wicked martinis.

11

Smoking is sexy. I really have no idea why we think this. I've heard it suggested that the source of this belief is film noir. In the subtler ways of the mid-twentieth century, black and white films used smoking to suggest both an invitation and the denouement to sex. In those films, women smoked while wearing elbow-length gloves, their cigarettes far from their faces in long, slim holders.

A woman smoking is confident, her own person. A woman or man who smokes in the twenty-first century is a rebel. A cigarette smoker is defying science and the entire medical community, playing Russian roulette with her life.

And that risk alone is a thrill.

Most people disagree. They find it disgusting, repulsive, something that drives them to shun another human being. And I can't argue. The smell on your breath or in your clothing, in a room or a nice car, is very unpleasant. Of course, film noir comes with sleek soundtracks and seductive visuals, but so far, there isn't an odor track layered into films.

You can watch those elegant clouds of smoke that look the same as the beautiful white clouds displayed on a daily basis.

You can watch the fancy exhales and listen to the slightly deeper voice of a smoker and think it's all so seductive. Smooth female skin and nicely painted lips, a man with a bit of stubble and tousled hair are enticing. No film has ever flashed a blackened, hardened smoker's lung, and only rarely has the camera lingered in the hospital room of an emphysema or lung or throat cancer patient. Films from the forties and fifties never show haggard, dried up husks of human beings pinching the butt of a cigarette, spewing out rough wet coughs.

Smoking is relaxing. And that's not just something sold in black and white films. It's the truth. The act of inhaling and blowing out smoke occupies the mind, it often delays the tongue from lashing out, giving the smoker a deliberate and careful demeanor.

I love smoking. I hate when I do it so often that it interferes with my running. I hate thinking about what it's doing to my body. I mostly try to believe that the limited amount of smoke I inhale is no worse than what everyone is inhaling around the clock from car emissions, and all the other gunk the human race is spewing into the air, much of it invisible. At least with cigarette smoke, I can see what I'm getting into.

I love the look of smoke moving languidly around me, the slow, gentle dissipation as the air absorbs it, like a magic trick, disappearing right before my eyes. I love the meditative focus on my breath—inhale, exhale. Anyone who has ever listened to a guided meditation soundtrack knows the rhythm of it. Inhalation…exhalation. Rest for a moment. Inhalation…exhalation.

Although it looks sexy in films, most people don't think it's at all sexy in real life. But I don't do it because I want to look sexy. Trying too hard to look hot makes you look anything but that. A little effort is fine. Subtle effort. Or at least effort that appears subtle even if there's a lot of groundwork with salon visits and cosmetics and clothing that has to come first.

Rarely do I get looks of desire when I'm smoking. I get looks of disapproval and disgust. I get looks of annoyance that often swell to anger that I would dare to pollute another's space, and self-righteous rage that I would pollute my own body. Possibly they think I'm a drain on the healthcare system, spiking costs that get spread like creamy butter across their own hospital bills and insurance premiums.

I think some men do like to watch a woman smoke. They see the defiance and the desire for risk. They know you're likely to do other risky things. They know you don't give a shit what other people think of you if you're willing to stand in an alley, ostracized and alone, drawing smoke into your body where the chemicals sit forever, slowly wreaking their havoc.

Maybe it doesn't bother me like it does most people because I don't think a lot about the future. I'm thinking about what I want and how I'm feeling in the moment that's surrounding me at any given point in time. I can't see my lungs, I don't have an ugly, phlegmy cough. There are no visible effects aside from the odor of my breath and my clothes, which I try to manage.

Smoking is alluring. It says that you have time to stand around doing nothing. Maybe that idleness suggests you're wealthy. It says you don't care, you want what you want. I've met a lot of people while standing around smoking a cigarette. It makes for easy conversation.

Sometimes I wonder if the people who say it's nasty and gross and stinks are conflicted. They know all those things, they fear the health repercussions, but inside, they want to do it too. They want something to occupy their hands, and they want to relax and let their minds drift as easily as the smoke. They wish they lived in a time when we were all ignorant of what inhaling smoke directly into our lungs would do to us.

They do see that it looks sexy, that it's a nice thing to do after making love. That it's a weapon saying—*keep your distance*. That it's a ritual and a pacifier in every good sense of that word. They want to be in a noir film, their hair impossibly glossy, their lips silky smooth, their skin flawless, wearing clothes that look as if they were stitched for their body alone, standing beside a strong, intelligent, quiet man or a smart, confident, mysterious woman. They want that odorless smoke curling around them, covering them with an aura of immortality, and for some reason I can't completely explain— money.

12

Thinking about that extra martini and kissing Rafe preoccupied me the entire next day. I'd woken after only three hours of sleep thinking about it, wondering if the desire for a cigarette had been my undoing more than the martinis.

I opened my eyes in the dark and recalled how he'd slipped icy cold fingers up my shirt, leaving a trail of goose flesh, his hand moving so fast I thought I might have to bite his tongue to stop its progress. I'd resisted that knee-jerk response and eased away from him, swinging myself around, grabbing the handle of the door, and opening it all in one dizzying pirouette. The sudden change in position caused him to stumble as if I'd literally ripped the rug out from under him. Or maybe the martinis caused him to stumble, as they had me.

When morning came, I shoved the memory out of my head and stood in the shower under an unnecessarily cold rush of water, trying to pummel my skin into something that felt less pulpy and ready for the trash heap. I deliberately turned my thoughts to Arlinda and our other clients. I thought about Trystan's desire to know me better, and all the people throughout my life who'd said I was cold and standoffish and all those other things that are supposed to be considered negative traits.

But are they?

I turned off the water, dried my hair, dragged on a nice pair of skinny jeans and a long white sweater, dashed the minimal amount of makeup across my face, and went into the kitchen to see what might settle the waves in my stomach.

The fridge contained a single boiled egg in a bowl, several cartons of yogurt, and a few slices of bacon. I also had butter and half a loaf of nine-grain bread that would make crunchy, settling toast. A single banana sat on the counter. I peeled it and ate it. Potassium was better than comfort. I drank two glasses of water and headed out the door.

The moment the elevator doors closed, carrying me up to our offices, I was assaulted with the memory of that kiss. It hadn't been bad. Kind of nice, actually. But the guy disturbed me. He wasn't someone I wanted in my life in that way, not under any circumstances. And then there was Vic—she needed to open her eyes. All his flirting with me hadn't been a game after all.

Rather, it was a different kind of game, new rules, new objectives, and all of that. Figuring out what that game might be crowded out my other thoughts.

Sitting at my desk, I gazed unseeing at the profile information and personality test results for three new clients. I re-filed old photographs into new folders, moving them around with no real purpose in mind.

I left work early. On the subway, I thought about Rafe, trying to figure out my next move.

And all the time I was thinking about him, all the time I

was trying to sort out what he might be after, there was a whisper inside of me saying it hadn't been the three martinis that made me kiss him. I'd kissed him because I was tired of their unsettling behavior, and honestly, bored with the weird dance the three of us had been doing for quite a few months.

I'd called his bluff, but I wasn't sure who had won. Normally, calling a bluff makes you the winner. In this case, I could imagine his gleeful smile. I could imagine how he would treat me in the future, and it did not suggest I was the one holding the best cards.

He hadn't said anything when I spun out of his arms and opened the door into the stairwell. He hadn't followed me down. Maybe he wanted to take advantage of the freezing night air to sober himself a bit. Maybe he wanted to get re-oriented before facing the woman he theoretically loved. But the way the two of them behaved, and considering the stories I'd heard from my neighbor, Kent, it might all have been planned. I hadn't called Rafe's bluff at all, I'd stepped right beneath whatever noose they wanted to lower over my head.

I climbed the steps out of the subway tunnel and faced the onslaught of cold wind. I huddled inside my coat and tugged my hat down, so it covered the lower part of my ears. I walked quickly, dodging other pedestrians.

Because I was so busy making my way along sidewalks that were crowded despite the chill and descending darkness, I wasn't prepared to talk to Victoria. Yet there she was, standing at the railing, looking down into the lobby when I entered the building. I had the few moments it took to climb the stairs to think about how things might go.

As my foot touched the top step, she grinned. "How's the hangover?"

Did she not know? Or did she not care?

I can easily kiss or have sex with any man that interests me at any moment, but most people aren't like that. Most people in a relationship have expectations and feelings and even rules about their interactions with other people. Most of them have tender feelings that are horribly bruised if those boundaries are crossed.

"I don't usually get hangovers" I tugged off my hat and stuffed it into my coat pocket.

"Lucky you. I couldn't get out of bed. And I didn't, not until like ten-thirty."

"So, you just blew off work for the day?"

"That's the beauty of being your own boss."

"I think if I were my own boss, I'd be irritated at myself for slacking off when there was money to be made."

She laughed. "I don't believe that."

I smiled. I unbuttoned my coat and rested my forearm on the railing, turning to face her. "Did Rafe have a hangover?"

She shrugged.

"You didn't talk to him?"

"No."

"All day? How is that possible in a tiny apartment, working at the same desk?"

"Nothing to talk about."

I kept my eyes on her face. "He and I had a cigarette. On the roof."

She stared at me. I couldn't tell if that was news, or if she was waiting for the rest of the story, or she was disinterested. I felt she was winning, but I had to know. "Did he tell you that?"

"What if he did?"

"You two have an unusual relationship."

She smiled. "Yes. I think I told you we do."

Had she? I wasn't really sure. But since I'd observed it for so long, it wasn't as if I needed her to give me that piece of information.

"You seem nervous," she said.

"No."

"Then why are you staring at me like that?"

"I didn't think I was staring."

"You haven't blinked in like ten minutes."

I rolled my eyes at the exaggeration. I blinked.

"You look like you have something on your mind, something you want to say."

"Why do you think that?"

"You play a lot of conversational games," she said.

"Do I?"

"So, what do you want to say?"

"Nothing."

"I thought the same thing last night, you know."

"Thought what?"

"That you wanted to say something. Have you changed your mind about the day trading?" Her face lit up at this possibility, her cheeks sprouting bright red spots over the bones, her eyes shining as if they were filling with tears.

I laughed. "You can't let that go. Why is my decision so important to you?"

"Because it's obvious that you want money."

I stared into her eyes, stared deep into her, stared until she took a step back.

"It's obvious from the way you talk about your clients. I can tell you're jealous of us and you—"

"I'm not a jealous person."

"You want what your clients have. Money. And lots of it."

"Doesn't everyone?"

"Not really."

I considered whether this was true. She was probably right, only because most people wouldn't do the things required to acquire large sums of money, which might suggest they don't truly want it.

"You should at least let me show you what it's like, how easy it is. And fun. It's a game. It's not like you have to make some kind of commitment. This isn't a pyramid scheme."

"I never thought it was."

"Okay. I shouldn't have said that. But let me show you."

"I work when the stock market is open. I'm not sure I could manage."

"Call in sick."

Why not? Wouldn't a day without facing the bitter cold and slick sidewalks, as well as the germs swimming in the stifling air of the subway, covering the handrails, and spewing out of noses and mouths be pleasant? A few hours of freedom? "Yes, I think I will."

She clapped her hands. I expected her to start jumping, adding the enthusiasm of her entire body to the hand clapping.

We agreed I'd come to her apartment at five-thirty Monday morning. In a few hours, I had an appointment to photograph Arlinda at a dinner party in her home, so I wouldn't even need to call in sick after the weekend. I'd mention it to Trystan as comp time.

I was strangely excited about learning how to buy and sell stocks. It never hurts to learn new things.

13

I was eager to see the rest of Arlinda's penthouse.

The place did not disappoint me.

Because I arrived forty-five minutes before her six guests, telling her that would allow plenty of time to get my equipment arranged, which took no time at all, she offered to give me a tour. I followed her through a sleek, high-tech kitchen, five bedrooms, six bathrooms, a formal living room and dining room, a study, an entertainment room, and a fully equipped yoga studio and weight room, the two spaces divided by a sheer white curtain. The *apartment* was larger than most houses and didn't feel like an apartment at all.

She chattered the whole time as if we were well-acquainted girlfriends, not client and photographer. My work meant to capture all her flaws while she ate and talked with her senior staff over a dinner prepared by a part-time chef. He only worked for her when she gave parties, and not even always then, because Arlinda adored cooking. It satisfied her soul, she said.

"I'm not one of those people who has a fancy kitchen just for show. Time disappears when I'm preparing a meal, even if it's just for myself. I love the combination of freedom and precision that comes from experimenting while still following a recipe."

She continued to talk about cooking, how she'd done it as a child, how it was something that never got old, how going to a market to choose fresh fish and high-quality meat, filling a basket with good produce was the highlight of her week. Cooking, she said, was almost as good as sex. When I laughed at her analogy, she didn't smile.

By the end of her speech, I almost wanted to take up cooking. She did indeed make it sound seductive. As I followed her through the other rooms, drinking in their tranquil and satisfying color schemes, the well-designed, comfortable furniture, and very clearly feng shui-d arrangements of art and objects and furnishings, I thought about food.

As someone who devours and relishes food, why didn't I like purchasing the ingredients and preparing a nice meal? Why was a restaurant almost always my first choice? It might be laziness. It might be a simple lack of experience. Possibly it was influenced by my mother's cooking, which she treated like a religious ritual. I suddenly saw my mother in a new light. I understood why she treated meal preparation with such reverence, since Arlinda had a touch of that as well. But my mother's brand of religion and the labeling of fancy food as borderline sinful might have turned me away from standing near a cooktop or seeing myself in her apron.

"I know the apartment is enormous for just two people," Arlinda said. "But I like to have space to breathe and think. I don't like feeling crowded."

"I can understand that."

"Even in my head."

I looked at her, but she didn't meet my eyes. I understood that desire even more than her desire to sink into food preparation, but nothing needed to be said.

She rested her fingers on my arm. Her short, unpolished nails made her seem like an average, easy-going woman, not someone who had launched a multi-million dollar advertising empire.

Finally, we settled in her living room. It was huge but didn't feel stiff or overpowering, even with the white leather sectional large enough to seat eight people and the glossy white grand piano—not a baby grand, but the whole nine yards. Windows lined one wall, narrow and covered with pale yellow drapes. There were touches of yellow throughout the room. It was a color I would never have considered for any kind of décor beyond a washed-out paint for the walls, but it made the room light and cool in a pleasant, not bitterly cold, way.

I had the camera set on the tripod for photographing her while she talked about the purpose of the dinner and told me a bit about the guests. During the meal itself, I would move around the room, keeping myself in the background. I'd worn a cream dress and camel-colored boots to help me blend with the creamy paint on the walls. Since the dining room had double doors leading from the living room, it would be simple to get a fair number of photographs from the other room where I'd be virtually unnoticed.

While I pressed the shutter release, taking close-ups of her face, she explained that this was a kick-off for their annual planning. She'd invited the six people who reported directly to her. They would discuss what had gone well the previous year and what needed improvement—everything from client relationships to employee satisfaction to upping their design game.

Talking about her agency transported her mind to another realm, and there was no longer a flicker of self-consciousness on her face regarding the oversized camera lens staring at her. The rapid click of the shutter was a steady backdrop to her words, like rain tapping the windows during a quiet dinner.

I took far too many pictures, as I had when I first met her, captivated again by her presence. The artfully created streaks of blond and bronze hair glimmered in the muted light. The electric blue sheath dress and identical blue high heels were stunning against all the white furniture.

When the bell chimed, announcing the arrival of all the guests en masse, I settled into a chair near one of the windows. She'd explained earlier that a limo had picked up her employees and brought them all to her building, whetting their appetites with sparkling wine on the drive over.

As her guests entered the living room, Arlinda introduced them, rattling off their names so quickly, I knew I wouldn't remember. But I didn't have to remember their names. I had eyes only for Arlinda, and I kept all my thoughts on her. She mingled with her guests while they nibbled appetizers, then led them to the dining room. I captured her smiling, frowning, laughing, holding a glass to her lips, and placing food on her tongue. I took pictures of her standing, then taking an aloof position in her chair. She leaned across the table to listen more intently to her vice president of new client acquisitions make a point about being more aggressive, and I snapped several more.

Their voices flowed around me, painting a world I knew

nothing about, but which sounded fascinating. All things interest me, and it seems that no matter what possible career crosses my path, I find myself thinking it might be something worth experimenting with. Obviously, when these desires strike, I immediately recognize that I'm not qualified for most positions. There are areas of life where you can bluff, where confidence takes you a long way—social media or photography come to mind. But once things get technical and require study or education, bluffing isn't a viable option.

Still, I wondered what kinds of positions were available at her agency that might fit my eclectic mix of skills. A job that paid more than I was making now. At the same time, balancing my income against the pure pleasure of capturing expression and gestures that people didn't expect, the thrill of discovering that sliver of a moment when they let their guard down and I could show something remarkable—it would take quite a bit to lure me away from that.

When the main course was cleared away, and cups of espresso were carried into the room prior to dessert, I packed my camera into the bag. I was overloaded with pictures of Arlinda. Taking more would make Diana's job more difficult.

Yes, there are a thousand, a million expressions to be captured on the face of any human being, but Diana had to find some kind of focus and theme. Inundating her was not helpful. She'd mentioned this several times. I already knew she'd be bringing it up again when she received all the images of Arlinda.

I stood just outside the dining room doors, sipping a glass of water, listening to them talk. Conversation had moved away from business and onto a rather lively discussion of ex-lovers. All of them flushed with wine, they talked over each other, laughing at their breakups—painful at the time and now fodder for dreadful stories. They joked about the profoundly disturbing idiosyncrasies of their exes, the bad habits, and the all-too-common need to control. They recalled failures in bed and the unbearable obsessions that had seemed enjoyable at first and grew tiresome and unacceptable and sometimes downright terrifying when the rest of the relationship deteriorated.

Cherry, the woman who headed up the HR department, grabbed Arlinda's wrist. She hooted and threw her head back, nearly tipping over her chair in the process. "I remember that guy you were with when you started the agency."

Arlinda's expression hardened so fast it looked as if her features had been poured like quick-drying plaster into a mold.

This was new. I longed for my camera. Why had I removed the lens, packed it away, and left myself with my arms dangling uselessly by my side? The most telling expression of the evening was slashed across Arlinda's face.

"Showing up at work, getting down on his knees and wrapping his arms around your legs." Cherry laughed harder. "Such adoration. And so degrading. What made him think anyone would want a guy with so little self-respect he cried in public and begged you to be his wife?"

Arlinda pushed her chair away from the table. "That's enough, Cherry."

Cherry laughed. "It was ages ago. Surely you can laugh about it after all this time."

"If you want to talk about ex-lovers, stick to your own stories."

Cherry pinched her lips into a tight bud, widening her pale

blue eyes that were fringed in such thick, dark mascara, they looked like some kind of sea creature. "So sensitive. You're always so sensitive. You were happy to laugh at everyone else's disasters, but yours are off-limits? We mustn't ever forget who's in charge, right?" She smiled. "Probably not what I should be saying. I'm talking too much. Too much lovely wine. But I feel like telling the truth, for once. After all, aren't we here to hash out what needs to change? How can we improve if we have to walk on eggshells?"

I stepped back into the living room and grabbed my bag. I slid my phone into the pocket of my dress and returned to the doorway, keeping myself mostly out of sight.

Arlinda glared at Cherry, her lips tight and drained of color. Across her forehead, just below her hairline, was a thin sheen of perspiration. "My personal life has nothing to do with the future of the agency."

"But this isn't about your personal life. It's about you as a person."

Arlinda stood. I pulled out my phone and snapped a picture. As if I sensed what was coming, I slid my thumb across the screen and tapped to start filming.

Arlinda picked up her half-full glass of red wine and tossed the contents at Cherry. The wine arched gracefully through the air and landed on the front of Cherry's silky white top. Cherry looked down. She studied the stain and slowly raised her head. "You'll pay for cleaning this up."

Arlinda walked past me and disappeared through a side door into the hallway. Her guests silently picked up their coffee cups. As the dessert plates were carried into the room, every single one of them looked nauseated. Nauseated and filled with a longing to escape.

14

Trystan was not in the habit of requiring work on the weekends. Occasionally our clients requested weekend meetings, but as much as possible, he handled those himself. When he suggested he and I meet for a drink on Saturday at five, I knew updating him on the results of Arlinda's photography session was a smokescreen. He was as dogged as I am, and he was not going to let our two aborted conversations about my standoffishness die a natural death.

I'd thought a lot about the things he'd said, but I still couldn't figure out what he was after.

We sat across from each other in a room that was so dark most of the light came from the shimmer of streetlights refracted by the rain outside. The glow turned the window beside our table into a rectangle of light that shone on our cocktail glasses and the stone slab filled with cheese, grapes, flatbread, and candied walnuts.

Trystan was drinking something frothy that I'd already forgotten the name of. In front of me was a martini with three olives, one of which I'd already eaten. I smeared blue cheese over a piece of flatbread and ate it. He did the same.

All we'd talked about so far was the weather. We'd managed to stretch that topic from the moment I sat across from him all the way through the ordering of our drinks and the cheese board and their arrival. I wanted to laugh that we'd managed to find so many things to say about rain and New York City, the forecast for snow and the temperature, traffic problems, and winter clothing.

Now we sat in silence.

He stirred his drink. "How is your weekend going?"

"Good."

"Any plans for later this evening?"

"No."

"Young, single, living in New York City, and you have no plans for Saturday night?"

"I like to see how things unfold."

He gave me a look that made me think he'd interpreted my words to mean we might be spending the entire evening together. His look of shock turned nervous, worried that meeting for drinks had communicated something he hadn't intended. He picked up his drink and swallowed some, his Adam's apple straining over the icy cold slush. He recovered quickly. "How did last night go?"

"It went well."

"More details, please."

"I took too many photographs. She's very photogenic."

"But of course, that's not the point," he said.

"Of course." I knifed off a large wedge of brie and spread it across a small piece of flatbread. I sipped my drink before I ate it.

"This is what I was referring to," he said.

"What?"

"I'm trying to discuss our client, and you're acting as if her behavior and the results of the photography session are a state secret."

"I thought you wanted me to talk more about myself?"

"That was a general statement. You tend to be closed off in a lot of ways."

"I'm really not. I just think it's wiser to not splatter your thoughts all over everyone else."

"What are you afraid of?"

"I'm not afraid of anything."

"Then why is it wise to keep things to yourself?"

"Why do you think?"

"I think that belief is typical when someone is afraid—of betrayal, of being hurt."

I laughed.

"This is a serious conversation."

"We're off track, don't you think? You wanted to know about last night."

"I also want to know about you. I want a warm, supportive team environment, and there's been some tension the past few months. Since you came on board, to be honest."

"I can't say anything about that because I don't know what it was like before I joined. But I can tell you I'm not tense at all."

"Perhaps you're making others on the team tense."

"Are you tense?"

"No, but I wasn't—"

"Diana doesn't have a tense bone in her body."

"True."

"So this is about Stephanie, not about me at all."

"I didn't say that. I asked you about a meeting with a client, and I expect a report, not one-word answers."

"I can give you all the details."

"Please do."

I gave him a rundown of the evening, leaving out the grand finale. He didn't comment. He nibbled grapes and sipped his drink.

When I was finished, he leaned forward, clasping his hands and resting them on the table. "Thank you. To my earlier point, I also don't expect you to be secretive about the rest of your life."

"I don't think employers have a right to know all about their employees' personal lives."

"There's a big difference between knowing *all* about your life and knowing absolutely nothing. Our whole reason for being, our sole purpose is to assist our clients in becoming their best selves. Part of that is open, honest interaction with other human beings. It's critical that we trust each other, that there's harmony so our clients can focus on their needs, not pick up a negative vibe from our internal politics."

I nodded. I ate an olive. He'd been talking in circles since the moment he first said I was too closed off.

I would never reveal the things he wanted to know. Settling back against the chair, I turned my gaze toward the bar, giving him a rather sketchy, untrustworthy vibe with my refusal to meet his eyes.

"I trust you." I turned back, smiling. "I trust the others on our team." This was a bold-faced lie. I didn't trust Stephanie at all. But as much as I trust anyone, whatever that word even means, I suppose it was truthful to say I trusted Diana. And Trystan, to some extent.

The problem is, trust means putting your well-being into

the hands of another person. I don't do that. Not with anyone. Trust means you believe you're intimately familiar with the character of another person. My beliefs are more along the lines of—you never know what someone else might do, especially given the right circumstances. So how can you really trust anyone ever if you know without a doubt that human beings are utterly unpredictable?

Trystan gave me a look that said he didn't trust me either. Not when it came to telling the truth. "We would enjoy our work more, the environment would be more satisfying if we had closer relationships."

"I enjoy my work quite a lot."

"Are you sure the others do?"

"That's not my problem. If someone doesn't like what they're doing, they should find a new job."

"That's harsh."

"See, you're getting to know me better."

He laughed, but he didn't look at all happy. "Is there a reason you prefer to keep yourself separate?"

It occurred to me, as if I were a clueless sixteen-year-old just waking up, that he might be hitting on me. Why hadn't I considered that before? He had a very warm way with women, but especially with me. There was nothing flirty about his behavior, and I'd never felt him standing too close or staring at me, but these questions, this sudden interest in my personal life was bizarre. There was something else behind it.

"Business is business," I said. "I can enjoy the company of other people without telling my life story."

"Maybe people want to know your life story. To understand you better."

"Doubtful."

"Why do you say that? Most people are interested in knowing the people around them."

"You get to know people by listening to them talk about the here and now, by observing what they do. More people should try it. You learn a lot more than you do by listening to stories of the past that are revised and polished to make someone look good."

He ate some cheese and took a sip of his drink.

I felt I'd finally forced him into a corner where he had to give up or else risk coming across like a bit of a creep. He chose to give up because he took two more sips of his drink and picked up his phone to check the time.

I'd been thinking all day about whether it was my job to mention the altercation at the end of Arlinda's dinner party. It felt strangely private—as if I'd been invited to join an intimate gathering where I was an invisible presence, a non-entity. I wondered how Arlinda would feel about me breaking that anonymity that was supposed to surround my photography sessions. Would she see me as someone she couldn't relax with? Would she put up barriers that made her photographs less useful and therefore, my role less important? Only if Trystan told her what I said, breaking my trust as it were.

At the same time, she was not at all secretive or reluctant to say what was on her mind. Blunt and open. But she'd been clearly unhappy with someone talking about a private moment in her past. Still...I was there doing a job. And Trystan was supposed to coach her to the heights of success and personal satisfaction. Didn't he need to know everything we could possibly learn about her?

"Something interesting happened," I said.

"What's that?"

"Last night…" I glanced across the room again, checking my final decision in my mind.

He took a long sip of his drink, then set it down out of his line of sight.

When I looked back, he held my gaze and waited.

15

It felt like we slipped out of time as Trystan looked at me. His eyes told me nothing. His mouth, a faint shadow at the edge of my vision as I stared into his dark brown, almost black eyes, took on the shape of something much more personal.

I described the scene I'd witnessed in Arlinda's dining room. Admittedly, I added some dramatic flair. I might have even described the expression on her face as one of intense betrayal rather than the slightly more objective description of clenched lips and the hardness in her eyes.

It seemed important to embellish the story. Often, if you don't witness something yourself, it's hard to pick up on the intensity, the incredible drama of it all, when another person describes a situation. Without the accompanying silence of the other unsettled guests, the shattered calm, the sudden sobering that seemed to flood the room, someone who wasn't there wouldn't understand how shocking it was. Without feeling the heat coming off Arlinda, smelling her rage, and seeing the sudden lack of concern for her fate that overcame Cherry, recounting the event would have fallen on the ground with all the energy of a rotten peach.

Trystan moved his drink back to its place directly in front of him. He touched the sides of the glass but didn't raise it to his lips. He almost seemed unaware of what it was. His hair and eyes looked equally black in the dim light of the bar. Against the lightly tanned skin of his neck and face, not yet fading after his winter vacation in Florida, and his crisp white shirt, open at the neck, he looked like he was ready for a photoshoot himself—the cover of GQ.

As I studied him and thought about his pleasing physical appearance, I wondered why I'd never been attracted to him. Possibly because I'd been so wrapped up with Gavin when I first met Trystan. Or possibly because I saw him as Tess's friend, nothing but a ticket to a better job. I didn't want to disrupt my interesting job until I was bored with it, or something else very nice landed in my lap. Being attracted to him was not something I should even allow to pass through my mind until that time came.

Still, the practical side of things rarely keeps my body from taking on a mind of its own, from longing for a good-looking man who's interesting and a little mysterious—shut off might be a good way to describe it. But even having these thoughts, even with my current unattached status, I felt nothing stirring inside. It was a good thing…still, surprising. "I wondered whether I should keep what happened to myself." I paused for a moment. "Since I was there in a position of trust…" I let my voice trail off and smiled.

He didn't seem to make the connection to our discussion of trust.

He said nothing.

"But if it helps with your assessment of her," I said. "If it gives you a topic to explore with her, I thought you might want to know."

He still said nothing.

I sipped my drink and waited. The silence stretched, and the sounds of the people around us, drinking and laughing, shouting to be heard above the music, filled the space and seemed to wrap itself around the two of us.

Finally, he spoke. "I'm not sure what I'm supposed to do with that."

"It allows you to see another side of her. That's all."

"What side is that?"

I sipped my drink and ate the two remaining olives. I was tired of the conversation and tired of him. Maybe that's why I'd never been attracted. He could be quite dull at times. I remembered what Tess had told me about him, his insistence that he had no weak areas except that he wasn't very good at golf. As if that were unique. A character flaw.

"She comes across as very open and blunt and what-you-see-is-what-you-get," I said. "But she's not."

"I don't think you can conclude that, based on what you described."

"She obviously was okay with other people talking about their exes, but it was off-limits for her. And it sounded like there's history. Cherry implied Arlinda's double standard could be an issue at the company."

"You're way off base."

I shrugged. "I just thought I'd mention it."

"Are you trying to undermine my opinion of her?"

"Why would I do that?"

"I'm not sure. That's what I'm trying to figure out."

I downed the rest of my drink. "Am I excused?"

He looked shocked at what I'm sure he saw as rudeness and insubordination. "I'm getting a very negative vibe from you," he said.

I wanted to laugh but decided I'd pushed it far enough. I did love probing people's secrets with my camera. "I'm just confused." I offered him a polite smile.

The server stopped beside our table. "Another round?"

"No thanks," I said.

Trystan gave her a single undetermined movement of his head, which didn't communicate anything, but she read the mood and left quickly. He pushed his drink close to the edge of the table and folded his arms across his chest. "What's going on with you?"

"Nothing."

"Describing that incident with Arlinda sounded catty."

"That's not how I meant it. But if you think it's irrelevant, I won't mention it again."

"It feels like you're trying to tarnish her in my eyes."

I laughed. "Really?"

He maintained his serious expression.

"I'm ready to get going," I said. "I don't think we're having a very productive conversation."

"Agreed." He didn't move, didn't uncross his arms.

The server returned with the bill and placed it near Trystan without saying anything.

I grabbed the black folder.

"I've got this," he said.

"No. I do." I slid my hand into my bag and pulled out my wallet. Still clutching the folder, holding it out of his reach, I managed to remove some cash from my wallet and place it inside the folder.

"Be sure to expense that," he said.

I put the folder on the edge of the table, the corner of a twenty sticking out.

"I don't like you paying," he said.

"Maybe it's better we forget about the past hour. No receipt. No expense report."

"I hope you'll tell me if there's anything going on with you. I like having you on the team. I enjoy working with you. You're a great asset to the company."

"Thank you. And I like working with you." I slid out of the booth. I picked up my coat and bag and walked away, feeling his eyes watching me leave.

I hadn't lied about one thing—I *was* confused.

16

Portland, Oregon

I drove to the store and picked up eggs for my mother. I drove to the church to drop off three boxes of peanut butter cookies she'd made for a bake sale. I drove myself to the dentist and back home. I did lots of driving with my temporary license folded inside my purse. None of the destinations were fun, but I did like driving, and I liked doing it without my father snapping orders in my right ear.

Finally, the official plastic driver's license arrived with my photograph gleaming on the front.

During all the time I'd waited for the real thing, my father had said nothing about buying me a used car. I couldn't figure out whether he'd forgotten about my request, had decided girls shouldn't have cars, which would not be surprising, or was stalling to see what I did about the situation. I also would not put that past him.

Sometimes, when my father and I were in one of our battles, I wondered if he actually liked our fights. My mother never argued with him. My brothers mostly worked around him, ignored him as much as they could, tried to appease him in most areas, so they'd have better odds winning more important battles. My brothers thought I wasted a lot of time and energy trying to get the upper hand with our dad.

Being the unquestioned chief of your kingdom had to get old after a while, issuing dictates and not getting any pushback. It would start to feel like you were working with robots. I didn't think my father liked robots, and for that reason, maybe he relished these power struggles with me. Maybe he was disappointed when I dropped things and followed my brothers' example. My father wanted my obedience in the end, but I don't think he minded taking awhile to get there.

Not that my mother was robotic. She was just an easy-going person and thought it was her god-ordained purpose to go along with my father. She didn't do that in a weary, put-upon way. She genuinely agreed with his beliefs. She didn't dispute his view of the world. I think she liked being relieved of the burden of making difficult decisions. Besides, she was interested in other things—the garden, reading historical novels and biographies, going to her book club to discuss all of this. She liked cooking and doing things for her kids. She didn't need to be in charge. And every so often, she quietly wondered whether the Bible was sometimes confusing or contradictory. She was also happy enough that my father seemed certain about what that book said and what it meant.

My father was washing the car when I approached him. The hose dangled from his hand, the attachment removed so that water flowed gently out of the nozzle as he lovingly rinsed soap off the hood and front fenders. I took the large sponge out of the bucket and began soaping the back. There was never a need for genuine scrubbing with his car because he washed and dried it by hand once a week. Grime didn't accumulate that fast.

Because of my somewhat unusual propensity for cleaning, I sometimes gazed with envy at our neighbors' grimy cars, longing to drag a sponge back and forth across the metal, wiping it clean and seeing a remarkable difference for my effort.

"Don't get too carried away there," my father said. "I'm rinsing as I go because I don't want soap sitting on the paint for more than a minute or two."

It was quite clear to me that he was rinsing as he went. That's how he always did it, and that was clearly his method now, but I wasn't going to point that out and start an argument before we reached the main battleground.

"I've had my license for seven weeks now," I said.

He nodded and moved the hose to the side of the car, letting water flow over a spot he'd missed on the fender.

"You were going to think more about when I'm getting a car."

"Was I?"

Standing outside his line of sight, I gave him a snarly look. It was impossible to believe he didn't remember. Of course he remembered. So I'd been right—he did enjoy the sparring. It was the same as the dirt-encrusted car—the more you can see the results of your efforts, the more satisfying it is. When he had to verbally wrestle me into submission, he believed he was doing his job. He was shaping a child into the creature god desired. One who never talked back, one who followed directives out of the fear of hell rather than her own belief system. A daughter who was passive but smart, although those traits rarely come in a single package.

Maybe he hadn't said he would think about buying me a car. I honestly couldn't remember. I hadn't intended to lie about it, but if he hadn't said it, he should have, and in my mind, that counted as saying it. "The boys—"

"Let me stop you right there. The boys have nothing to do with you having a car."

"It's not fair that they got one, and I don't. And I already know that life isn't fair, so you don't have to explain that to me."

"Watch your tongue."

I dropped the sponge into the bucket. Soapy water splattered across my jeans, and a small cluster of bubbles landed on the side of the car. I wiped it with my hand.

"Please wash that spot and rinse it." He handed the hose to me.

"I wiped it off."

"You left grease from your fingers."

"My fingers aren't greasy."

"Human skin has oil in it. You know that. You might not be able to see it, but it's there. It's just like greed. You might not see the grease on the car right away, but it will show itself as something ugly soon enough."

His analogy missed the mark, but I had to keep my attention on what I wanted. I needed a car if I was going to have any freedom during my last year of high school. And it was absolutely unfair, even if life was unfair, for the boys to get cars while I was stuck running errands for my mother. Unfairness comes from the world at large, but this unfairness was completely under my father's control. He acted as if it had nothing to do with him. One way or another, he'd acquired used cars for all three of my brothers.

As water dribbled out of the hose, washing off the soap where I'd scrubbed away my oily fingerprints, I tried to think of a new strategy. I should have worked it through before I spoke to him. I knew better than anyone that complaining about unfairness went nowhere with him. I'd heard that lecture all my life, and here I was complaining about unfairness when all that did was cement him in his position.

He stood watching me rinse, saying nothing. I could feel that any minute he was going to remind me not to waste water, but so far, all he'd done was stare at the spot I was cleaning.

"What do I need to do to get a car?"

"A car is a big responsibility."

"I know that."

"And it's not to be used for selfish purposes. We're servants of others. Your brothers helped your mother a lot. Maybe you weren't paying attention to that aspect. They ran errands, drove you to school, and helped drive people to church who were too old or incapacitated to drive themselves. They drove children to Sunday School, whose parents weren't believers. They were of service."

"Okay."

"Knowing you as I do, I'm not convinced you would use a car for God's purposes."

Once again, I was backed into a corner. He had a point. I wasn't thinking about driving other people around, picking up children who were lured by snacks and art projects, and playing with other kids before the lessons of our church were imprinted on their malleable brains.

I wanted to drive myself far away from church as fast as I could.

"You have nothing to say?" he asked. "Usually, you're talking before I can get the words out of my mouth."

I couldn't say a word because he was right, and I was losing the battle. I did not want to become a chauffeur for Pure Truth Tabernacle. Even if it meant I would never sit behind the steering wheel of my own car until I left home.

"I could earn money for it."

He took the hose out of my hand. "That's enough."

I wasn't sure if he meant rinsing the car, our conversation, or both.

"At least you're truthful. I've always appreciated that about you, even if I fear for your soul. I have no objection to you earning money. You can do extra chores around the house. You could babysit. Most girls your age are eager to take care of small children."

I held his gaze. I was not eager, and he already knew that.

He sighed. "So, yes. If you want to earn money for a car, I'm not going to stop you. As long as you keep your grades at the level your mother and I expect."

That was a no-brainer for me. Schoolwork was easy. "So you won't help me at all? The boys got cars, and I don't because I'm a girl."

"That's not the reason. It's because you have a contrary heart."

I think he believed I might repent in the hopes of getting a car. At the same time, as he'd said, he knew me too well. That was never going to happen, and I needed to figure out how to make some cash. A lot of cash in a short amount of time.

17

New York

The moment the idea came to her, Stephanie knew it wasn't a good one. She should dismiss it immediately, but it wouldn't let go of her. It floated through her thoughts in the middle of Pastor Mike's sermon. It lodged in her brain and blocked out everything he had to say about the fifth chapter of the book of Ephesians. It lingered through the offering collection and the final songs.

As she walked down the side aisle and out the back of the building to the narrow concrete steps where Pastor Mike stood greeting each member of his flock, taking a moment to make genuine eye contact, the idea pressed so deeply she felt a headache coming on.

She walked down the remaining steps of the former market where the Church at the Heart of the City held Sunday services, mid-week Bible studies, prayer circles, community dinners, and served the homeless large cups of soup and rolls on Sunday evenings.

The idea sparked at the base of her skull—the dinosaur

brain, some would say—had quickly become a compulsion. An obsession. Something that made her seem small and petty and was decidedly ungodly, but she could not *stop* turning it around in her mind.

Who would know? It would be her secret. Something to confess in prayer later, but the doing of it wouldn't hurt a soul.

She was going to walk by Alexandra's apartment and see if she could find out what that woman was up to on a Sunday morning. For all she knew, she'd see Eileen and Alex together, heading out to brunch. At the same time, maybe that's why the idea didn't seem too terrible. The chances of catching Alex coming or going from her building on an icy cold Sunday morning were slim to nonexistent. And that's where the compulsion came in—despite the low odds, she didn't think she'd be able to relax at home if she didn't make the effort.

It had happened before. That time, it hadn't been deliberate. On the spur of the moment, it had seemed less shameful. She knew where Alex lived because she'd followed her to the subway after work, settled into the car behind Alex's, and then watched her get off the train, following at a distance up the stairs and onto West Fiftieth and up one block to her apartment building. Twice.

She hurried away from the church steps.

She rode the subway with her mind in a blank state, her Bible stuffed into her oversized bag so it wouldn't taunt her about what she was doing. There wasn't really anything wrong with observing Alex's apartment. Where did it say in the Bible that you couldn't take notice of another person's life? In fact, there were a lot of directives that seemed to imply the opposite. A Godly woman needed to watch out for her enemies, for the wicked. They waited around every corner to bring her down.

West Fifty-first Street was quiet on a Sunday morning. There was very little traffic, making it feel almost desolate. Adding to that sensation were the small trees planted along the curb, all of them without a single leaf. The sickly gray color of their bark made them seem close to death.

A few pedestrians were scattered along the sidewalk on both sides of the street. They carried takeout coffees and bags of pastries. One guy wearing a plaid flannel shirt as a jacket and a blue beanie the color of his shirt was clutching a burger bag with both gloved hands, already wanting lunch even though it was only eleven-twenty.

As she should have expected, the door to Alex's building was closed.

Stephanie stopped a few buildings away and leaned against one of the sad little trees. She pulled her scarf more tightly around her neck and pushed her hands deep into the pockets of her coat.

Maybe her subconscious mind had known this idea would come to her, because she'd dressed for extra warmth that morning, pulling on a turtleneck with a thick wool sweater over it. She'd worn her lined leather gloves that were too thick to wear when she had to use her hands for anything more than grabbing a railing or a subway pole. Normally she chose the thinner ones that allowed her hands to carry out simple tasks such as taking cash from an ATM or buying a cup of coffee.

Her clothing kept her warm and the adrenaline of hoping to see something, anything, that would help her get the upper hand with Alex raced through her, making time pass quickly. She stood there for close to an hour and a half before she was rewarded.

The door to the building opened, and Alex stepped outside. She wore black leggings and expensive-looking black leather boots that covered her knees. Her coat was also black and came to the middle of her thighs. She wasn't wearing a hat or gloves, and she'd left the coat partially unbuttoned. Stephanie shivered violently, imagining the cold snaking inside the coat, gripping her hands and ears, piercing those leggings, no matter how thick they were.

While Alex stood with her attention fixed on something across the street, Stephanie moved off the sidewalk into a recessed doorway. It would be easy enough to duck inside if Alex headed in her direction.

After a few minutes of staring at the opposite side of the street, Alex sat on the top step and pulled something out of her pocket. She put a cigarette between her lips, snapped a lighter, and inhaled when the flame caught the paper and tobacco.

Stephanie gasped. It was too cold to sit on a concrete step and smoke a cigarette. Alex must be freezing, yet she looked completely relaxed, unfazed by the temperature. Stephanie watched, transfixed as Alex pulled smoke out of the cigarette and held it inside. She exhaled with languid grace as if it were the most pleasing substance in the world that she was easing along her throat, drawing into her lungs.

It was remarkable that she managed to make such a filthy, deadly habit look enticing. She looked content. She looked as if nothing in the world was troubling her, and maybe that was the case. Alex was always calm, smiled easily, even when the smile didn't come anywhere close to her eyes, even though her smiles often appeared at inappropriate times.

Anyone would be fascinated by her. Trystan clearly was. And Diana. And Eileen.

Tears filled Stephanie's eyes. She yanked off one of her gloves, freeing her fingers to wipe the tears away. Worse than the situation at work, the impossible situation in which she felt her career was walled in by brick and mortar that stood in a twelve-foot high circle around her, was Eileen.

It became clear to her, watching Alex, that Eileen did not respect her mother. Even though Stephanie shouldn't be comparing herself to a girl closer in age to her daughter, she couldn't help herself. The fact that Stephanie and Alex worked side-by-side made Alex seem like someone that Eileen might look at through the same lens as she did her mother.

In that lens, Stephanie would come up short. Her daughter had never admired her. Instead, she saw a woman who had no courage, no flair. She was limp and weak and drab. Her clothes were unremarkable, alongside her hair and minimalist approach to makeup, when she bothered at all.

She'd never done anything bold or outrageous. She was a victim, abandoned by Eileen's father, her whole world encapsulated in their small apartment and the tiny church where she spent too many evenings and weekends. Her job wasn't a fascinating career. She was an administrative assistant with a few extra responsibilities.

Maybe she'd misinterpreted the Bible. Just because women were supposed to be submissive didn't mean she couldn't have personality. Just because you weren't supposed to over-emphasize the importance of your physical appearance, didn't mean it wasn't important at all. Pastor Mike's wife was loud and opinionated, she wore bright red clothing and carried outrageously large purses.

What would Eileen say if Stephanie changed the type of clothes she wore? Stephanie still purchased clothes as if she was a single mother scrimping to raise a child on her own. She had plenty of cushion now. It didn't have to be this way.

What would Eileen say if Stephanie went out more? Although where that would be, she had no idea. What would Eileen think of her if she looked for a new job? Craziest of all, what would Eileen say if Stephanie took up smoking? It did look relaxing. And it didn't have to be done to the point of causing cancer. An occasional cigarette couldn't hurt, Alex proved that.

18

Victoria offered me coffee and a hard-boiled egg when I arrived at her apartment at five-thirty in the morning. She said a light breakfast of solid protein was important for staying on my toes while I followed the wild ride of the stock market.

I asked for Tabasco sauce for the egg. She didn't have any. She did have some homemade salsa, so I dipped my paltry egg in a small dish of that and ate it standing near her dining room table. She did the same, although she didn't eat the salsa.

Watching her eat that egg felt like watching an enormous lizard devouring the egg of its prey. Her eyes glittered, and her fingers pinched the rubbery white like they were claws. I had to look away before she got to the yolk.

Rafe wasn't home. I wondered where he'd taken himself to in the early dark hours of a Monday, but I didn't ask, and she didn't volunteer the information.

We settled into the side-by-side ergonomic chairs. Victoria moved the mouse to wake the computer and began opening windows, talking a mile a minute to explain how it was done.

Apparently, I needed a minimum of twenty-five-thousand

dollars to get started with a trading account. Twenty-five-thousand dollars allowed you to make trades up to one-hundred-thousand dollars at most places. "That's not a problem for you." She gave a short, sharp laugh. "I see what nice clothes you have, and I've seen the building where your office is. Rafe thinks you're doing just fine, more than fine. He said he bets you've saved a lot."

I kept my gaze on the screen, waiting for her to finish assessing my financial condition, about which she knew absolutely nothing. Of course, I had quite a bit tucked away, and I could easily slice off a piece to get started day trading. Still, I hadn't realized it would require so much. They certainly had never mentioned that before. When they offered to make a few trades for me to prove their expertise, they'd used a few hundred dollars. A few hundred dollars of their own cash, not mine.

"You have to spend money to make money, right?" She giggled softly.

She went on to explain that the first step was to sign up with a brokerage firm, advising me on the choices, followed by her opinion on which one I should select. She went over the hours day traders normally worked—an hour and a half or so when the market opened and the last hour of the day. "That's when there's the most movement so you can scoop up positive returns more easily, although it's certainly not guaranteed. Also, the point of day trading is you never leave a purchase riding until the next day. You sell everything before the market closes at four Eastern time—that's why it's called day trading."

"Clever," I said.

"Are you making fun of me?"

"No."

Her fingers tightened on the mouse, and she moved it furiously. She leaned forward, peering at the screen, trying to locate the cursor that was floating among her brightly colored charts.

It was more complicated than I'd realized. I understood why she'd made such a big deal out of showing me how it worked. Half the things she said sounded like she was speaking a foreign language. I recognized the words, and some of them I understood perfectly, but not in this context —*liquidity, margins, volatility.*

She informed me that I would need to read up on business news if I wanted to succeed. She showed me how to look for stocks that had frequent price changes, such as technology companies, and how to buy small amounts. It was important to know what kinds of events triggered movement in particular stocks that you were interested in. I would need to set up a spreadsheet with all the stocks that interested me, adding a few every day. This way, I could purchase small amounts—a few shares here and there, and my nest egg would grow.

This was not simply tossing a ball onto a roulette wheel and calling out red or black. It wasn't even sitting at a poker table and making decisions about when to draw.

My mind wandered back to the eggs we'd eaten, and then I missed the next things she said, my thoughts consumed by the gnawing in my stomach. Eating the egg with that delicious salsa hadn't been half bad, but I wanted more.

Next, she started rattling on about foreign exchange markets and futures trading. "We'll go over some of that next time."

I already knew—there would not be a next time. What sounded easy was no such thing. Yes, it appeared to have potential for making a lot of money, and it had the thrill of risk. You could do well working only three to three-and-a-half hours a day. But they would be grueling hours, clutching the mouse like she was. And that didn't include time spent doing research. She'd gleefully left off that part of the equation.

I could barely manage sitting in front of my computer for one hour a day. When I had desk work, I was constantly getting up and going to the break room, outside for a smoke, or into Diana's office for a chat. I was not cut out to stare at a screen for two hours straight, especially if I had to keep my thoughts sharply focused on the numbers and graphs shifting in front of me. They were mesmerizing, and my mind drifted elsewhere.

I'd thought day trading, any kind of so-called investing in the stock market, was simply gambling dressed up to look important. All it involved was choosing a company that had an intriguing name, buying a few shares, selling them as soon as the price went up, making a few bucks on each trade, spreading it out across enough companies that you made serious money every day.

What Victoria had described wasn't gambling after all. Well, it was still gambling. But it was roulette with a large dose of a history class on the side. A class taught by a dull instructor who focused on nothing but the dates and places of various wars without digging into any of the interesting bits of human drama.

I let her keep talking while my mind wandered back to my current job. The money was nothing like Victoria claimed they made, but it was good. And except for those times sitting in front of the computer, I was happy. Photographing clients didn't even feel like work. I felt alive when I was capturing the expressions of Trystan's clients. I liked watching them and deciding when it was the right moment to snap a photo. I liked shooting video. I liked going to dinner parties and restaurants where I was supposed to photograph them in their *natural habitat*.

It was fascinating to show clients their photos and video footage. Witnessing their reactions was as good as watching a reality TV show. I couldn't tear myself away.

I liked getting clients to relax in front of the camera, and I liked catching them by surprise. In some ways, it was the perfect job for me because I could do what I do best—watch people and observe how they interact with the world and each other.

As I studied Victoria's profile, I imagined myself photographing her. I wondered why I'd never thought of doing it. She had an interesting face that was fully exposed by her short, spiky hair. The shape of her small ears was delicate, and the series of piercings that ran up the curve of her lobe looked elegant rather than heavy and clunky with metal as some do.

Although she was the definition of quirky, she was smart and really quite beautiful. Not that being less intelligent and average looking would give Rafe a pass in how he treated her, but I couldn't understand why he was so lacking in appreciation. Was he simply one of those men that needed to prove himself, or find someone new on a regular basis, or needed the ego-massage of conquest, or whatever it is that drives some men?

"Rafe doesn't appreciate you," I said.

"Yes he does."

"You're not being honest with yourself."

Without turning, she took a deep breath and said, "You don't know him. We value each other, and we work well together. We're in love, so we choose to overlook inequalities."

It was the strangest description of love I'd ever heard.

"Pay attention, or you aren't going to learn this," she said.

"I wonder if you—"

"I don't need your advice on my relationship with Rafe. Stop talking about him. Concentration is critical here."

I let my mind drift again, and she believed I was concentrating, just as she believed Rafe loved her.

19

Since I'd taken the entire day off and my day trading lesson only lasted a few hours, I went to the Museum of Natural History. I'd never been, but everyone raved about it. I wandered around looking at unusual insects, the bones of dinosaurs, and Native American artifacts.

There was too much for one short visit, so I tried to limit my curiosity for this round. I left in the early afternoon and ate lunch at a hot dog stand. While I chewed sauerkraut and zesty stone ground mustard on my beefy hotdog, I thought about my morning lesson in trading stocks for easy money.

I still didn't understand why Victoria was so keen on my learning all the details. Trying to figure out why she cared so much was driving me crazy. I felt like I was lost in the center of a life-sized brain-twisting puzzle. In some ways, she gave the impression she was lonely and wanted a colleague. I supposed Rafe didn't meet that need, but she'd raved about being her own boss. Why the sudden need for a co-worker? Maybe they were tired of each other—working together and living together and having a relationship is a lot of togetherness. It might feel, after a while, as if you couldn't breathe. Even one of those things had the power to suffocate me.

I tossed my hot dog wrapper, took a long gulp of water from my bottle, and started walking toward the subway.

After several minutes sitting on the train and watching people salivate over their phones, I pulled out mine. I sent a text to Kent, asking if he was free for dinner. At first, he'd been very firm that he wasn't going to get involved in whatever game Rafe and Victoria were up to, but he'd finally caved. He'd told me a little about their interaction with Nick, the previous tenant in my apartment.

He'd explained Nick's weird relationship with the two of them—Victoria coming on to Nick, then Rafe following Nick around almost to the point of stalking. It definitely sounded strange, but there was more to it than that. A lot more. Otherwise, I wouldn't have a letter addressed to Nick from the New York City field office of the FBI sitting in the drawer of my bedside table. I wouldn't have had Victoria dancing around me, straining to get her hands on that letter.

Kent replied before the train reached the next station.

Kent: *What's up?*

Alexandra: *How about I bring over some sushi and stuff for martinis?*

Kent: *Ok.*

I locked the screen and held the phone on my lap. A tiny smile danced across my lips. My phone buzzed, and I opened it to read Kent's new message.

Kent: *BTW, if this is about digging for more dirt on our neighbors, just a reminder I'm all tapped out.*

Alexandra: *You're awfully suspicious of a friendly offer to provide dinner. AND drinks.*

Kent: *Ha.*

Alexandra: *No strings.*

Kent: *Not likely, but sushi sounds good. And you make a killer martini.*

I smiled, reading his choice of adjective for my martinis.

Alexandra: *Seven?*

He replied with a thumbs up.

I slid my phone into my bag and returned to watching the people around me. It was mid-afternoon on a Monday, and still, the subway was over half full. Some of the riders were dressed for work in an office, and I tried to imagine whether they'd left early, were going in super late, or had been fired from their jobs. It was impossible to tell from their faces. They wore masks of privacy, unwilling to reveal the slightest detail about their lives.

At home, I showered and changed into navy blue leggings and a pink crop top with a navy blue camisole underneath. The blue of the camisole was visible through the loose weave of the top. I wasn't trying to hook up with Kent, but as I'd wandered lazily through the day, I noticed myself thinking that wasn't completely off the table.

Still, it wasn't my primary objective. My gut was nagging me that I had to understand my bizarre neighbors before they did something that would seriously disrupt my life. It's hard to describe that feeling. It was most likely simple self-preservation. They were just too…eager. Like puppies hopping around me all the time, wanting something, but never able to communicate what it was. Puppies want games and pats, so maybe they weren't like puppies. They were more like crows hopping around, moving ever closer, looking for dead flesh.

I ordered the sushi to be delivered between six-forty-five and seven. Absolute freshness was more important than ringing Kent's doorbell promptly at seven. I put vodka, vermouth, and a jar of olives into a grocery bag. I wrapped my martini glasses in towels and placed them gently beside the bottles.

While I waited for evening, I sprawled on the couch and scrolled through a few websites giving advice and insights on day trading. I wasn't sure why I was bothering. I'd made my decision. It might have been the lure of more money refusing to release its grip. I could almost feel it brushing against my fingertips, if Victoria was telling the truth.

It might have been that I wanted to get one up on her and Rafe. If they talked more about it or turned up the pressure, I wanted to sound like I knew what I was talking about. The question was, did they? If they really made that much, why were they still living in an adequate but less-than-ideal apartment? Even mine was nicer than theirs with its street view and French bedroom doors.

When I told them I'd made my final decision against becoming a day trader and they could stop going on and on about it, how would they respond? They'd been harassing me about it since the day I met them. It was always about how they wanted to help me. But why? Except for a few dinners together, and Victoria's mildly stalking presence in my photography class, they hardly knew me.

The sushi arrived at five minutes to seven. It couldn't have been more perfect. I carried the food and drinks down the short hall, relieved that neither Victoria nor Rafe popped out to ask where I was going. It was like living next door to a life-sized cuckoo clock.

I laughed at the image and knocked on Kent's door.

When he opened the door, I held out the bag of sushi and stepped into his minimalist apartment. Immediately, I felt a sense of lightness and calm. No wonder he liked the lack of decor and furniture. It was soothing. Although in my mind, it would be better to have a house with a few rooms decorated in that style while the rest of the house was filled with the normal accessories of living.

"Do you ever think about getting more stuff?" I said.

He shook his head. "My mother was a hoarder."

"And you went for the opposite?"

"You have no idea what it's like to live with stuff crowding you, falling down on your head, piled in your bedroom so that you feel like you can hardly breathe. When I wanted to shower, I had to clear her tchotchkes from tourist shops out of the bathtub." He opened the cabinet and took out two plates. He put the plates on the table and went to work breaking apart the bamboo chopsticks provided by the restaurant. He placed them on the napkins while I opened containers and arranged the food.

We sat at the table, martinis glistening in front of us, and the rolls and sashimi on our plates looking like jewels— minimalist food for a minimalist guy. I wondered if that's why the thought of sushi had popped into my head when I'd offered to bring dinner.

We ate and talked about movies. Kent talked about work, and I told him about Arlinda. I described how she'd tossed that dark wine onto an expensive blouse. He didn't know her and he never would, so telling him the story didn't matter. I spoke about her as a client without mentioning her name or the agency name.

He leaned toward the opinion that the work we did with Trystan was more or less bullshit, and he wasn't shy about letting me know that. He was right in one sense, but it was still a harsh thing to say. Not everyone was as together and focused as he was. Some people need fitness trainers, and others think it's a waste of money. Some people use mentors —it's considered a standard practice in the business world and other fields. I suggested that people value mentors because mentoring is free, but the minute someone like Trystan wanted to charge for his insight and expertise, it was bullshit? Kent laughed and said nothing more.

It seemed to me that we helped our clients, but maybe Kent was right. Maybe they would have figured it out on their own if they put effort into it.

After we cleared up the remains of the food, I mixed a second round of martinis. Sitting in the living room, I let my gaze fall on his shaved head. I'd never been with a man who shaved his head, and I wondered what it felt like. As he talked about his brother-in-law, a cop, I watched the movement of skin on his skull. The more I looked at it, the more I wanted to run my hand across it.

At the same time, I was thinking about the brother-in-law, wondering how close he and Kent were. I didn't need to get mixed up with a guy who was related, even if it was only by marriage, to a cop. Not that a street cop had anything to do with investigating murders, but it made me cautious. It's best to keep a wide distance between myself and anyone who might become curious about me for any reason at all. Maybe that's why Trystan's prying questions had disturbed me. He'd made it sound like it was all about social interaction, all about the workplace, focused on strengthening our team. But deep in my gut, it felt like someone wanting to know too much about me.

"Are you close to your brother-in-law?"

He shrugged. "Not really. He hangs out with other cops. My sister hates that he's a cop. Or so she says. She worries all the time. But I'm not sure she's telling the truth." He laughed. "She worries, sure. She's scared, and she won't shut up about the danger. It's the first thing she tells people—*David's a cop.* And she always sounds like she's bragging. She mentions that even before she mentions their son. I guess cops make women feel safe. They think their man is tough, and that turns them on."

"Do they really make women feel safe?" Surely that wasn't the case for all women. He was basing his opinion on one woman.

He took a sip of his drink. He didn't answer. I think he felt my eyes fixed on his skull.

"Why are you looking at me like that?"

"Like what?"

"Staring. Like you're studying me." He laughed. It wasn't nervous though. He laughed as if it was genuinely funny.

I put an olive in my mouth and sucked on it, tasting salt and vodka. I liked that he didn't always feel the need to respond or chatter about nothing. I liked that he laughed instead of getting edgy and defensive about me staring. Then I decided I was actually quite drawn to his stoicism, including his refusal to get involved with speculation about Victoria and Rafe.

When our glasses were only half empty, and we both had one olive left on our skewers, he put his arm around my shoulders, pulled me toward him, and we started kissing.

After a while, I placed my hand on his scalp, and it was as smooth as it looked. It felt strong, and I realized the lack of hair was also a minimalist thing. When his hand slid up under my sweater, I leaned into him and held the back of his head. Before long, we were walking toward his bedroom, leaving our half-finished drinks behind, even my olive.

20

With the dubious promise of day trading still hovering in the back of my mind, no longer dulled by the martinis I'd had with Kent, I had a flash of insight on the subway ride to work the next morning. It was an insight that should have been glaringly obvious from the beginning—all of our clients were hugely successful. All of them came to us because they craved more. More money, more status, more satisfaction, more power…More. More. More. It's the human condition.

Woven throughout our clients' profiles were the secrets to their success so far. It was possible I could figure out a way to accelerate my accumulation of money. There had to be standard rules for success. I wasn't inclined to read a self-help book looking for an answer, but I had real-life information a click away.

Every aspect of life has common rules. There are well-defined methods for lifting weights, standard practices that are effective in changing the shape of your body by controlling the amount of weight lifted and the number of repetitions, by managing what you eat, and even the optimal times of day for ingesting the largest portion of protein.

There are rules for photography. Hadn't I taken a class that precisely outlined what some of those rules were? Light doesn't change, and the aspiring photographer learns to use it to her benefit to capture the best image, following proven practices.

Common rules for running and relationships, cooking, and putting on makeup are outlined in books and TV shows, online articles, and amateur instructional videos on YouTube. Everything has rules. Of course, you can break them—some things are better served with broken rules, but some broken rules will literally kill you. Rules for flying a plane come to mind. And so do guidelines for killing people without getting caught.

But with all that instruction available to the human race, rules for success are a little more elusive. It almost seemed as if people who achieved the highest echelons of income wanted to keep their rules a secret. They were often vague about how they got there. One obvious method for achieving great success was being born into a life of privilege, where your relationships were curated from birth, on through to private schools and elite colleges, and into jobs that weren't advertised on Craig's List or company websites.

It was clearly too late for me to be born into a wealthy family. I couldn't tick the college checkbox since my college career consisted of a few years taking whatever classes interested me rather than working toward a degree. But I was certain there had to be other guidelines I could follow.

Sitting at my desk, I decided to start with the most obvious among our successful clients—the most recent. I would comb through Arlinda's psychology tests and bio information with a new filter, looking to find something I hadn't seen before. Instead of trying to get insight into her life to see where she needed Trystan's assistance, I'd look for insight into my own life.

It might seem strange to look at a stranger's life trying to figure out your own, but there had to be something in there that explained how, and maybe why, she'd achieved the kind of success that had purchased that gorgeous penthouse apartment, while the rest of the people seated at her table during her dinner party were occupying subordinate chairs and most likely did not own the penthouses in their buildings.

Usually, we looked at our client's profiles trying to find out what was holding people back. I'd do the opposite—what had pushed her forward that was holding me back? Maybe what I read would turn on the proverbial light bulb in my brain.

At our next photography session, I would arrive armed with questions for my own future. Arlinda was eager to talk— we'd chatted easily during our early photo sessions, and with little prompting, she opened up. Most people like to give advice, they like to tell their stories of success and failure both, given the opportunity. I would become her eager student.

I closed my office door and settled at my desk. I unlocked the screen, logged into the database, and pulled up Arlinda's profile folder. It contained the photographs I'd taken so far as well as the tests and questionnaires she'd responded to when she began working with us. I hadn't actually read much of it because that was apparently Stephanie's new job. It wasn't critical for me to read the details before taking pictures.

Usually, I was more interested in Diana's contribution to building our client profiles—the interpretation of micro expressions that helped me figure out what I needed to focus on during future photography sessions. She and I hadn't yet gone over the photos I'd taken of Arlinda. I picked up my phone and messaged Diana asking if she could meet in an hour to review photographs. She responded with a smiling face and a thumbs-up emoji.

The aptitude and personality tests were tedious reading. I was bored after the first page of the Myers-Briggs test. I clicked to the end and read the summary and the assignment of traits outlined in that widely used tool—extrovert or introvert, intuitive or sensing, thinking or feeling, perceiving or judging. Arlinda had been identified as an extrovert with a strong bent toward the intuitive side of the scale. She was also labeled feeling and judging. There was nothing to be learned from this because, according to those who believe the test offers a great deal of insight into what kind of career one would excel at, the traits are considered inborn characteristics. All the test does is help you know and understand your own psyche.

In other words—we're pre-programmed to be teachers or business leaders, artists or salespeople. I wasn't sure if I believed that. But some might be pre-programmed with the personality characteristics of a killer, so maybe it is true.

Whenever I skimmed past those tests for a client, I wondered at their lack of self-insight. I didn't need a test to tell me anything about myself. I figured it out by noticing my own inclinations. Maybe they'd also done that, and they simply took the tests out of a desire to be cooperative, to make sure Trystan and his team knew them as well as they knew themselves.

The other aptitude tests were equally unhelpful in identifying any kind of rule that I might adopt to propel myself toward a higher income at a faster rate. I closed the files and turned to the essay questions that had been developed by Trystan and Diana.

Forty minutes later, I was finished, and I had a pretty good idea what set Arlinda apart from me, aside from the differences in our upbringing and life experiences.

I threw on my coat and took the elevator to the lobby. I walked quickly to the coffee shop a few blocks away and bought two foamy, chocolaty coffee drinks. I glanced at the scones and croissants and decided the coffee was enough. The drink alone was like a mid-morning dessert.

At eleven, I was knocking on Diana's doorframe. Her door was wide open, her back facing me as she preferred to orient her desk toward the window. This way, she avoided glare on her computer screen and was able to glance out at the sky whenever she paused in her work. I would have loved regular peeks at the clouds or the brilliant blue on a clear day, but I didn't like the thought of my back to the door, exposed and unaware of anyone watching me work or sneaking up on me.

She invited me in, and I settled in the chair beside her. We talked about what we'd done over the weekend. She didn't ask about my *sick* day, and I blurred the boundaries of my weekend to tell her I'd had dinner and drinks with my neighbor. She asked whether he and I were falling for each other.

"Already fallen," I said.

She laughed. "That's a very succinct way to describe it."

"Nothing else is required." I hadn't meant fallen in the way she'd interpreted it, but she wouldn't understand an explanation that it had nothing to do with love. Any attempt to explain would be misinterpreted as coldness and possibly as slutty behavior.

"It sounds like maybe he's fallen harder than you have," she said.

"Probably." I wondered if she understood a lot more than I realized, given her insight into micro-expressions.

We talked a bit more while she pulled up the photographs of Arlinda. She took me through the progression of what she'd seen in the pictures taken during that first evening I'd spent with Arlinda. She pointed out that Arlinda had started off with an expression that suggested she was self-conscious. Not in an uncomfortable way, but as if she was performing for the camera, and for me. Shortly after, Diana pointed out, Arlinda's expressions had changed. The shift in her eyes as well as other minuscule tells indicated she had progressed quickly from wanting to impress me to forgetting the purpose of our meeting as she got caught up in whatever we'd been talking about.

The photographs from the dinner party were quite different.

Those images showed a woman who wanted to maintain control of the conversation. They showed a woman holding herself back from connecting with anyone, revealing little beyond superficial hints at intimacy, viewing herself as quite separate from her team.

I marveled that as much as I pride myself on my ability to read people, I hadn't been aware of this. The only exception was the control she exhibited when she shut down the conversation about the man who proposed to her in front of her staff. Other than that, I'd had the impression she was relaxed and engaged with her executive staff. She'd seemed to feel warmth and affection toward them. Although, it's possible I wasn't really paying attention, caught up in giving my energy to manipulating the camera and making sure I was aware of the difficult lighting in a room set up for a dinner party.

Diana pointed to various shifts in the muscles around Arlinda's mouth and eyes and even her chin that said she wanted to be sure everyone knew that the agency was her baby, that it belonged to her. Then she said something that surprised me a little.

"Arlinda looks a little bored."

I laughed. "Tossing a glass of wine doesn't suggest boredom."

"Unless she was looking to liven things up."

I recalled the conversation that led up to her splashing her wine on Cherry. Boredom had nothing to do with it, but I trusted Diana. She hadn't been wrong before.

21

Victoria was waiting for me in the lobby when I got home from work. A look of madness consumed her face, and I didn't need micro expression interpretation skills to see that. She was seated on the backless iron bench facing the doors. That bench was the epitome of discomfort. She was going to make absolutely sure I didn't glance up the stairs, see her on the landing, and change direction before she could catch me.

She stood and walked toward me. "Where were you this morning?"

As I approached the stairs. I felt her right behind me, close enough to drive a knife into my back, her Ugg boots clumping on the tile as if Sasquatch were following me. I started up the stairs, but she grabbed my scarf, nearly strangling me. I turned and took hold of her wrist. "Don't do that."

"I'm trying to talk to you."

"And I'm trying to get to my apartment, so I can relax."

"I thought you were coming over this morning."

"I never said that."

"But I assumed—"

"You shouldn't. Never assume what other people are thinking or planning. Isn't it fairly obvious that you might get it wrong?" I began climbing the stairs.

"Are you mad at me?"

"I don't appreciate being strangled."

"Why didn't you come over?"

"You showed me how day trading works, and that was enough. I have a job. I can't spend every morning getting lessons on the stock market."

"I thought you were interested."

"I was. And now I know a little about it."

"I thought you were planning to become an investor."

I turned and started up the second flight of stairs to our floor.

"Wait. Why won't you talk to me?"

On the landing, I stopped and unwound my scarf. I unbuttoned my coat. I pulled off my hat and ran my fingers through my hair to relieve some of the static generated by wool rubbing on hair. "I'm not going to become a day trader."

"That makes no sense. I thought you wanted more money."

"I also want to enjoy my life, and sitting in front of a computer all the time isn't for me. I'm glad it works for you." I dug my keys out of my bag.

"I thought I explained that you don't have to do it all day."

"Victoria. Please stop. I don't want to do it. I'm tired of telling you that."

"You don't get how much we make."

I shrugged.

She pulled her phone out of her pocket and tapped through her photos. "Here's a picture of the brownstone I told you about. *Our* brownstone."

"If you own such a great home, why aren't you living there?"

"Just some paperwork and stuff. Closing escrow. And some painting and other things that need to be done before we can move in."

I nodded.

"Did you see it?"

"Yes."

"Do you have any idea what a brownstone costs?"

"That's irrelevant."

"If you don't believe we really own it, you can look it up. It's a public record."

I moved closer, holding her gaze.

She gave me a weak smile. "So anyway…"

I waited for several minutes. Her eyes filled with tears. Finally, she spoke. "Why are you doing this? What's wrong?"

"I don't care about your brownstone. I'm glad you have a place you like. I know everything I want to about day trading, and I'm not interested in doing it. Don't talk to me about it again. If you do, then we won't be seeing each other any more." I turned and stuck my key in the lock.

"I was…we're trying to help you."

"I don't need help."

"It seemed like you wanted to earn more money. I think you do want that."

I left my keys hanging out of the lock and turned back. She was not going to let it go, and the only way out of it was to change the subject. Or go inside and close the door, but first I wanted something from her. "Can you give me Nick's contact information?"

"Why? Do you still have that letter?" She moved closer. Her eyes seemed to jitter inside her skull as she looked at me.

"I just need his cell number."

"Why?"

"That's not your business," I said.

"Yes it is."

"How is it your business?"

"Because you don't know him."

"It's two simple questions—do you have his number, and are you going to give it to me? Otherwise—"

"Otherwise, what?"

"I'm going to go inside and get comfortable and eat some dinner."

"Do you want to come over?"

"No thanks."

"I have a nice bottle of—"

"No thanks. Will you give me Nick's number?"

She shook her head.

Her behavior was very unsettling. I was tired of her erratic moods and her demands, but there was a constant battle inside because I couldn't let go of my need to figure out what was going on. I didn't understand why she refused to give me a phone number. Did she think I was going to harass the guy? A more likely explanation was that she thought I would ask him about her…about Rafe, and she didn't want me to hear what he had to say. Of course, this possibility poured fuel on my curiosity. Didn't she realize that?

For a while, I'd honestly forgotten I had the FBI's letter to the former tenant of my apartment. I'd taken off for vacation and never asked the building manager if I could have Nick's new address. Now, it seemed worth a shot to ask Victoria for his contact info one more time. She was easier to get in touch with than the building manager who had defined hours posted on his door, and most of those hours were during the workday.

She took a deep breath and smiled as if we were having a completely different, friendly conversation. "I don't get why you want to talk to him."

"You don't need to get that." I opened my door and pulled out the keys. "Are you going to give me his number?"

"I can't."

She turned and was inside of her apartment so fast I hardly had time for a second breath.

I went inside and closed the door. I adjusted the temperature and began peeling off the rest of my outerwear. I dropped everything on the couch and sat down. I pulled off my boots and let them fall beside my feet. I was overcome by a desire to lie down and close my eyes. But doing that after work never paved the way to a pleasant evening.

I forced myself to my feet, put each article of clothing in its appropriate place, and changed into yoga pants and a long-sleeved top. I rolled out my mat on the living room floor and did ten minutes of poses to quiet the sound of Victoria's craziness rattling around inside my head.

Quite a few people have said *I'm* a little crazy. People like to throw that word around at anyone who's different from them, and different in a way that makes them uncomfortable. But I genuinely believed there was something not right with Victoria. Her behavior was unpredictable in a bizarre way. It sometimes seemed as if she was acting out a script that someone else had written for her. At those times, I wondered if Rafe was exerting a lot more control over her than I'd realized. At other times, she almost seemed to be responding to imagined voices in her head. The things she said didn't always fit together from one sentence to the next.

What was going on with her? What was happening inside that apartment? Inside that head? Part of me desperately wanted to find out, another part wanted her to go away because she was making my own head ache.

22

Portland, Oregon

My father had been clear that he was not going to stop me if I wanted to earn money to buy a car of my own. This was monumentally unfair. It was also manipulative. He didn't think I was capable of earning that kind of money and he wanted to provoke me into trying to prove otherwise, while he watched to see if it could be done.

A used car would cost thousands of dollars if I wanted something that wasn't going to die at every corner. It seemed an almost impossible amount of money for a sixteen-year-old to accumulate on her own.

I surely wasn't going to make that quantity of money with the rare babysitting jobs I had. Watching children, as every single teenage girl in our church, and half the girls in my school seemed to be expected to do, hadn't worked out well for me. I thought the brilliant, curious, uninhibited little ones should be given more than the average amount of freedom to do whatever pleased them, as long as it wasn't life-threatening. Most of their parents did not agree, and they shared their opinions of me freely and widely. I was the babysitter of last resort, the one they called when no one else was available, and they absolutely had to keep an appointment.

Although I couldn't see it on his face, I could feel my father's internal smirk when he said I was free to earn money for a car. I still wanted to know why he was depriving me, but it didn't seem worth the effort. He'd dodged the question every time I asked, and I wanted a car more than I wanted an answer. It wasn't as if he was fair in his other decisions, so the unfairness in this situation shouldn't have surprised me. It did, but it shouldn't have, and I was annoyed with myself for not seeing it coming.

After our conversation over a bucket of soapy water, I holed up in my bedroom for the rest of the weekend. When my mother came to check on me, I told her I wasn't feeling well. She took my temperature. She made me chicken broth. She brought me an extra pillow. She wondered if it was nausea or a headache, and I told her I just felt light-headed. She wondered if we should go to Urgent Care.

Finally, I kissed her cheek and said I thought I needed to rest, and the broth would help me relax, and the extra pillow would help me sleep. She stepped out of the room and latched the door closed. For most of my life, my father had wanted our bedroom doors partially opened at all times to make sure we didn't get up to no good in a private space, but once my two oldest brothers left home, the rule hadn't been enforced as consistently.

Still, when either of my parents encountered a closed door, they cracked it open. Now, I was thrilled with this benefit of claiming to be ill. All I really wanted was time to think. I had to figure out how, alongside school and all the required church activities, I was going to find time to make money. I needed a pathway to my own income that didn't take an enormous number of hours and also paid well.

I sorted through the options for most kids to earn money —babysitting, pet care, yard work, part-time jobs. The babysitting was obviously out, and none of the others really offered much more earning potential. A part-time job would be difficult to manage with evening and weekend church activities.

After sipping most of the broth, I curled up and fell asleep. The afternoon light coming into the room, the warm, mildly salty comfort of the broth, maybe even the extra pillow caused me to have a strange dream. It involved soapy cars, all of them beautifully glistening in the sun, all of them offering freedom to a new driver. Throughout the entire length of the dream, I was running a large sponge over glistening red and blue and silver painted metal, wondering if the car I was washing was really my own. It wasn't clear. Things never are clear in dreams.

I don't understand people who get insights into their lives from dreams, who believe a vivid dream resolves a problem that's been plaguing them. All I get is a bunch of fanciful stories that are disconnected and confusing.

When I woke, my first thought—trying to force-fit the dream into my life as so many people at my church liked to do—I wondered if it was telling me I should wash cars to earn money. But really, I think it was the broth and the angle of my head from that additional pillow and the frustrating conversation while my father washed his own car that created the dream.

It wasn't some magical answer from a mysterious god,

concerned about how a teenage girl would acquire extra cash.

But what happened next made me wonder if there was something to it after all.

I got out of bed, pulled up the covers, and brushed my hair. As I stared at my reflection, my gaze wandered to my desk reflected behind me. Sitting on the corner of my desk was a folder that I'd avoided for over a week. Inside were colored fliers and envelopes and instructions on picking up the candy bars that each member of our youth group was supposed to be selling to earn money for church camp.

I picked up the thick sheet of paper with luscious photographs of the candy bars—plain milk chocolate, dark chocolate, and both choices with almonds. They were delicious. When I'd sold them the previous years, I'd purchased at least one candy bar a week for myself. They cost three dollars a bar. It wasn't clear how much of that money went to the church, but people were always happy to buy them. Some eagerly waited for those candy bars every year. One of our youth group leaders had done an excellent job choosing a company that knew the pleasure of good chocolate. The candy bars sold themselves. All you had to do was look at the photograph and you knew these were a cut above.

I was pretty sure people would pay five dollars each, possibly more. I could pay myself a nice commission for selling that candy.

It wasn't as if I would be taking money from an organization that helped the homeless or supported kids' programs by selling chocolate. It was for camp. The money enabled one-hundred-fifty teenagers to ride a bus into the mountains where we slept in rustic cabins, ate mass-produced food, sang songs, played volleyball, swam, and, of course, listened to preachers.

I know some people, most people possibly, would consider my plan stealing. But I wasn't intending to take any money from the church, and no one would be forced to buy an expensive candy bar. In a way, it was my commission for doing free labor to pay for a church camp I only enjoyed during playtime and after dark. The rest was boredom and misery and sitting in non-air-conditioned meeting spaces that consisted of a roof and wood benches. We sweated in the afternoon heat, swatting mosquitoes while some guy stood in front and talked about how the Bible applied to our teenage lives.

There was nothing in the Bible that said I couldn't earn a commission if I found a way to sell a lot more slightly over-priced candy bars than anyone else.

23

Stephanie sat at her desk, staring at her computer. The screensaver had come on, bringing up images of planets and galaxies across the black surface. The shots from space faded to nothing as the minutes continued to tick past. The black nothingness reminded her how long she'd been sitting there, unproductive with both her work and her thoughts.

In a way, staring at that black screen was symbolic of her job. She'd tried talking to Trystan about her dissatisfaction with work, had tried pointing out that Alexandra had swept in and stolen the photography job that was supposed to belong to Stephanie, but he'd refused to recognize how it had been snatched away from her. It was so unfair. Thinking about the injustice made it difficult to breathe.

He'd promised the job to her, then flown off to Australia and come home with this woman following closely behind. Alexandra had moved into the office, been handed interesting classes and expensive cameras, and taken over everything while Stephanie sat staring at the blank screen of her life, trying to manage a job that was going nowhere.

Trystan thought he'd fixed things by asking Stephanie to do the initial client assessments, but she knew now that was a nothing job. It certainly hadn't gotten her any more money. It was almost humiliating, as if the others couldn't read the self-assessment summaries themselves. She was bored and unnecessary. Would they even notice if she left? Would Trystan bother to fill her job? She supposed he had to have someone do the work of entering data and setting up client appointments and…and what? He could arrange his own damn appointments.

Diana and Alex did the important, interesting work. Was some sort of age discrimination going on here? Trystan claimed Alexandra possessed an indefinable confidence, charm, allure, or whatever he called it, that made Alexandra perfect for the photographer position. But in Stephanie's eyes, the only traits Alex had were arrogance and good looks, and those good looks were partially a result of her age.

Any woman in her thirties was going to look better than someone like Stephanie, heading quickly toward middle age, if she wasn't there already. Something had to change.

She pushed her chair away from the desk. She started toward the door, then turned back and went to the window. Bringing up the subject of age discrimination might not be the best move. It was never a good idea to ask for something from a negative perspective, as if you were accusing the other person of doing something wrong. She didn't want to come across as a victim. There'd been too much of that already.

There had to be a better way, even if she knew in her heart that her age was definitely part of the problem. Her age and her beliefs. Alexandra was pushy and outgoing, flirty and *fun*

—which was what Trystan really meant by his euphemisms—because she didn't care one bit about behaving in a way that was pleasing to God. Alexandra did what she wanted, said what she wanted, and took whatever she felt like taking. Maybe she'd never actually taken anything, except the job, away from Stephanie, but that was her type. Stephanie knew that type.

As she thought more carefully about all that had happened, she realized Alexandra had indeed taken more. A lot more. Things Stephanie could never forgive her for, no matter what she believed about forgiveness. Alexandra Mallory had sucked the very atmosphere out of their cozy office with its devotion to improving others' lives. Alex had turned it into a place filled with suspicion and secrets. And if something didn't change soon, Alex was very close to taking Eileen away from her mother. That was the part Stephanie would never forgive.

She pressed her forehead against the window. It wasn't as cold as she'd expected. With snow threatening all morning, she'd assumed it would feel like a sheet of ice. The glass must be thick enough that it was absorbing the warmth of the building on this side. Or there was some strange atmospheric condition taking place. Maybe God was speaking to her, reminding her that miraculous and unexplained phenomena could happen at any time. There was a way to use Alexandra as surely as Alex had used Stephanie. And there had to be a way to cut her out of Eileen's life. It just hadn't been revealed yet. She had to follow each stepping stone on the path without looking too far into the future. Trying to see the end of the path was what caused you to stumble.

She straightened and placed her palm on the glass. It was still warm. She felt as if she were saying a prayer, looking for guidance on how to speak to Trystan.

Their last private conversation had been satisfying in a spiritual sense, but very dissatisfying for her career. The conversation had started out with Stephanie feeling ashamed for the way she'd lashed out at him, upset that he'd touched her when she was drunk. Embarrassed that he'd had to steady her when she was stumbling around. The conversation had ended well when he finally stopped resisting the idea of forgiveness and agreed to absolve her. Everything was good from that perspective.

But there was still something wrong. He valued Alex above Stephanie. The things he'd said in praise of Alex had nothing to do with photography. It was almost as if he considered that secondary, or not important at all. Maybe that's why he'd claimed to hire Alex for one amorphous role and then moved her to photographer, almost as if he'd done it mid-air as he was flying back to the United States.

He'd said Alex had superior *people* skills. That was a laugh. Alex was rude. She worked overtime to get all the attention focused on her. She lied. She was sneaky. Look at the way she'd managed to suck Eileen into her vortex. If taking advantage of a vulnerable young woman was considered a *people* skill, Trystan needed better discernment. Especially if he wanted to position himself as a guru who helped people reach their potential.

Stephanie knew far more than Alexandra about people and what made them the way they were. Most believers did. The Bible was where you got insight into the human heart. Trystan and Alex were focused on superficial elements.

She needed to use some of that Godly wisdom to make Trystan see how much he needed her. To make him see that *she* should be the photographer, that she *deserved* to be the photographer, that she had far more understanding and ability to capture people than Alex ever would. And he needed to see that Alex was ultimately going to destroy his consulting firm.

That was what she'd done wrong—she hadn't been aggressive enough. She'd thought they could work together, that there was a way to befriend Alexandra, but that was not the case. Stephanie had tried, but Alex's deadly tendrils were spreading farther, wrapping themselves around every living thing. When an organism grew out of control—a cancer, when it couldn't be pruned and tamed, it had to be cut out. Alex needed to go.

The other thing Trystan had mentioned was Alexandra's ability to take control of a situation. He felt that mattered quite a lot in dealing with their high-powered, very controlling clients. And it was the truth, in ways that he didn't seem to grasp—Alex had taken control of Trystan. He thought his admiration of her was about her ability to connect with their clients. It wasn't that at all. He was physically attracted to her, like all men probably were. He might not even realize it, but that's what was happening below the surface of his conscious thoughts. The God-given directive to procreate that consumed men and drove their behavior even when they were unaware was driving Trystan.

Slowly, she moved her hand off the glass. A handprint remained, the faint trace of her moisturizing lotion where her knuckles and the edge of her palm and tips of her fingers had been pressed firmly against the window. She would leave it. The outline would be a reminder of her insight. Now she knew what to do.

24

After Diana reviewed the photographs and discussed Arlinda's micro-expressions with me, Trystan and I met to plan the next photography session.

As it turned out, I'd misread his response to my telling him the story about Arlinda tossing her wine all over Cherry's blouse. Either that, or my abrupt departure from the bar, my willingness to stand up to him, had given him second thoughts. It was possible I *had* read him accurately, and then something changed. Maybe he was afraid of losing me. Despite his displeasure with my standoffishness or whatever it was that he didn't like about my admittedly anti-social behavior, he needed me. I knew that. I knew he liked how his clients responded to me, and I knew he saw that I added energy and attitude and confidence to his business.

Although he didn't admit he'd behaved as if I'd done something wrong, he clearly no longer thought the story was catty. He no longer questioned my motives for telling it.

"I've given some thought to what you told me about the dinner party." He said this without preamble as he seated himself beside my desk and surveyed Arlinda's photographs, which were open on my computer screen. "Is the video uploaded?"

"No. It's still on my phone. I had the impression you didn't approve of me shooting it."

He didn't look at me, didn't change his tone, or allow any regret to color his words. "I'd like to see it."

Clearly, he planned to pretend he hadn't reacted badly. He planned to pretend that we'd been in agreement all along, and I'd been doing my job in a way that was beyond what he expected. I didn't challenge him. It seemed to me that keeping quiet instead of poking at his mistake might give me the upper hand the next time he started prying into my personal life, pushing me to be someone I was not.

I opened the AirDrop app and moved the video off my phone onto the computer. As the file loaded, I thought about telling him he was lucky I hadn't deleted it based on his utter disinterest and disapproval. But I kept that to myself as well.

We watched the video without talking.

When it was finished playing, he spoke. "So, where do we go from here?"

"I was thinking it would be a good idea to photograph her at her condo."

"Why?"

"Because—"

"This is about her career. I don't think her home is an appropriate environment."

At least he didn't shut me down entirely. Of course, it wasn't the typical environment. We only ever visited clients' homes for dinner parties hosted for their customers and clients. "She opened that door by having our first meeting at her home."

"True. But she said—"

I cut him off, determined to get what I wanted. "I know what she said. But I think there's more going on with her than just feeling stagnated in her career."

"She came to us for help with her *career*."

"But if that's not the only issue, don't you think we should look at the whole person?"

I saw the flicker of a smile cross his lips. He liked that I was talking in the same terms that he used, mirroring the language he used to sell our services. He liked that I was pushing him in a different direction.

"Why do you think there's more going on?"

"Because of the video. It sounds like she doesn't allow her employees to speak freely. Any good executive knows that having people provide honest feedback is critical to not losing your perspective as a leader."

He nodded.

"Throwing your wine at someone is very personal," I said.

"I agree."

"It's almost violent."

"That's a stretch."

"Is it? She lost control of her emotions. She acted out physically."

"It sounds like a combination of a little too much drinking and a conversation that took a wrong turn."

"But there's a reason she reacted so strongly to what Cherry said, and I don't think it's just about how Arlinda interacts with her executive staff."

I began scrolling through the other photographs. We were silent as we studied the notes Diana had attached to each one, highlighting what we should notice about Arlinda's personality and the suggestion of what she might be thinking and feeling.

I had to suppress my own smile as the silence grew. He was clearly thinking about my proposal, and I was quite happy that he was buying my nonsense about the personal nature of the attack. I was probably right about it, but more importantly, I wanted an excuse to spend time in that gorgeous penthouse. And I wanted the chance to photograph a powerful and seductive woman in that exquisite environment.

Thinking about how much I would enjoy taking those photographs, thinking about my chance to pick Arlinda's brain thrilled me far more than any promised allure of money that might be plucked out of the stock market like nuggets of gold pulled from a mountain stream, glittering in a pan among the pebbles and mud.

Trystan pushed his chair away from my desk. He leaned back, staring up at the ceiling, closing his eyes against the fluorescent lights. "Going to her home feels like we're headed off track. Involving ourselves in parts of her life where she didn't ask for input."

"There are a lot of questions in our tests that ask for information that's not directly related to our clients' careers."

"Yes, but that's to give a complete picture."

"Exactly."

He straightened and opened his eyes. "We've always been very clear that these photography sessions are professional interactions. Meeting at her condo was her suggestion, but not something we should encourage. To go outside of what we've outlined as the process—"

"I'm not going to ring her doorbell and force my way

inside like I'm selling vacuum cleaners. I would suggest that since her home is something she clearly values, we thought more photographs there would be useful."

"Will they?"

"Yes."

"You seem very sure."

I *was* very sure. I knew that a longer conversation between Arlinda and me would bring out another side of our latest client. I planned to ask her what the wine tossing incident was all about, and that would reveal quite a lot, quite a lot beyond the photographs themselves. I did not plan to tell Trystan about my objective.

"I don't want her to lose confidence in us," he said.

"But you know I'm right, otherwise we wouldn't still be talking about it."

He gave a short laugh, unaccompanied by a smile. "I don't know that at all. I'm considering how she'll interpret it and trying to figure out if there's anything to be gained with your suggestion."

I didn't respond. I waited for him to figure it out. He was making an issue out of something that Arlinda would most likely not even consider. Sure, our introductory pitch explained our process, but it also said we customized our approach for our clients. My guess was that she would be flattered by the extra attention, and flattered that she was unique enough to require an alternative approach.

We all like to think we're unique. We like to think the processes that fit others don't apply to us. We like being one of a kind. We like being the center of attention. If we say we don't, we're lying to ourselves. I couldn't wait to spend a few hours alone with Arlinda. I was confident I would come back with information that Trystan would appreciate.

He stood and pulled the chair back to the opposite side of my desk. "Okay. You can give it a shot. But don't push. Make the request, and if she hesitates at all, have a back-up suggestion."

"Sure." I smiled, and he left my office without saying anything more.

25

As I rounded the corner headed toward my apartment building, the lobby doors swung open. Victoria stepped out into the cold evening air. I thought about the temperature because she was wearing strappy pearl-colored shoes with narrow heels. Her legs were covered in the sheerest of nylons, and her dress hung to mid-thigh, also a pearly off-white color, covered with beading, almost like a flapper dress. Her hair was tamed down from its usual spikes with a few pieces formed into curls around her cheekbones, as much as the short strands would allow.

She clutched her jacket around her and tugged on the ends of her scarf as if tightening it would keep her warmer. She wasn't wearing a hat or gloves.

It was cold—thirty-nine the last time I'd checked the temperature, possibly colder now.

Where on earth was she going? It was obvious she was freezing in those ridiculous shoes. And it was obvious she didn't want to be seen, the way she scurried like a roach, caught by the light and racing for cover. I expected her to pause and flag down a cab, knowing she couldn't go far in such unstable shoes, but she walked as quickly as the delicate straps and narrow heel allowed, ignoring the empty cabs that passed by.

Hunger gnawed at my stomach, insisting that paying attention to whatever she was up to was pointless and kind of silly, but a deeper part of me had to know. I had bangers to cook and potatoes to mash and fresh veggies for a salad in the fridge. I was looking forward to a glass of red wine to go with my comforting dinner.

Not following her was not an option. This was surely a chance to find out something about her that she didn't want me to know. Questions rattled in my brain—about her strange outfit that looked like something she might wear to a wedding, a wedding that took place in the early sixties or the tail end of the fifties, possibly a cocktail party during that same era. I wondered whether she was meeting Rafe or if he was even aware of her rush to leave the apartment.

I followed, hanging back far enough that I could quickly duck into a doorway if she turned. I didn't think she would turn because her head was bent against the cold, plowing forward with nothing on her mind but escaping the freezing temperature and soothing those feet that must surely already be aching and icy cold.

At the subway station, she turned and began making her way down the stairs, moving more slowly now as she tried to navigate steps and people pouring out of the station, not caring who they might trample on their way home from work.

She got on the E train. I tugged my hat over my eyebrows and re-wound my scarf, covering my mouth and nose so that I looked like a woman in a white knitted burkha. I got on the same train, keeping to the far end, turning slightly, so only my profile was visible, if she happened to look.

When she got off, I followed again. Two blocks later, she stopped outside a club. It was windowless with a padded door, the thick faux leather held in place by huge brass tacks. She unwound her scarf and stuffed it into her pocket. She unfastened the top button on her jacket and grabbed the door handle with knuckles so red I could see them from where I stood, dark and raw under the lights around the door.

The electric sign identified the club as The Moonlight Sonata. It looked very old and very dull, and when the door opened, I heard the unmistakable voice of Frank Sinatra. She stepped inside, and the door closed slowly.

I stared at the closed door, trying to decide whether it was worth the risk to follow her inside. The size of the club wasn't easy to determine based on the exterior of the building. I hadn't seen any people, only a glimpse of a narrow, dark hallway, so I had no idea whether it would be easy to get lost in a crowd. Of course, if this were a crowd that favored Sinatra and door construction popular in the sixties, I would likely stand out no matter how many people were inside. So would Victoria, for that matter.

I clapped my gloved hands together, trying to keep out the chill that snaked across my wrists from the place where my coat met the top edges of my gloves without a tight seal to keep out the cold.

Standing there for an hour or more, waiting for her to come out, would achieve nothing. I still wouldn't know what she was up to, and she would likely see me. Not to mention I might freeze to death.

I turned and started back toward the subway station. Below ground, it was warm enough to pull off a single glove and tap the name of the club into my phone. The website was clearly out of date, lacking any of the modern features that made a website work well on a mobile phone. There was a single home page and a few links to static pages with the lunch and dinner menus.

They positioned themselves as a *gentlemen's club*. Their presentation was so old-fashioned, the person providing content for the website clearly wasn't aware that gentlemen's club was now often a euphemism for a strip club. There was no mention of membership requirements as gentlemen's clubs had required in the past.

From what I saw, and inferred from the menu, it was simply a full-service bar and restaurant that offered a lot of steaks and breaded fish and other heavy food on tables covered with thick white cloths. None of the photographs along the top edge of the home page showed any women, a single non-white face, or anyone under the age of sixty. Most looked to be well past that age.

I slid my phone back into my bag and tugged my glove onto my hand. I found a bench and sat down, waiting for the train to arrive.

Victoria was more of a mystery than ever. Was it possible she had some elderly, secret financial advisor she met there? But why would she go to a club instead of an office? Was she hiding something from Rafe? And why would she dress like that? Her clothes made it seem more like she was looking for a rich sugar daddy, trying to persuade an aging man she was like the girls from his past.

26

It made no sense that our building manager had so-called office hours Tuesday through Saturday, from ten a.m. to noon. During four of those days, nearly everyone in the building was at work. This meant a clogged toilet or drain, a leaking window, or an invasion of roaches all had to be borne until the weekend unless you were lucky enough to catch him coming or going.

The roaches were the worst. It sounds substandard to mention our building had roaches. It sounds like the place was a slum, but it was not. It was a very nice older building—clean from the lobby to the funky but well-kept rooftop garden. Roaches were everywhere in New York. It said nothing about your cleanliness. I'd been told it was the density and the readily accessible curbside garbage.

So the ugly beasts bred and then needed sustenance for their brood. Roaches and rats live in the walls of rundown buildings as well as multi-million dollar condos. Roaches can flatten themselves to the thickness of a sheet of paper and enter a room in search of the smallest crumb—a hearty snack for their relatively small bodies. They invaded apartments and offices and restrooms all over the city, looking for nibbles and warmth, just like the rest of us.

I'd grown used to them and was not averse to smashing one with whatever available heavy object I could find, cleaning up the gooey guts with the sweep of a damp paper towel. But when the roaches came in a group, stronger methods were required. It had only happened to me once, but others saw them more regularly. Maybe I didn't keep enough staples in my cabinets. Maybe I was more religious than most about taking out my garbage.

I'd asked the manager why his hours were so unfriendly to working people, and he'd stared at me as if I were challenging his right to exist.

For this reason, I considered it my lucky day when I entered the front door that evening, and he was stepping out of his ground floor apartment. Before he could insert his key in the lock, I greeted him in a loud voice, meant to carry across the lobby so he couldn't avoid me. "Hi Brian."

He didn't turn immediately. It seemed as if he thought he could behave as if he hadn't heard me, that he thought he might manage to turn the other way and project total ignorance of my presence, escaping the building and his responsibilities. He lived there rent-free in exchange for maintaining the building and keeping the peace, whatever that meant. With the cost of rent, it was a very good deal for him. Most of the maintenance was done by people he hired. It wasn't as if he had to run a snake into an overflowing toilet.

"Brian! I have a quick question."

He turned slowly. He was a skinny guy with blond hair that hung to the middle of his neck, cut all one length, so he was constantly having to scoop it behind his ears. There was something about the way he made the gesture that caused him to look like a woman. He scooped his hair now as he turned. He gave me a sour look—overly red lips pursed just enough to make sure I knew he was irritated. "I'm on my way out."

"Do you have Nick Ressler's contact information?"

He looked at me as if he had no idea who I was talking about. "I'm Alexandra, in apartment 2A. Where Nick Ressler used to live."

He nodded. "I know who Nick is."

"Do you have his new address? Or his cell number. That would be easier."

"Easier for what?"

"I need to get in touch with him."

"Why?"

"I have something that belongs to him." I wasn't about to make the same mistake I had with Victoria, telling him I had a letter that he could then offer to forward. I wanted to talk to the guy myself. I got it that Brian wouldn't want to give out personal information, but at the same time, what I had wasn't really his business.

"I cleaned that apartment," he said.

The only way out of this, the only way closer to getting that cell phone number, which I was now certain he had since he hadn't denied it, was a small, convenient, undiscoverable lie. "It was stuck behind a baseboard."

He scowled. He shoved his keys into his pocket and folded his arms, looking very much like a scolding parent. "Why are you finding things stuck behind a baseboard? I hope you haven't damaged the building. It will affect your deposit."

"Yes, I know. But I didn't damage it. The board was loose.

I was actually trying to fix it."

"Don't fix things. If something needs fixing, you contact me." He started toward the stairs. "Show me."

"Not now."

"I need to inspect the damage."

"I thought you were going out?"

"I have a minute."

I gave him what I hoped was an embarrassed smile. It wasn't an expression I had a lot of practice with. "I haven't done my cleaning this week. I can't have you see it all messy."

His scowl deepened. "How messy?"

"Can I get his cell phone number?"

"I don't give out tenants' contact information."

"But I told you, I have something that belongs to him."

"Then give it to me, and I'll get in touch with him. You don't need to be in the middle of it."

I took a step back. This wasn't going as smoothly as I'd hoped. I should have foreseen it. Brian was suspicious of everyone who lived in our building, assuming we were always doing something illegal, always damaging and devaluing the property. You'd think he owned the building himself the way he fussed over making sure it didn't deteriorate on his watch.

"I don't feel comfortable doing that," I said. "The thing I found is personal."

He rolled his eyes. "It can't be that personal."

"I don't feel comfortable showing it to anyone."

He shrugged. "Then, I guess Nick is SOL."

He started walking toward the lobby doors. Speaking over his shoulder, he said, "I'll come by on Saturday morning to check the damage."

"It's not damaged."

"A loose baseboard is damage."

"Look," I hurried after him. "This is really important. I'm not going to give his number to anyone else. I'm not going to bother him. You could text him and ask if it's okay."

He paused as if he was actually considering this. "Why are you being so secretive?"

"I respect people's privacy too." I smiled, suggesting he and I were on the same team. "I understand there are laws you have to follow and all that. But I think he would want to hear directly from me on this."

This seemed to strike him. Maybe he liked the idea of both of us having the same ethical concerns. "I could do that. But it will be a few days before I get to it."

His hunger for power was etched in the creases around his eyes. It would take him four seconds to send a text message. The conversation just now had taken longer than it would for him to text Nick and pass on the contact information to me and check the supposedly damaged baseboard. I wanted to laugh. Instead, I bit the inside of my lip and waited.

"When I come by on Saturday, I'll check the baseboard and give you the number. *If* Nick okays it."

"Sounds good." I turned toward the stairs.

"In the future, don't try to fix anything yourself."

"I thought I was doing you a favor."

"You're not. This building has character and history, and it should be maintained properly."

I nodded.

He pushed open the lobby door. "Saturday."

As the door started to close, I called after him. "What time?"

The door shut, and he was gone. I couldn't decide whether

I was victorious or irritated. I was sure I'd get the number, but now I had to hang around all morning on Saturday, waiting for him to show up.

27

The same woman who had ushered Trystan and me into Arlinda's penthouse the first time we visited opened the door to me on Thursday evening. It was late—eight-thirty—so I was surprised to see her there. I'd taken a cab because I wasn't thrilled about walking to and from the subway at that hour. With the temperature dropping fast, turning the sidewalks to ice, breathing felt like inhaling tiny icicles.

Walking into Arlinda's home was like entering a spa. The air smelled sweet. It wasn't perfumed, just a light aroma that reminded me of a garden on a Spring afternoon.

The woman, dressed in a silky navy blue dress this time, but her hair slicked back in the same, no-fuss style, took my coat and hat. Her feet were bare, and her expression was neutral. There was no suggestion she'd met me before. Instead of asking me to wait, she led me into the living room.

A moment later, Arlinda appeared in the doorway. She wore jeans and a white top that skimmed her hip bones. Her feet were also bare, her toenails unpainted. With her hair in a loose ponytail tied with a white satin ribbon, she looked like a high school girl. It was clear she believed I was there to capture something undefined, and these photographs weren't about her appearance. I liked that she hadn't piled on the makeup and done her hair as if she was going to a photoshoot. I also liked that she looked approachable, eager to let things unfold naturally.

"Do you want a glass of wine?" she asked.

"I'm supposed to be—"

"Don't say you're working. This isn't the kind of work that requires a crystal clear head. I know a small glass of wine will help me relax."

"Sure. Wine would be nice."

"Chardonnay?"

I nodded, my mind drifting to Tess's cockatoo and his eager announcement every evening that it was *Chardonnay time.* I missed that bird. He was funny and smart. After having lived with him, no one ever offered me a glass of Chardonnay without Damien coming to mind. It almost seemed as if I heard his raucous voice in my head, drowning out the sound of Arlinda's words.

While I unpacked my camera, she left the room, returning a few minutes later with two very large wineglasses, each containing a small splash of wine. We clicked our glasses. It seemed neither of us felt obligated to offer a toast.

"So what are you looking for?" she asked. "Why the extra photographs? Am I that complicated?" She laughed and took a sip of wine before setting her glass on the coffee table.

"I think you're more complicated than most. So far, the clients I've worked with have all been men. Women are more complex, don't you think?"

"Absolutely."

"I was thinking we might take a few shots in each room, if

that's okay with you?"

"Whatever you say. You're in charge."

I absolutely knew I was *not* in charge. Despite her gracious attitude and her casual, girlish appearance, I could feel her drive and determination like she had steel for bones, the strength of it emanating from her body.

We started with a few photographs of her standing at the living room window, looking out on the glowing golds and reds of the city lights.

"You seem comfortable with a camera staring at you," I said.

She smiled at her reflection in the window.

"Are you used to being photographed?"

"Not really."

"A lot of people squirm. They pose in ways that make them look ridiculous because they're trying so hard to look natural."

"Are you supposed to be talking to me about your other clients?"

"I was referring to people in general."

"Maybe they care too much how they're perceived."

"It seems like you care how you're perceived."

"Why do you say that?"

"Why don't we go into the dining room," I said.

"Are you photographing me or my home?" She laughed and touched my arm gently as she moved past me.

"Both."

"You're very straight-forward."

"So are you."

"Why are you so interested in my home? You aren't casing it, are you?"

"Of course not. It's gorgeous, and it seems to be...I don't honestly know. I do love beautiful homes, so that's part of it. I'm always thinking about what I might want someday."

She smiled.

"But we were talking about you," I said.

We stood in the doorway to the dining room.

"Why don't you sit at the head of the table," I said.

She moved around and pulled out the chair, settling down as if she were at a desk rather than preparing to eat a meal. I decided not to point this out. She was right about the position she'd chosen—it would look forced if she pretended to be eating when the table was empty.

I dimmed the lights and turned on the flash attachment. I snapped a few photos, not paying much attention to what I was seeing through the lens since what I really wanted wasn't going to show up in a photograph. "You do care how you're perceived," I said. "You were furious at Cherry that night for talking about an incident that made you feel uncomfortable."

Her expression shifted, but she didn't look angry that I'd brought it up. I hoped I was reading her correctly. I didn't want our session to end prematurely. There were other things I wanted to talk about. One other thing, actually—day trading.

"I shouldn't have done that," she said.

"Why did you?"

"It's complicated."

She didn't respond as I continued to snap photos. We moved from room to room, talking about the camera and lighting and everything but her display of violence.

As we stood inside her workout room, trying to decide what was the best way to capture the room when she wasn't wearing workout clothes, I lowered my camera. "I caught it on video."

"What?"

"When you tossed the wine at Cherry. Have you talked to her about it?"

"It's not really any of your business." She said this calmly, and I didn't sense she was trying to put me off. It almost seemed as if she was testing to see how hard I would push.

"Were you embarrassed?"

She turned and faced me. "You know what? I can't recall what I was feeling. But I think it says more about Cherry than it does about me. I encourage people to express their viewpoints. She was dead wrong about that."

"It sounds like they don't all see it that way."

"When their viewpoints are nothing more than a list of complaints, when they get energy from complaining and don't offer solutions, I lose my patience. Cherry likes to complain. But a lot of people do."

We moved into her bedroom. It was done in shades of green, giving the feeling of being in a forest, even to the point of an entire wall painted in an abstract style to give it the appearance of a wooded area. I could imagine waking up in that room, feeling as if you were some sort of sprite who had slept on a bed of soft, earthy-smelling moss.

"Why didn't you like that man's proposal? It sounds very romantic."

She laughed. "At work? Where I'm trying to maintain authority, run a business? It proved he didn't know me at all. If he did, he never would have done that."

"Does anyone really know you?"

"Good question."

"I suppose the person who knows me the best is Serena."

"Who's Serena?"

"The woman who answered the door."

"Does she live here?"

"Yes." She gestured toward a hallway where we hadn't gone. "She has several rooms that are configured into a separate apartment, including a kitchen."

"So she's like a butler or something?"

"Oh, so much more." Her face flushed. "So much more. My personal assistant. Although I don't like calling her that, because truly, we're friends. We're closer than…"

I waited for her to finish. She gave me a strange smile, one that looked sad and confused…maybe. I wasn't really sure how to read her expression. I let the silence linger, but she didn't say any more. "Let's go into the kitchen," I said.

I'd saved it for last because her comment about cooking being better than sex had made me think it might be her favorite room. Part of me wanted to suggest she prepare something simple so I could really capture her feelings about it, but that seemed a bit too much. She'd already over-indulged me.

She leaned on the center island and looked at me, not smiling. "What do you really want, Alexandra?"

"I told you."

"No, it seems like you want more from me."

"I'm trying to understand you. To make sure we deliver what we promised in helping you move to the next place in your career."

"And what do you think that is?"

"That's Trystan's job to work with you on that."

"I imagine you have an opinion."

It was definitely not my role, and I didn't think Trystan would be happy if he found out I was talking to her about issues that were his sole territory. "A few things have crossed my mind, but I don't have a solid opinion."

"And what are those *things* crossing your mind?"

"My guess is that you're bored."

She smiled, encouraging me to keep talking, not disagreeing.

"And I'm pretty sure there's something else going on that isn't related to your career at all."

"And what is that?"

"I don't know."

"Isn't that why I'm paying you an outrageous amount of money? To answer that question?"

"I'm sure it will come out in your sessions with Trystan."

"What if it's too personal for me to discuss with a man?"

I had no answer for this. That's so rare for me, I felt my lips and cheeks freeze along with my tongue and my brain. After holding her gaze for a long time, I smiled. "Why don't you see how it unfolds. He's very easy to talk to." I was no longer sure this was entirely true, but it had been in the past, and it seemed to be the way most people felt about him.

She laughed. "How politically correct of you. I didn't think that was your style." She took a step closer. "So what else do you want? You seem very curious about me."

"I'm curious about most people."

"And you photograph them in their homes to satisfy that curiosity? Are you just a voyeur? Does Trystan know this?"

I laughed. "No." This was probably a half-truth at best, but she didn't seem to notice.

"Or has your curiosity not been satisfied at all?"

I placed my camera on the granite countertop. "I do love your house, and I hope to have something equally beautiful... eventually. Photographing you has made me think about my career, such as it is."

She nodded.

"It seems like people that are the most successful have something they build and own themselves."

"I think that's probably true," she said.

"Someone I know is trying to get me interested in becoming a day trader. I was curious what you think about day trading."

"Do you like studying the stock market? The economy? Business health metrics?"

"I've never done it, so I don't know whether I'd like it."

"That's the answer right there. If you had an aptitude for it, or felt passionate about those things, you would already be reading business journals."

"Maybe. But what do you think of day trading?"

"I don't know much about it. If you want to own something, you have to love it. My guess is that day trading works if you're passionate about it, and if you're just in it for easy money, it probably doesn't work all that well."

Her answer was so sharp and concise, I wondered why she needed Trystan's services at all.

28

It repulsed Stephanie to know that Eileen's improved attitude might be directly attributed to her friendship with Alexandra. Stephanie hated every smile that Eileen flashed her way, hated her easy-going mood, hated her eating habits that no longer bordered on an eating disorder.

At the same time, she loved that her daughter was returning to her former beautiful and generous self. That she seemed free of the damage that man had caused, free of her belief that she had to starve herself to skeletal proportions to succeed in a modeling career. She even seemed to be less driven in pursuing that career.

It was infuriating and baffling and heartwarming. Maybe this was a case of God using evil people to accomplish His will without their knowledge or cooperation. It had happened before, there were many biblical and post-biblical instances of it. Perhaps she should let go of her fury and enjoy the changes, reveling in the knowledge that, against her will, Alexandra was being used for a higher purpose.

That was a comforting thought.

When Stephanie had mentioned to Eileen that she was

considering refreshing her appearance, her daughter had been thrilled to offer advice. Tears filled her eyes, and she'd given her mother a hug. "That's great. You're a young woman still, you should be enjoying life, you should be dating and having fun."

Stephanie shrugged. "This is about my career. It's stagnating."

"That's great too. You have a lot to offer, and you shouldn't assume there isn't a great future for you just because you're competing with younger women."

"Am I? Competing with them?"

Eileen laughed. She touched her mother's wrist. "Don't get offended. You know it's true. We're all competing. That's how the world works. You have to accept it."

Stephanie wasn't sure if this was how God would view the situation, but it certainly was true that the world was throbbing with competition. It was everywhere. She just didn't know if it was healthy to get drawn into that. She shoved the thought away. For now, there was no other choice.

"If it's a competition," Stephanie said, "I would appreciate it very much if you don't mention this to your new friend."

"Alex?"

"Yes."

"I won't. Why would I do that?"

"She's very good at prying information out of people," Stephanie said.

Eileen laughed. "Whatever."

From there, Eileen had made recommendations—a makeup artist who would offer a consultation on how to transform her face, a stylist at the hair salon Eileen went to, and a personal shopper who would completely revamp

Stephanie's wardrobe.

"I don't think I can afford all of that. I was definitely planning on the haircut, but—"

"And color."

"I'm not dying my hair. That's phony. I'm proud of the wisdom that comes with gray hair."

Eileen laughed. "Thinking wisdom comes with gray hair is folklore."

"I'm not dying my hair."

"I think you'll be happy if you get some lowlights. They're subtle, but they'll add some life to your hair."

"There's plenty of life."

"Do you want to do this or not? You asked my advice."

"I can't afford a bunch of makeup and a whole closet full of new clothes. Just one or two things."

Eileen stood suddenly. She bent over the chair where Stephanie was sitting and wrapped her arms around her mother's shoulders. She pressed her lips against Stephanie's hairline. "Let me pay for it."

"No." Stephanie stiffened. She tried to pull away, but Eileen wouldn't let go.

"You've done so much for me…all my life. And I can afford to do something for you now."

"I can't let you do that. If you have extra money, you should be saving for the future. You won't be young and beautiful and wanted forever. Look at me." She laughed.

"I'll look at you in a few days, and I'll see someone who isn't hiding her beauty under hair that needs some care—"

"You can't buy or paint on youth, Eileen. You need to save your money. A modeling career has a very short shelf life."

"I know that better than anyone." Eileen squeezed harder.

"I have more than you realize, and I'm saving plenty. I want to do this."

Stephanie shook her head. She couldn't speak. Her throat was swollen with the threat of tears. Why had there been such an enormous change in her sulky, alienated, depressed daughter? She shook her head again. She wouldn't think about that.

"I won't let you say no. I'm doing this. It will help your career, and it will help you feel better about who you are, and that affects everything."

"My career isn't like yours. It's not about my appearance."

Eileen laughed. "It was your idea. And all careers are affected by how we look. You might not like it, but it's the truth."

"It's not fair that women have to deal with this."

"Men face it too. It's different for them, but it's still there." Eileen let go and moved away. She crossed her arms and smiled at Stephanie. "I'm doing this. You'll feel better, and I promise that will change everything. And you know it's true, or the idea wouldn't have come to you."

The idea hadn't just come to her. It was given by God, but Eileen would probably roll her eyes at that. It was terrible to take that kind of money from your child, but maybe that was also part of God's plan. Maybe she needed to let go of her pride. And maybe Eileen doing something good with money she'd earned posing in ways that were not pleasing to God was also a good thing. Maybe this was a redemption of sorts. For Eileen and for herself.

She nodded. "Okay. But I don't want you going overboard. I don't need a whole closet—"

"You need to get rid of the old. All of it. You won't feel

better if you're only looking good fifty percent of the time. And that includes lingerie." She laughed. "Definitely that needs changing. And do not give one more thought to the cost. I'll go with you. A mother-daughter adventure into feeling great. To looking as good on the outside as you are on the inside. Am I right?"

Stephanie laughed. She felt like Eileen's school project. At the same time, her heart was bursting with happiness for the anticipation of all that time they would be spending together, for Eileen's support and enthusiasm, and yes, for the thought of a haircut that would make her look younger and clothes that would cause people to give her a second look.

"And you need to lose the cross," Eileen said.

"No."

"It's like you're screaming at the world that you're judging them. It takes away from everything else."

Stephanie took the base of the gold cross between her thumb and forefinger. She lifted it away from her breastbone and held it tightly as if she expected Eileen to rip it off her neck. "I'm not betraying my—"

"You aren't betraying anything. If God requires you to wear that thing, then it says He's awfully insecure. It's the first thing people see, and it makes them form an opinion of you."

"That I trust—"

"No." Eileen stepped behind her. She lifted Stephanie's hair off her neck and undid the clasp. She reconnected the hook and placed the necklace gently on the table. "It's like you're advertising. Spirituality should be in the things you do, in the look on your face. You know I'm right about that too."

For the first time in decades, Stephanie wondered why she'd always worn the cross. What *was* she trying to say? Was she so uncertain about her standing with God that she felt she had to make sure He knew she was putting Him first? She wasn't going to try to figure it out right that minute. Her daughter did have wisdom, despite the lack of gray hair. Where had she acquired all these insights?

At the end of the day on Thursday, Stephanie sent a message to Trystan. She didn't want to talk to him, didn't want to explain or stumble into her usual habit of making excuses, saying too much, so she waited until she stepped out of the elevator into the lobby. She pulled out her phone and sent a message that she needed to take Friday off for personal business. He responded with a thumbs up.

***

Friday began with a massage that Eileen said would help her relax. It seemed like yet another waste of money, but she was trying to follow her daughter's lead. She'd asked for help, and Eileen was taking care of her. It felt quite nice.

When the day was over, she had a hair cut with faint red and blond streaks that blended closely with her natural light brown. Her hair felt silky and soft. It swung around her neck like angels were brushing their wings across her skin. The new lingerie made her literally feel, and look, ten years younger. Her eyes were bold and warm, and her skin glowed. They each carried two shopping bags. The rest of the clothes and shoes would be delivered on Saturday.

It felt so much more wonderful than she'd imagined. She felt like a new person, a woman young enough and confident enough to compete with Alexandra and Diana. A woman who would deliver a strong message to Trystan—he wasn't going to underestimate her any longer. And he wasn't going to keep her handcuffed to a calendar and a spreadsheet while the other women were free to explore their creative interests.

29

Brian knocked on my door at eight o'clock on Saturday morning. That was fine with me. I'd already finished a short run and taken a shower and swallowed two cups of coffee, a bagel with cream cheese, and five slices of bacon. I couldn't imagine how most tenants would feel about an inspection of their apartment at that hour on a Saturday morning, but if Brian meant to unsettle me, he lost the first round.

Not wanting the broken baseboard to look fresh when he came snooping around at the supposed property damage, I'd pried off a section of baseboard right after I'd spoken to him a few days earlier. It had not gone well. I'd thought the board would easily pop loose along the seam where two boards had been joined. The boards had been sealed together with far too many coats of paint over the years. As old paint and newer paint grabbed and pulled from various layers, the aging wood had splintered slightly when I pulled it free.

I wasn't sure I could convince Brian that the board had come loose on its own. I'd stood staring at it, trying to figure out how I was going to explain it. Finally, I'd decided to blame it on the roaches, making it his fault for not having the place sprayed on a more regular basis. Once I had him on the defensive, there was a decent chance he'd back down and not argue over the details of how the board came loose. It wasn't guaranteed, nothing ever is when you're trying to manipulate someone, but the odds were in my favor.

I opened the door and stood back. He walked in as if he owned the place. Immediately his gaze traveled around the living room, pausing on each of my three pieces of furniture, darting to the framed black and white photographs on the walls, and then roving toward the kitchen, unconsciously nodding approval when he saw the spotless, uncluttered countertop.

"You're very neat," he said.

I shrugged.

He walked toward the doors leading to the bedroom and peered through the opening. My bed was made, the comforter pulled tight, the pillows covered in shams, standing plump and upright as if they were there for show, not for my comfort at night.

"Where's the loose board?"

"It was only partially loose. I don't know if I said that."

He glared at me. "You said it was loose."

"There were two or three roaches a day coming in and out of there. So I had to pull it away a bit to really spray it."

"Let me see."

I went into the bedroom, stopping near the wall where the tiny closet was located, and pointed to the floor. "It's creepy when roaches come into your bedroom. It gives me nightmares." I shivered dramatically.

"They don't usually go into bedrooms. They're looking for food."

"They probably just wanted to be warm."

"Were you eating in bed? Did you leave food out?"

It was a rather personal question, and I didn't like the too-interested look he gave me as he waited for my answer.

"I don't eat in bed."

I did occasionally drink a martini or a glass of wine in bed, but he didn't need to know that. Roaches were not interested in alcohol.

"Not ever?"

"Not ever. It's disgusting."

He nodded eagerly. I felt like I'd won the lottery for getting a difficult person on my side.

"I agree," he said. "And no matter how careful people think they are, they always leave crumbs. They think they clean up, but they don't. The smallest crumb can bring them like an army."

"I know."

He knelt on the carpet and picked up the splintered wood. He held it in place against the wall. "It's not too bad."

"No."

He leaned the wood against the wall and stood, rising like a ladder being unfolded, his long, narrow frame bending awkwardly in the small space between the foot of the bed and the wall. "I'll have to come back with tools to fix this."

"That's fine."

"I don't know if I have time today."

"No rush," I said.

"It's not going to look right. To do it properly, I'd have to pull back the carpet, and I can't do that when there's furniture in the room."

"I'm not worried about it."

"Good, because you don't have a choice."

He walked out of the bedroom, and I followed.

"I'll let you know when it's a good time for me to fix it."

Clearly, a good time for me didn't enter into his thinking. "Okay." I walked around him and stood in front of the door. "Did you hear back from Nick?"

He tipped his head and studied me. "What's the big secret? That space isn't large enough for anything that important."

"What did Nick say?"

He stared at me, waiting. I did the same.

"It had to be something like a credit card or maybe some cash," he said.

I remained silent.

"Don't play games," he said.

"Did you get in touch with him or not?"

He moved closer. It was obvious he wanted to try to get out without giving me what I wanted, but he was too uncomfortable to lunge at me in an effort to open the door.

"Why are you making this difficult?" I said.

"Why are you?"

This was ridiculous. I needed Nick's phone number. I needed to find out why the former tenant had rushed out of New York City, fleeing back home just to escape from my neighbors. I had to know why he was in contact with the FBI. There had been several nights where I'd seriously considered opening the letter, but once it was open, I couldn't give it to Nick. And my reason for getting in touch with him, for getting him talking to me about Victoria and Rafe, was that letter.

It felt as if Brian was the one who wanted to play some sort of game. I knew Nick had said *yes*. Brian's delivery of a refusal would have been swift and final.

Brian was not a very attractive guy. I'm drawn to long hair on a man, but the way he wore his gave me the creeps. His overly red, freakishly shiny lips made me slightly ill. But I needed him to cough up that cell phone number, and it was starting to look like I was going to have to persuade him to do what I wanted in the way that works ninety percent of the time.

I relaxed my shoulders and gave him a welcoming smile. I moved away from the door. I was ready to take a step toward him.

He reached into his pocket and pulled out the torn flap of an envelope. He handed it to me. "Have at it. I don't know what you're up to, but I don't want to get involved."

"So, he said it was okay?"

"Yup." He grabbed the doorknob and pulled the door open. "You better be careful," he said.

As he stepped into the hallway, I followed him. "What does that mean?"

"I'm not a moron. I felt you trying to flirt with me. I'm not that kind of guy, and if you think that will get you any special favors here, you're dead wrong."

I smiled. "I don't want any special favors."

He laughed. "Right. Girls like you always want favors." He took a step toward the railing. "If you'll provide permission for me to get into your apartment, I think it's better if I fix that board when you're not here."

"No problem," I said.

It really wasn't. I didn't want to see him any more than he wanted to see me.

"I'll leave a note with the day and time when I'm coming

by. Don't worry, you can trust me not to look through your things."

Until he'd said it, I hadn't thought it would be an issue. Now, it sounded like I was going to have to work my schedule around his until the board was fixed to be sure I was at home when he showed up. But I had Nick's number. And from now on, that letter would stay in my bag everywhere I went.

When Brian was gone, I grabbed my phone and sent a text to Nick. I told him I lived in his old apartment, gave him my first name, and said I had something that belonged to him.

30

Walking into the office on Monday morning, Stephanie didn't feel quite as fabulous as she had when she and Eileen walked out of the department store late Friday afternoon, headed to dinner at a cozy Italian restaurant to revel in the success of their day.

It was one thing to have her daughter who had engineered the makeover, and the women paid to update her appearance, gushing over how incredible she looked, how the impression she was delivering to the world was something entirely new and powerful. It was something else to consider facing the startled looks of her boss and co-workers, wondering at the sincerity of their words, fearing they might be mocking her and marginalizing her still.

Would they see this as the pathetic attempt of a woman past the prime of her life trying to be someone she was not? Would they think she'd lost her faith? Worse, would they assign unflattering motives to her updated appearance?

She shivered as she rode up in the elevator. Normally, the small enclosure felt too hot, forcing her to start peeling off winter clothing as it rose slowly past the floors below theirs.

She hadn't worn a hat, afraid of mussing her new hair. She rubbed her ears gently, trying to ease the numbness. Her hair, soft and silky, slid over her fingers. She smiled. Who cared what they thought? As Eileen had said a hundred times—this was about how *she* felt. This was about recognizing in her own eyes that she wasn't old, that she had a lot to offer. And although she'd never breathed a word of this to Eileen—this was about showing Alex she was a force to be reckoned with, and forcing Trystan to recognize that Alex was barely past girlhood. Stephanie was a stunning woman with character and depth.

How had she forgotten that her daughter, with a face and figure that allowed her to have a career in modeling, embodied Stephanie's genetic code? It had been so many years since Stephanie had seen herself as attractive, she'd completely forgotten. This was God-given beauty. As long as she didn't use it for evil or put herself above other people, she could enjoy the face and bones and flesh that God had given her. There was nothing wrong with it at all.

She opened the outer door to the offices and stepped inside. The best way to approach this was to find some private entertainment in the shocked expressions she was sure to encounter.

She ran her hand down the curve of the slacks over her hip. The fabric seemed to have been cut from a pattern that had been created from her own body. They fit so well, she hadn't been able to stop looking in the mirror as she was getting ready, constantly returning to the mirror to pose from a new angle. Finally, she'd blushed and felt overcome with shame as she became aware of her vanity. It might take longer until the inside of her fit with her changed appearance.

A woman who looked like she did now was not someone who walked around bathed in shame.

Still, she'd forced herself not to check the mirror again before leaving the house. As she walked to the subway, she turned her head away from the windows. She dismissed the sense that several women and two men had given her a second glance when she boarded the train.

Inside the small suite of offices, the important thing was to act normal. No pausing in doorways to see who noticed her. No lingering in the small lobby area, hoping someone might come out and break the ice. If she had to sit at her desk unnoticed for most of the morning, she would go mad, but that's what was required. Parading herself around would add fire to her self-conscious feelings.

She didn't want to create a scene and definitely hoped to avoid all of them seeing her at the same time, feeding off each others' responses while she felt as if she were standing on a stage, sweating under a too-strong spotlight.

Moments later, heading to the break room for her second cup of morning coffee, she walked slowly, feeling comfortable and pleased with the way she moved through the space around her. The surrounding silence told her that only Diana had arrived so far. When Alex was there, a hot energy filled the place.

After putting her lunch bag in the fridge, she poured steaming coffee into a pale blue mug and added a bit of cream.

"New outfit?" Diana's voice from the doorway was warm and approving, as Diana's voice usually was.

Stephanie breathed a silent prayer of thanks that Diana would be the first to see her new look. She turned.

Diana's mouth opened, and her bracelets clinked in the silence as she lifted her hand to her cheek in a gesture of surprise. "Wow."

Stephanie tried to smile, but it felt stiff. How was she supposed to respond to that? It was a compliment, she could feel it in Diana's tone and see it in the look of approval that filled her eyes, but it was the kind of comment that didn't pave the way for a casual response.

"You look great, Steph."

No one in the office had ever called her *Steph*. She felt a surge of tears, an overwhelming gratitude toward her daughter for creating this transformation, and a feeling that perhaps not all of the world was set against her.

Diana smiled. "I didn't mean to make assumptions. Are you okay with a nickname?"

"Yes. It's fine."

"You really look great. I love your hair. And that belt. Don't tell me where you got it, or you might find someone copying you." She winked.

"My daughter took me on a shopping trip."

"How sweet. I love it."

Stephanie touched her belt, willing herself not to look down and study the dark brown leather and pewter buckle that was formed by two hands clasping each other. It had been ridiculously expensive. She reminded herself to stop thinking about that. Her daughter loved her. Wasn't their new connection exactly what Stephanie had longed for these past years when it seemed as if their relationship was crumbling into a thousand pieces? Now, they'd crossed an invisible bridge from mother and daughter into a friendship of sorts. All because of a visit to the hair salon, a manicure, and a day of shopping. It was truly miraculous.

Trystan appeared in the doorway. Diana moved out of his way and went to the coffee pot. She re-filled her mug and turned to leave.

Trystan raised his eyebrows. The discomfort was obvious on his face. Especially after her violent reaction to his solicitous touch a few months ago, it was clear he didn't want to cross a boundary by noticing, much less commenting on her appearance. But in his typically smooth way, after only a moment of hesitation, he found the words easily. "You look relaxed and happy. You must have had a good weekend."

"Yes, I did."

"Good. I'm glad to hear it." He left without taking a mug of coffee, seeming to have forgotten why he was there.

When Diana followed him out of the room, Stephanie sighed at the release of tension. It would be okay. Over the coming days, Trystan would look at her differently, and she would be able to approach him about her job in an entirely new way. And now, no matter what vitriol Alex tossed at her, no matter what mind game she chose to implement, Stephanie was ready for it.

31

There was a flash of cream and chocolate past my doorway, shoulder-length shiny brown hair that seemed custom-colored to match the outfit. I leaned sideways from my desk, but I couldn't see who she was. No one came into our offices unless there was a client meeting, and those were rare. We almost always held them at the client's office.

Who was she? I hadn't heard any voices besides our usual team.

I pushed my chair away from my desk and went to the door. The hallway was empty. I stepped out and walked to the break room. The lights were off, so it had been at least ten minutes since anyone was in there when the sensor lights timed out. All the office doors were closed. I tried to remember if I'd heard a door close when I was straining to see into the hallway.

I checked the conference room and our lobby area. Nothing.

I couldn't believe I'd imagined seeing her. There was clearly someone there who had now disappeared. I knocked on Diana's door.

"Come on in."

I opened the door.

"What's up?" she said.

"I thought I saw someone in the hallway—a woman I didn't recognize. I wasn't sure if there was a meeting I'd forgotten about, but the conference room is empty."

"Maybe Stephanie."

I shook my head. "No."

She tipped her head toward the door, indicating I should close it. I did, then moved closer to her desk.

"I don't mean to gossip, but I didn't want her to overhear and think I was making too much of it. Stephanie has a… how should I put it…a new look. Although it seems almost more than that."

"A new look?"

"Haircut. Highlights. Makeup. Clothes. The cross is gone."

I stared at her. That cross defined Stephanie. Maybe it didn't do that in others' minds, those who weren't as soaked in religion as I'd been, but it had caused me to form an opinion before she even opened her mouth the first time I met her. She'd lived up to my early impression in every way— judgmental, sneaky, easily offended.

The cross was a fixture around her neck. I'd wondered if she slept with it on, trusting that if she strangled herself on that 18-karat gold chain, the cross itself would save her from an ugly death.

I couldn't imagine that exquisite haircut on Stephanie's head. I'd seen only a flash, but it looked like a three-hundred dollar cut and color. The kind that makes you look like you were born with favorable genes. The kind that looks like you might be suitable for the cover of a fashion magazine. The gorgeous hair I'd glimpsed and Stephanie's gray-streaked, untrimmed brown were clashing in my mind.

"Why?"

She shrugged. "I have no idea. A new guy?"

"Maybe."

"Although actually, I didn't get the impression it was only about a guy. It seemed more dramatic. Like she's decided to become someone different."

"That's interesting." Of course, I wasn't the only person in the world who liked to become someone different, changing how I'm perceived, trying on different hair or makeup styles as easily as I change my clothes. Although I was somewhat unique in using those tools to tweak my appearance for a specific situation. Stephanie struck me as someone who liked being who she was. She might be bitter about it, mostly bitter because she wanted everyone else to adhere to her view of the world, but she never struck me as wanting to fit in.

In fact, that was the other thing about that cross. She *wanted* to be in your face, telling you she was different, advertising that she wasn't going to do what anyone else expected.

As I thought about this, I wondered if we were more alike than I'd realized. I laughed.

Diana leaned back in her chair, the seatback flexing with the pressure of her body as it was designed to. "What's so funny?"

"I'm just trying to put it together."

"She looks great. I'm not surprised you didn't recognize her."

I nodded.

She glanced at her computer screen. "I better get back to it."

"Sure." I moved toward the doorway. "Lunch?"

"I can't today."

I went into the hallway and closed the door softly. I stood there for several minutes, willing Stephanie's office door to open so I could see for myself. It remained solidly closed. This too was slightly different. Often when she was working, she kept it partially open, wanting to be aware of everything happening around her—another similarity between the two of us.

I thought about texting Eileen to find out what she knew about it, but that would probably come across weird and slightly creepy. Still, I needed to know why Stephanie was trying to transform herself. People don't do things like that for no reason.

Stephanie's door remained firmly, defiantly closed. I returned to my office, leaving my own door open wider than usual, adjusting my chair and nudging my desk to an angle that offered a better view of the hallway.

After that, it was difficult to concentrate.

I considered simply knocking on Stephanie's door, but I didn't want her to know I was so desperately interested in her. And there was no logical reason why I might ask to speak to her. In fact, I rarely approached her at all. We avoided each other—she was as put off by me as I was by her. Her threatening email from a few weeks earlier crept forward from the back of my mind. I was sure she still planned to undermine me, or worse, as soon as the opportunity presented itself. Was her change part of some effort to do that?

Her email message had been dense with text—only four paragraph breaks in a letter that looked capable of filling three printed pages.

Most of it had consisted of Bible verses repurposed in an attempt to pretend they were her own words. She had no idea how familiar I was with all those words, most of them embedded into my memory like tiny thorns.

In the end, her message had been this—

Eileen was possessed by the devil, and I had no idea what I was walking into, befriending her as I was. If I continued to spend time with her, my life would take a turn for the worse. The implication was this bad turn would be some kind of vengeance from god, there was a vague description of dark angels, but the instrument would be Eileen. According to Stephanie, Eileen craved money, and she would find a way to extract it from me, stopping at nothing to get it. I should be afraid. *Very afraid.*

Of course, the email hadn't stirred any fear in me. Not much does. I suppose if I were facing the end of a gun or felt the tip of a knife prodding my throat, my body would respond with an extreme rush of adrenaline. I would experience an intense awareness of the present moment and racing thoughts of how I might escape, but fear? No.

Over the years of my childhood, my family had gradually learned that I didn't feel fear like they did. They knew I had an iron rod of self-preservation running through my heart, but I wasn't afraid. It angered them, worried them, upset them, and most of all, terrified them.

I think my father believed I was born with something evil in my heart. It was difficult for him, because I think he loved me and hated who I was all in the same rush of confused emotion.

I pushed my father and Stephanie's threats of dark angels

out of my head. I watched the video of Arlinda tossing her red wine onto Cherry's silky white top. It was my tenth viewing. There was something to be learned from that scene, but it still eluded me.

Finally, I was so agitated by my thoughts refusing to turn away from Stephanie, I grabbed my coat and bag and went outside. I walked to a small park a few blocks away and stood shivering, smoking a cigarette. Stephanie's transformation was disturbing. Maybe because of her melodramatic threat. Until then, I'd forgotten about it. Now, it seemed I shouldn't have done that. I'd thought I had her figured out, but maybe not. I had no idea why she was mixing things up, and I wasn't sure how it would impact the comfortable balance of power in Trystan's tiny but fierce consulting firm.

I returned to the office, opened the outer door, and came face-to-face with Stephanie. She stood in the center of the lobby, sliding her arm into her coat. She looked like an entirely different person. If Diana hadn't told me about the change, I was sure that for half a second, I wouldn't have recognized the woman standing in front of me.

Her face was re-shaped by expertly applied makeup. She'd obviously had some lessons from Eileen. Her eyes had come alive, and their color appeared richer. They weren't coated in dark colors, made up for dramatic effect, but they drew your attention to them as she stared back with a yearning look. It was something I hadn't seen in her eyes before. To me, she'd always looked ready for a fight.

Her skin was smooth and had a nice color. Her eyebrows were perfectly shaped, adding to her alert, intelligent expression. Her hair was sleek, framing her face and neck in a way that made her look closer to thirty than fifty.

The blouse, pants, belt, and boots were obviously expensive. Each item fit her beautifully.

I stared, knowing I looked rude. Shocked. It wasn't something I usually thought much about—trying to avoid rudeness—but now, I was intensely aware that the situation required a compliment. Still, none rose to my lips.

Setting the new image alongside her insistence that Eileen was obsessed with money made me wonder if the threats in her email had been projecting something in her own heart onto her daughter. The new look had cost a considerable amount of money. Did she think she was some sort of avenging angel herself? You never know with deeply religious people who have more than a passing belief in the intertwining threads of biblical prophecy, the paranormal, and their own bad feelings.

My thoughts seemed paranoid on the surface, but there was no doubt in my mind she was planning a significant change in direction. Her appearance was only the first step. That email threat had spoken for itself. Nothing had happened to make me think she no longer believed the things she'd written.

What on earth was she after?

32

Portland, Oregon

My father had shaped me into a savvy saleswoman.

Or maybe that skill was innate.

To sell something well, you have to believe in it with all your heart. If not that, you have to believe with all your heart that the person you're selling to needs that item more than life itself. So maybe the secret to effective selling that flowed through my bloodstream had been fed from several directions.

Every time the church doors opened, I was being sold to— told how my life would have meaning if god were at the center of it, told how desperately I needed forgiveness, told that my very existence was in jeopardy, warned about eternal torment. It was a superb sales job, and for most of my peers, it worked. You could say that in my case, the sellers didn't know their audience. They were operating from a one-size-fits-all mentality.

My father tried to sell me the same things, taking a more personalized approach by pointing out how my specific traits doomed me to a life of suffering. He had anecdotes from my own family that illustrated why it was critical to buy into the Bible and the need to repent.

At the same time, I was always selling to my father, although more subtly. I wanted him to purchase my arguments for personal and psychological freedom. I wanted to win. Which I suppose means that in my case, it wasn't about selling, it was about playing a game.

At any rate, I thought I had a good idea of how I would sell those candy bars for five dollars apiece. I figured I needed about ten thousand dollars for a car. That meant five thousand candy bars, with a two-dollar commission to me on each one.

First, I had to find a new, larger pool of customers.

Although there were many people in our community who were familiar with the teenagers ringing their doorbells every spring, carrying order forms and samples of candy, I couldn't approach them. They were ready-made buyers because they loved the candy, and a respectable number of them wanted to support teenagers in whatever we did—especially if it kept us out of trouble and taught us good values. Why they thought selling was a cherished value, I never figured out.

But most of those people would remember the price of the candy from previous years.

And that dilemma brought me right back to my initial problem. How was I going to expand beyond the streets within walking distance of our house when I had no car? I could tack a few sales opportunities onto the end of the errands I ran for my mother several days a week. But going too far afield would raise questions about why the gas was disappearing from the tank so quickly, and why I was taking two hours to pick up a carton of eggs.

I sat in the backyard on the swing tied to the branches of an oak tree that had a trunk as thick as a small car itself. I let the swing glide gently while I closed my eyes and felt the breeze on my cheeks and eyelids, stroking the edges of my nostrils.

I supposed I could hitchhike, although that was forbidden, and the risks of it weren't lost on me. I could take the bus or ride my bike. My bike seemed preferable, although kind of difficult with a backpack full of candy samples and brochures. Still, I needed a plausible reason to take my bike to do my candy selling.

My mother would question the need. She would worry about my safety, riding alongside cars. She might even want my father's input on whether it should be allowed.

I pumped my legs with full force, opening my eyes as I began to fly higher, rising up so close to the branches and leaves above that I felt like I was about to join the birds, busy with their nest-building.

Telling a lie that I was involved with some other activity at church—reading to people in rest homes or working at the soup kitchen invited exposure.

After swinging as high as the ropes would allow before growing slack, feeling the air cool down as dusk approached, I finally decided that something close to the truth was the best. Something that would distract my mother and blind her to the details, overriding her usual concerns.

I slowed the swing and got off. I went into the kitchen where she was chopping carrots for stew. "I wondered where you were. Will you please peel those potatoes?" She gestured with her elbow.

I picked up the first potato and the peeler, pulling it across the already scrubbed skin. "I was swinging."

She smiled. "You haven't done that in a while."

"I know. And it gave me an idea."

"What's that?"

"I'm thinking about summer camp. They were saying the cafeteria needs upgrades, and they have extra prizes for people who can double last year's candy sales. If you double your sales, you get a sweatshirt and a stuffed bear."

She laughed. "That doesn't sound very motivating for girls and boys your age."

"It's a nice sweatshirt, with a hood and pockets. Also, the one who sells the most gets a cash prize."

All of these things were true. It felt as if the church leaders had set it up just for me to be sure I was inspired to blow all of my peers out of the water with the amount of candy I sold. The previous year, unmotivated by the prizes, as I usually was, I'd sold fifty candy bars. It was the minimum expected. I'd briefly considered selling forty-nine, just to see what they did, but in the end, my father decided on the spur of the moment one night that he wanted to eat one, so he made an impulse purchase.

"I don't know if I agree with that," my mother said.

"With the prize?"

"Cash."

"You said the bear wasn't great for kids my age."

"Yes, but—"

"Kids my age like cash."

"Oh, sweetie. Please don't say that. It sounds…crass."

"Anyway, I'm going to try to win."

"That's good, I suppose. It's good to set goals."

I placed the peeled potato beside her cutting board and started on the next one. There was a bad spot near the end. I shoved the tip of the peeler into the potato and dug out the chalky, decayed black stuff, smoothing it until all that remained was the healthy vegetable. "Not really for the cash. Although I wouldn't mind it." I smiled to myself. A hundred dollar prize was not going to get me much closer to the car I wanted. As this thought passed out of my mind, I saw a huge flaw in my plan. How was I going to explain to my parents that I had earned enough cash to buy a car.

It felt like someone had carved a hole in my stomach, dug in with a peeler in the same way I'd scooped out that ugly black stuff. I'd been so excited about the potential for making a lot of money, so excited that my plan fit under the structure of the church fund-raising program that my parents wouldn't be inclined to question my enthusiasm. How could I have missed the most obvious point? I hadn't thought for a single moment about explaining how I'd earned all that money.

33

New York

Only seconds after I got over my shock at seeing the new Stephanie, I managed to give her a compliment, although it sounded fake and limp in my own ears. I was certain she heard the same qualities.

"You look astonishing." I should have chosen a less flamboyant word. To make up for the lapse, I added a smile that I was absolutely positive looked genuine.

She smirked and muttered *thanks*. She yanked her coat around her and headed out the door without saying anything more.

Sitting in my office, I stared at the computer screen. Trying to avoid being consumed with figuring out the meaning behind my co-worker's dramatic change, my mind drifted back to my conversation with Victoria.

I'd insisted I did not want a job where I spent most of my day sitting in front of a computer. And yet, there I was. That's where I'd been since I came in that morning, and that's where I was likely to be throughout the afternoon. It's what I did on far too many days. Although I wasn't tied to my desk, unable to even blink as I focused every fiber of my brain on constantly shifting charts and cascading numbers, I was still staring at a computer.

I opened a web browser and skimmed the news. I found myself gravitating toward financial news as if Victoria's insistence that I had to understand the companies I invested in had taken root. Without any real interest, I was poking around to see who was doing well, and which companies provided inadvertent hints that their stock might be poised for a drop.

Of course, I discovered nothing like that. I didn't know enough about business or any of the industries I was reading about to guess what problems might cause drops and which ones might result in a steady-state, or even growth. I clicked away and read a bit of celebrity gossip.

Finally, I closed the browser, stood, and went to the window. I stared out at the bleak sky and tried to think. I loved taking photographs. So far, I never got tired of trying to get my subjects to relax, to forget I was there, to expose their internal lives to my camera. How had I ended up spending so much time pouring through dull test results and reading self-impressed essays? I wanted to be with people face-to-face, listen to them preen, and analyze in their own words.

At first, reading about their secrets and reviewing their self-analysis had been entertaining. Now it had become research, all the life taken out of the people we were studying.

I wasn't sure a single thing I'd read in our files had ever influenced the way I'd taken a photograph. I wondered whether I should tell Trystan I was bored. Whether I should see if he really needed me in the office reading all these documents. Didn't I deserve to work only when I was actually taking photographs? Listening to Diana's interpretations was interesting, but other than that, my position didn't seem to require me to show up at the office from eight to five most days.

As I stood there, I became aware of Stephanie's voice—the same slightly pleading tone as usual. So…that part of her hadn't changed. Yet. But as I listened, her tone changed after all. Her voice grew louder, and with the volume, more confident.

"A dinner meeting would be better," she said.

I moved quietly across the room and paused just inside the doorway, out of sight from where she was standing.

"I prefer to keep business during business hours," Trystan said.

Stephanie laughed. Her laughter sounded different. She sounded truly amused, not trying to sound that way while inside she was angry or upset. "Since when?"

"Since I try not to intrude into your evening hours and I expect the same respect for my time."

"Half the photography sessions and client meetings take place in the evening," she said.

"Yes, but that's to accommodate our clients. Talking about internal issues should be done during the workday. Why don't we arrange lunch on—"

"I don't want to be confined to a lunch hour, or feel like you're looking at the clock when I'm trying to talk about something important to me."

"We can take an extended lunch hour, Stephanie."

"I prefer dinner."

"It's not—"

"You were thrilled to have Thanksgiving at my house. On a holiday. That was an intrusion on personal time."

There was a moment of silence. She sounded like another person entirely. She was aggressive, and she wasn't going to back down. What *issue* involving our team did she want to talk about? Was she going after me again? Memories of her accusation that I'd been flirting with a client, memories of her sneaking into Trystan's office, going through his things, passed through my mind. Was it more of the same, or something new?

Was she hitting on him? Her tone didn't suggest that, but her tone didn't suggest anything I'd known about her up to this point. It was apparent she wanted something very badly. Was the makeover all about trying to change her relationship with Trystan? If that was the case, her attitude made no sense. But she wasn't a person who demonstrated a lot of skill in dealing with people. Maybe she had the idea of going to dinner with him, coming on to him, and now that he wasn't interested, she was handling it poorly.

"I don't understand why dinner is necessary," Trystan said. He sounded frustrated and more than a little confused.

"Because this is important to me. It's my life we're talking about, and dinner means you're taking it seriously."

I ached to know what she'd said before I picked up the words of their conversation. Why was she talking about this in the hallway? She could see my door was open. Did she not care if Diana or I heard this demanding dinner invitation? That, too, was different.

She was normally secretive about most things, not blasting her thoughts down the short hallway, unconcerned about someone else joining the conversation.

"If you're worried about the cost, I'll pay," she said.

"I'm not at all worried about the cost. And I'm not allowing an employee to pay when it involves your work here."

"Whatever. Does Wednesday at seven work?"

"I'd have to check my calendar."

"I'll wait."

She said something else, but I didn't catch the words as she and Trystan headed toward his office. A moment later, I heard the door close.

34

Stephanie took a cab to the restaurant she'd chosen. It felt good to be in charge. Most of the time, especially with men, she was the one going along with the other's suggestion. It was starting to look as if Eileen had been right. Her daughter's wisdom was both startling and slightly intimidating.

The new look was absolutely giving her a new-found confidence. It was almost eerie. As if she were a snake who had changed its skin and became a creature to be respected for her venomous power. She shivered at the unfortunate comparison to the creature God had chosen to deceive the human race. But still, it was true. She no longer felt people were staring at her, unspoken critical and condescending thoughts shimmering in their eyes. It might be different the first time she went to church. She would face a different kind of criticism there, but for now, it felt quite good.

There were several minutes during her conversation with Trystan when she'd felt sure he was going to win. She'd feared she would wind up agreeing to lunch. The timing of the meal would make her feel rushed, and she wouldn't get a chance to fully express how she felt or tell him why she deserved a better role in his company. He would brush her off and give her another bone to play with. She would never get a third chance.

Not only had she chosen the restaurant, she was getting there early so he would have to seat himself on her terms.

She would be careful with alcohol. One glass with dinner was her pre-determined limit. She didn't need a repeat of Thanksgiving. She needed a clear head and an unwavering focus on what she wanted. On what she *deserved*. She'd even prayed about the situation and was filled with certainty that God was on her side.

She'd worn a red dress. It was a bit extreme to choose the most shocking and attention-drawing color there was, but she felt divine in it. The dress hugged her body in a way she'd never experienced. It was cut low in the front, but not so that it showed too much and whispered suggestions that were not what she intended. Low enough to make her look like she wasn't uptight and ashamed of her body. It had long sleeves that came to points over the backs of her hands, scooped higher on the underside of her wrists. The hem was irregular, with one side cut above her knee and the other hanging below. Of course, Trystan wouldn't see that. Neither would he see her higher-than-normal black heels. But that wasn't the point. The point was how she felt inside—utterly fantastic. Still, quite a few people had looked at her as she entered the restaurant.

The chair was comfortable. It was an armchair, providing a bit of warmth as she settled into cushions that were soft yet still offered good support, so she didn't have to work too hard at maintaining good posture.

When she was offered something from the bar, she'd ordered sparkling water with lemon. The drink was already sitting in front of her. She wanted to move the utensils, rearranging things to absorb the nervous energy twitching in her fingers, but she resisted. A woman who wore a red dress, who had silky, youthful-looking hair partially swept up on the back of her head, didn't fiddle with utensils like a child.

She turned, looking out the window at the people passing by. The placement of the window in relation to her chair allowed her to see them from their shoulders to their knees. It was a strange view, but she enjoyed the rhythm of it, the not-knowing how old any of them were except by what they might reveal in their gait or by their clothing. In winter, there wasn't much to see—a lot of overcoats and hands shoved into pockets.

"You beat me." Trystan's voice cut into her thoughts.

She turned too quickly, and for a moment, the room spun. She regained her equilibrium. "Thanks for meeting me."

He gave her a curious look and settled himself in the chair across from her. The server placed the napkin on his lap and took his order for a martini.

His drink choice was irritating. It made her think of Alexandra, although Alexandra was at the root of the conversation they were about to have, so there was no sense pretending she didn't exist. She loomed over everything, dictated the division of responsibilities, set the mood for their office, and in many ways, maybe entirely, she was the reason for Stephanie's changed appearance.

Did that mean she owed her new-found confidence to that woman? It didn't seem fair. She shoved Alex's smirking face to the back of her mind.

"Have you already ordered for us?" Trystan said.

"No. I wouldn't assume to order—"

"I just thought…since everything else was arranged." He opened his menu. "So, what should we have?"

They were silent as each studied their menus. Stephanie chased away the pressure to speak, to mutter over the different selections, working her way to her decision out loud, as if seeking his approval for whichever way her appetite leaned. With anyone else, she would have done that. With another woman, talking over their indecision felt like a friendly ritual. Maybe with a date or a husband it was the same, but right now, talking too much would be to her disadvantage.

So far, she seemed to be right. Trystan was not his usual, ultra-smooth self. He seemed off-balance and uncertain of how to treat her. Good. He deserved to feel like she did much of the time. Yes, he was her boss, but he no longer got to control her life the way he had. He no longer got to lie and skate around his promises as if he'd never made them.

He ordered steak with a side dish of potatoes. She ordered gnocchi, which would provide the comfort of pasta without the mess of trying to wrap long strands around a fork and getting them into her mouth, inevitably slapping sauce on her chin. They both ordered the beet salad to start. Stephanie asked for a glass of Pinot Grigio, and Trystan said he'd stick with his martini for now.

Would he order a second drink later or had suggesting he might simply been a polite dismissal? Maybe the conversation would be over in ten minutes, and they would be forced to spend an awkward hour plodding their way through the rest of the meal. But the fear of that happening didn't make her regret her insistence on dinner. Already, Trystan seemed less tense, less concerned about the time or the speed of the service. Or, for that matter, what he had to drink. She hadn't considered this. Was alcohol likely to make him more inclined to listen carefully to what she had to say, or less? Was this how men felt when they were in charge, wondering whether to buy a woman a second or third drink?

They made small talk about clients and the weather until the salads arrived.

Trystan stabbed a yellow beet, put it into his mouth, and chewed. "So, what do you want to discuss regarding your role?"

"I'm bored with my job." The words surprised her. She hadn't planned to be so blunt. And she hadn't even taken a sip of her wine yet. The strong statement must have come from some other place deep inside where her new personality was taking root.

"Bored?"

"Yes."

"I'm not sure how to respond to that."

"You could start by asking what might make my work more interesting."

He took a bite of his salad, followed by a sip of his drink. "I'm surprised to hear that you're bored," he said.

"Why?"

"I find our work fascinating. I had the impression everyone felt that way. Proving once again, it's never a good idea to make assumptions." He smiled as if he wanted to get her on the same page, as if they were a team in this.

They were not a team. He was the boss, and she was the under-valued, marginalized employee. She was not going to fall into making him feel like everything was okay when it wasn't. "*Your* work *is* fascinating."

He studied her, his expression confused.

Was he pretending not to understand, or was he truly not sure what she was talking about? He was a perceptive man. He made his living—a very nice living—understanding people, reading between the lines, or looking below the surface; however you wanted to put it. Surely he'd heard the inflection in what she'd said. And above it all, he surely knew that scheduling meetings and presenting summaries of their clients' needs was not absorbing, fascinating work. She rarely got to meet their clients face-to-face. She never got to do anything to actually help clients advance to a new level, to see the look of appreciation and feel their gratitude for helping them break through psychological barriers.

The job she did could be performed by artificial intelligence. A machine could compare a client's calendar with Trystan's and propose three dates, allowing the client to finalize their choice via a text message.

The silence between them continued. She wasn't sure if he was trying to figure out what to say or if he was waiting for her to speak. Or, was he hoping she would get so frustrated she would resign? She felt her lips part with the sudden realization that might be what he wanted. Maybe he'd recognized the same thing she had—that her job could be done by a robot. He no longer needed or wanted her.

The main course arrived. The disruption eased the stiffness of the empty moments that had passed between them. When the server was gone, Trystan cut a piece of steak and looked carefully at the exposed meat. Still holding his fork and knife, poised for another cut, he spoke without looking at her.

"What do you want, Stephanie?"

"I want the job that belongs to me. The job I deserve. It was my idea to make the photography a core part of what we offer, and I would be very good at it. You said it would be my job."

"I'm sorry that didn't work out the way you'd hoped."

"The photographer job belongs to me."

"That's not how things work."

"So I can just be the meeting scheduler until I'm ready to retire? That's all you think I'm capable of?"

He ate a piece of steak, still avoiding eye contact. He took a sip of his martini. He'd hardly had any. In fact, she wasn't sure he'd had any after the initial taste. His water glass had been refilled twice.

Things were slipping out of her control. Why was it so easy for other people to say what they wanted and walk away happy with the results of a meeting? She felt like she was crawling through wet cement. There was no way out. Maybe this *was* all she was capable of. It certainly seemed that way in his eyes. And more importantly, why wasn't God on her side after all? Did He disapprove of her new clothes and hair? Everyone else got whatever they wanted, and she was left with all of that wet cement hardening around her.

"Maybe you should explore other options," he said.

"What does that mean?"

"Don't ask questions you know the answer to. It's annoying."

Now she was *annoying*. She felt ill. She pushed the half-eaten plate of gnocchi away from her. She took a sip of wine. There wasn't much left in the glass. Her limbs felt heavy, her head had a slight ache, and her throat was dry.

"Are you firing me?"

"Not at all. I sense your frustration, and I'm trying to help."

"Why can't I be the photographer?"

"We already discussed this."

"Not completely. There's nothing Alexandra does that I can't do. And if you gave me half a chance, you'd see that I can do it better. She doesn't have some magical rapport with clients. I could do the same, you never even let me try."

"And I already told you, I'm happy with her work."

"It's not fair."

A flash of irritation crossed his face.

"I don't mean to whine about this, but it's not fair that someone with no experience got that job when it was my idea. You might not have thought about this, but my relationship with God, my study of the Bible, has given me far more insight into human nature than Alexandra has."

"It's better if we stay off the topic of religion."

"We don't need to discuss religion, but it's the truth. And if you don't mind me saying, I think you might have a blindspot with Alexandra. She's very self-absorbed. Surely you see that I have the maturity to understand a lot more about human nature. I listen, I pay attention, and I have a certain amount of wisdom that she—"

"I'm not going to discuss it anymore. I expanded your responsibilities, and I'm sorry if you're not happy with that. Your feelings are a little disturbing. We can't communicate that attitude to our clients." His expression had settled into a deep frown, bordering on anger.

"None of our clients know how I feel."

His plate was suddenly empty. How had she not noticed he

was finishing his meal so quickly? He took a sip of his drink and pulled his wallet out of his pocket. As if drawn by a magnet, the server appeared beside the table. Trystan handed the card to him, and the server disappeared.

"So that's it? I don't get the job, and dinner is over?"

"You pushed your plate away. I assumed you were finished."

"What about dessert?"

He gave her a look of such pity she thought she might cry. Her refreshed appearance hadn't done anything for her after all. She was the same person as always, trying to pretend she was someone different, and he'd seen through it. All her confidence melted.

Trystan paid the bill. He escorted her to the lobby and helped her with her coat. "Can I call you a cab?"

"Yes, please."

When the taxi arrived, she didn't thank him. He owed her. She made it home and up to her apartment and into her bedroom, closing the door before the tears began to flow, ruining her makeup.

35

I arrived at the office early. Although I hadn't overheard Stephanie confirm her Wednesday evening dinner with Trystan, she'd slipped out of work before four o'clock the previous day, so I was pretty sure he'd agreed to meet her that night.

After the coffee was made, I settled down in my office. The door was wide open. Instead of facing my computer, I sat in the guest chair, which offered a better perspective on anyone passing by. I sipped coffee and waited, feeling a bit like a spider at the center of her web, all eight of her eyes watching for the slightest movement. Stephanie was not going to get into her office without me seeing her.

At ten minutes to eight, I heard the outer door open. I sat forward. A moment later, Diana passed by. I heard her in the break room pouring coffee, and then she was in my doorway. She took a sip from her mug. "Why are you facing your desk?"

"Getting a different perspective."

She laughed. "You already have a different perspective."

"I probably do."

She turned away. "Talk later." She moved out of view, and I heard her open her office door.

Five minutes later, Trystan came in. He rapped his knuckles on the doorframe as he passed by, but didn't look in, saying *g'morning* as he passed out of view.

It was ten minutes to nine before I heard the outer door open for the third time. Stephanie never came in this late. Dinner had either been so marvelous that she no longer believed she had to impress anyone with her early arrival, or it had gone badly, and she also no longer cared what anyone thought, but in a different way.

I stood and went to the doorway. She passed by. She was wearing brown leggings with chocolate brown boots and a white shirt with the tails out, hanging almost to the middle of her thighs. Her hair was down and loose.

"Hi," I said.

She ignored me. She went into her office and closed the door.

I put down my mug and followed her, knocking firmly.

There was no response. I knocked again.

"I'm busy." Her voice was loud, ensuring there was no chance she wouldn't be heard through the closed door.

"It's Alex. Do you have a minute?"

"Nope."

I knocked again.

"I said, I'm busy."

I knocked a third time, hoping all my knocking wouldn't bring Trystan or Diana out to see what was going on.

The door swung open. "Are you deaf?"

"Oh." I stepped back, trying to look contrite. "I'm sorry. Just trying to be friendly. Trystan said he wants—"

"Is this a cult? We all flutter around and do whatever *Trystan wants?*"

I laughed.

Her face remained serious. Sullen. She started to close the door.

"Can we talk for just a minute?"

"About what?"

I glanced to the side, implying that I didn't want to be overheard.

"I don't think we have anything to talk about," she said.

"I wanted to apologize."

That got her attention. She went to her desk. I stepped inside and closed the door. I sat across from her, scooting the chair close to her desk. "I should have asked if you want coffee." I started to stand.

"I don't want coffee. What did you want to apologize for?"

"I don't think I gave you a proper compliment regarding your new look."

She stared at me.

I waved my hand in front of me, gesturing toward her new shirt, her hair and face—the makeup lighter today, but still carefully done. I was sure it was Marc Jacobs or some other high-end brand, and trying to figure out how on earth she could afford it tormented me. I didn't know her salary, but I was confident it was quite a bit lower than mine. Maybe Eileen had decided to start spending her inheritance.

"You look great," I said.

"Thanks."

"Don't say it like that. I mean it. You look ten years younger."

She glowered at me.

"Except when you make faces." I laughed.

"I don't appreciate you laughing at me. If that's all..." She looked pointedly at the door.

"I'm not laughing at you."

"Now you're going to lie right to my face? I'm not an idiot."

"I wasn't laughing at you. I was trying to tease you. You look like you don't believe me."

"I don't."

"I truly mean it. Honestly." Truthfully, I did mean it. Of course, I wanted to use the compliment to find out about that dinner, but it wasn't flattery for that purpose only. I was sincere in believing and saying that she looked good. That she looked younger. She no longer had that disapproving, hateful air coming off her like cheap perfume. As if the change in her appearance had shifted something inside her.

"I'm not used to you telling the truth, so it's hard to know," she said.

"I'm usually honest about what I'm thinking."

"No, you're not. Only when you think it will get you something."

I was surprised she'd read me so well.

"So, what do you want now?"

I pushed myself out of the chair. "I was trying to be nice, Stephanie. I really mean it. You look good. That's all."

"Thanks. I guess."

"Everyone noticed."

"You're talking about me behind my back? Gossiping about how awful I used to look?"

Why was she so difficult? In her constant paranoia, she hit upon the truth quite often, but it was a little pathetic. I have my own forms of paranoia, so I don't tend to view all paranoia as pathetic, but in her case, it was. She seemed to work from the assumption that people didn't think well of her. I couldn't imagine going through life with that kind of monster breathing in my ear.

"No one is talking behind your back," I said.

She snorted.

I wasn't getting anywhere trying to soften her up. I might as well cut to the heart of things and see what happened. "How was your dinner with Trystan?"

"How did you know about that?"

"I overheard you making plans." I placed my hand on her desk and leaned toward her. "Don't look at me like that. My door was open, and your voices were quite loud."

She looked like she didn't believe that either, but said nothing. It was the truth. Maybe not the genuine truth of how I'd heard, but factually, it was true.

"It was fine," she said.

"It's good to talk to him one-on-one every so often."

"Why?"

"To make sure you're getting what you want."

"You never have a problem getting what you want."

"It's a priority." I smiled.

"You're so cold. I can't believe how cold you are."

"There's nothing cold about going after what you want. Everyone does. And why shouldn't we at least try? Why just let life happen to you. Don't you think?"

"It's not so easy for everyone to go after what they want. Most of the people on this planet don't get everything they want. They don't even get half of what they want. A tiny fraction—"

"But that doesn't mean you shouldn't try, if you have the opportunity."

She glared at me.

"Is there anything I can help with?" I said.

"What does that mean? Like you have more power here, and you can affect my job?"

"I don't have any power. Just offering to help."

"You can't."

"Were you happy with how your discussion went?"

"None of your business."

I smiled. "Okay."

"Is that all you wanted? To pry into my life? You have to know every little thing that's going on?"

"I came in to apologize. Your new look makes you look more professional. I hope you don't take that as an insult. Our clients dress up, and I think they have confidence in us when we do the same. So I'm sure, in some way, it will help your career. Whatever it is you're looking for."

"We'll see."

I moved toward the door. She wasn't going to tell me anything, but she'd said enough. There really wasn't anything going on that affected me. She probably didn't like that Diana and I had the more interesting jobs. She didn't like setting up meetings. It wasn't interesting, and there was no satisfaction in the work. Maybe she was like me—not thrilled about sitting in front of a computer all day. It was possible she'd realized on some level that she didn't provide the same polished impression as the rest of us. As a result, she was kept locked in a closet away from our clients' eyes, and she'd decided to do something about that.

36

Two minutes after I stepped into my apartment, there was a knock on the door. I'd already taken off one boot. I began to ease the other off my foot. There was a second knock. I thought about calling out that the visitor should chill, but I wasn't sure they would hear.

I removed the other boot and went to the kitchen. I filled a glass with water and took a few sips while I waited for the third knock. It came, and I went to the door.

When I pulled it open as far as the chain lock would allow, Rafe was standing with his face pressed into the opening. The pressure of his skin and bones against the wood frame distorted his face, making him look like the monster in a horror movie. The aroma of pizza filled the space, pushing its way into my apartment while the chain prevented Rafe from doing the same.

"What's going on?" he said.

"Nothing."

"I have pizza."

"I noticed."

"And wine."

"Good for you."

"Can I come in?"

"Why?"

"Isn't it obvious?" He grinned, his face still bent into an odd shape, cutting off the edges of his smile so his teeth seemed more prominent.

"You want to eat pizza and drink wine with me."

"Yep. I know you haven't started dinner because you just got home."

I suppressed the shiver that they always seemed to know when I was home, even when I didn't encounter them on the landing.

"Are you going to let me in?"

"I'm trying to decide what I feel like eating."

"Aw, come on. Everyone always feels like pizza."

"Do they?"

"Absolutely. As soon as you smell it, that's what you want, even if you weren't hungry."

"Where's Victoria?"

"She had to go out."

Had she made the frigid trek to the gentlemen's club again? Had she worn the same useless shoes, the same fussy dress? Or did she have several similar outfits? Maybe she was all in pink this time instead of pearl and silver. "Out where?"

"Not important."

"To you, or to her? Or you just don't want me to know?"

"She's meeting some people for a drink. What's the big deal? Why so curious?"

That was a laugh, given their extreme interest in my comings and goings. I wondered if what he'd said was the truth, whether she had friends who hung out at that club. I realized I should have gone back and checked out the place after I'd seen her there, gotten a feel for the atmosphere instead of making assumptions based on the photos displayed on the club's website, which could be ten or twenty years old for all I knew.

"So, can I come in?"

I considered the leftover soup I'd planned to eat for dinner. I considered the fact it was Friday night. I wondered what time Victoria was coming home and whether she would then be part of the pizza party. Most importantly, I remembered that kiss and Rafe's attempt to insert his bony fingers inside my bra. Surely he was here without Victoria at his side so he could figure out how much more he could get. He was a greedy, needy guy. But a needy guy might be more willing to talk than his anxious, more cautious girlfriend. It was nothing I couldn't handle.

I slid the knob of the chain out of the slot and opened the door. "What kind of wine is it?"

"That's all you care about?"

I went into the living room and grabbed my boots off the floor. "I'm going to change my clothes first. You can find glasses and plates in the kitchen."

"It's a Syrah."

I opened the door to my bedroom.

"Do we really need plates?" he said.

"Yes, we really do. I'm not eating out of the box." I stepped into the bedroom and closed the door behind me, not that the French doors gave much privacy.

In the bathroom, I changed into a black tunic and black leggings. I put on Ugg boots over my bare feet. Keeping my feet bare, or even wearing socks, would suggest I was comfortable and ready to relax with him. I wanted to be comfortable, but I didn't want him to know that. I opened my bedside drawer to see if I had any roofies. One remained, but I wasn't sure that was the right way to go. I wanted him to talk, not pass out. I'd have to handle his physical aggression myself. Hopefully, it wouldn't be an issue. I closed the drawer and returned to the kitchen.

The wine glasses were half-filled with glistening red liquid. He'd even found a votive candle, placed it in the center of the table, and lit it. Folded paper napkins were tucked under the edges of the plates, and the pizza box was near the edge of the table, the top poised to open away from the candle.

We sat down, and he lifted the box lid. The steaming combination pizza was piled with chopped mushrooms and olives, thin slices of onion, green peppers, and Linguica. He pulled a slice away from the others and took a bite. Strings of melted cheese fell in a long ribbon onto his plate.

"Mmm."

"No toast?" I picked up my glass and took a sip of wine.

"I figured we were both hungry."

"A toast is always nice. It's civilized."

He grinned. Gripping the slice of pizza in his left hand, he picked up his wine glass. "Cheers."

"To neighbors," I said.

"Sure. Sounds good." He took a sip, put down the glass, and bit into the pizza.

"So, who was Victoria meeting tonight?"

He didn't meet my gaze. "Why do you wanna talk about her?"

"I was curious."

"Just some people."

I nodded as if this was a fascinating revelation.

"How's work?" he said.

"It's good."

"Boring?"

"Not at all. Photographing strangers is fascinating."

"So you said."

"I think Victoria likes taking photographs too. She loved the class we took together."

"Did she?"

I nodded. "She was very excited about it."

"Okay, well, she doesn't have a job as a photographer, so I think she's over the excitement. You can't all be Annie Leibovitz."

"No, we can't." I took a bite of pizza. After a moment, I added, "None of us can."

"Is that what you think you are? An artist?"

"In a way."

"I thought you took corporate pics," he said.

"There's still an art to capturing a person's essence."

"Not sure I agree, but I'm not an artist. I've taken some great pics of Victoria on my phone. We should compare. See whose looks better. Getting a good photograph is mostly about luck."

"So it sounds like Victoria didn't tell you much about our class. Good photography takes some planning."

He lifted another slice of pizza out of the box. He finished drinking his wine and refilled the glass. He glanced at mine, saw there was quite a bit still there, and put the bottle back on the table. "Vic said you picked up the knack of trading really fast."

"I'm not sure how she'd know that. I didn't do any actual trading."

"She said you're a natural."

"How do you define a natural?"

"Someone who has good instincts."

"That's vague."

"Someone who isn't afraid to take a chance, but is smart about it."

I nodded. I nibbled on the crust of my pizza and took a small sip of wine. I steered the conversation away from trading, and away from work in general. It wasn't hard to do. All I had to ask was what sports he liked to watch on TV, and he took it from there.

Two slices of pizza remained, and the wine bottle was nearly empty.

"Should we sit on the couch?" He picked up the bottle. He held it up to the light and tilted it to see how much was left.

"I have a bottle of Pinot Noir," I said.

"Or you could make martinis."

"Not tonight." I went to the cabinet and got out the bottle of wine. I opened it, finished what was in my glass, and poured a bit more.

He followed my lead, splashing the remainder of the Syrah into his glass, swallowing it quickly, and holding out the glass for a refill.

In the living room, he sat far too close on the couch. Without a preamble, he placed his hand on my thigh and massaged it. "I think we want the same things," he said.

"Are you and Vic breaking up?"

"Not at all."

I moved away. "Then what the hell are you doing?"

"She gets me."

"You told me that."

"It's true. She's cool with whatever." He took my wine glass out of my hand, placed both glasses on the table in front of the couch, and flung himself on top of me, pushing me onto my back.

I laughed. "Get off me. You're being ridiculous."

"You liked that kiss I gave you. I think I would say you loved that kiss."

"Get off me. Now."

He sat up.

I ran my fingers through my hair to get it off my face and picked up my glass. "Why don't you tell me what's going on?"

"You have conditions?"

"The way you and Victoria behave is bizarre."

"Why?"

"I don't have the impression she knows what happened between us."

"Oh, she knows."

"And she doesn't care?"

He shrugged. His glass remained on the table, and he stared at me with hungry, craving eyes, waiting for me to stop talking so he could carry on.

"And what's with the constant pressure over day trading?"

"What do you mean?"

"Why are you so hell-bent on getting me to try it? Sometimes I have the feeling you're running a pyramid scheme, but I can't figure out how day trading fits with that."

He laughed, a short, rough sound. "You ask a lot of questions for a chick with no guy in her life and a job taking pictures for some prick who thinks he's a guru or whatever that guy is."

"Did you ever think that maybe I don't want a guy in my life?" This was a debatable point. Of course, I liked the companionship, the sex, but I didn't see it as critical to my survival. Rafe seemed to think that made me desperate. It didn't speak well of his own self-esteem if he thought I would be interested in a guy who was already connected to someone only because there was no one else.

"Every chick wants a guy."

"Where did you get that information?"

"I just know it. I understand women," he said.

I smiled. It was clear this was going to be the same circular conversation I always had with him. I was not going to find out why they had such a weird relationship, and I was not going to find out why they were obsessed with getting me to change careers.

I stood. "I'm tired. You should head out."

"But—"

"Now."

I grabbed the pizza box off the table. I walked to the door and opened it.

To his credit, he stood and moved toward me. I shoved the box into his hands. "Thanks. Good pizza. Nice wine." I nudged him into the hallway and closed the door.

I truly was tired. I'd wasted too much time trying to find out what they were up to. I was tired of them, tired of whatever game they were into, and tired of thinking about it.

37

In an orchestration of bad timing, Brian had left a note saying he'd be by to fix the board in my bedroom at nine-thirty on Saturday morning. At nine-twenty-four that morning, I finally received a response from Nick Ressler. I opened the text. He asked how I'd gotten his number. I'd assumed Brian had told him he was giving it to me once Nick approved. It sounded as if Brian hadn't asked him at all.

I laughed. I heard the key in the lock. I went to the door and was standing a few feet away when it opened.

Brian took a step back. "Why are you here?"

"I didn't have plans this morning."

"It would have been better if you were out."

"Why?"

"So I can work without interruptions."

"I'll stay out of the way." As if to prove my word, I returned to the couch and texted Nick to let him know how I'd gotten his number.

It was a surreal sensation, texting him with Brian only a few feet away—Brian, who apparently had tried to set me up, to start me off on the wrong foot with Nick. It was rather a big risk on Brian's part, compromising his position of trust. Maybe he figured that guys who have unmentionable secrets hidden behind baseboards aren't going to file a complaint about their privacy being compromised. I explained how I'd gotten his number.

Nick: *How can I help you?*

Alex: *Do you have time to talk. In about an hour?*

Nick: *About what?*

Alex: *It's hard to explain in a text message.*

Nick: *Try. You can use a few messages.*

If I told him about the letter, he would simply provide his new address and ask me to forward it. At this point, it was possible I'd gotten him in trouble since the letter had been sitting in my drawer for a few weeks. I should have dealt with it sooner, and I hoped it didn't mean he would be arrested or something. No FBI agents had come to my door, so maybe it wasn't even that important. Maybe it was just a follow-up. Maybe he'd already heard from them via phone or email.

Alex: *I have some questions about Rafe and Victoria next door.*

Nick: *Such as?*

Alex: *If we could talk, it would be better.*

The sound of a hammer pounding wood erupted from the other room.

Nick: *I'm confused. Brian gave you my number for this?*

Alex: *It would be easier to talk.*

Nick: *I don't know you, and I have nothing to say to you about my ex-neighbors.*

Alex: *I'm worried I'm in trouble.*

Nick: *Why?*

Alex: *Please can we talk? There's another thing—I have something that belongs to you.*

Nick: *I cleaned that place completely. I didn't have a lot of stuff.*

Alex: *I really need to talk to you. I'm not going to tell you what I have until I talk to you.*

Nick: *If I didn't know it was missing, I probably don't care about it anymore.*

Alex: *Oh, you'll care.*

Brian's hammering stopped, then immediately started up again, much louder this time. It sounded as if he wanted the noise to drive me out of the apartment. I had the impression he'd opened the bedroom door wider to make sure he interfered with whatever I was doing. What was he doing in there? It should only take a few strikes to replace a baseboard.

Nick: *Fine. Whatever.*

Alex: *I'll call you at ten-thirty.*

I slid my phone into my pocket and settled my head on the back of the couch. I closed my eyes and listened to the thud of the hammer. Surely he would be finished before my scheduled time to call Nick.

The hammering stopped. No sounds came from my bedroom. I didn't think he would go looking through my things while I was sitting right there, but I was overly conscious of the silence. It was easy enough to check on him. My bag, the letter and roofie safely inside, sat on the floor beside the couch.

Finally, Brian emerged from the bedroom. "All fixed."

"Thanks."

"It better not happen again."

"It won't."

"If you see more than a few roaches, you need to tell me."

"Absolutely."

He went to the door and let himself out without saying good-bye.

At ten-thirty, I called Nick.

He answered immediately. "So, what do you have that you think belongs to me?"

"I need to know why you moved out of here so suddenly."

"Was it sudden?"

"I had the impression you had an issue with Rafe. And Victoria."

"You *had the impression*?"

I hoped Kent wouldn't be pissed, but there was no way to leave him out of this. "Kent told me you had a thing with Victoria. And Rafe kind of stalked you, or something."

He sighed. "Ancient history."

"I've had an issue sort of like that, in reverse. Rafe keeps hitting on me. I think Victoria knows, and she doesn't care. I feel like they have an agenda, but I can't figure out what it is."

"I'd avoid them if I were you."

"That's all? Why?"

"*Why* isn't really important. Just stay away from them."

"Easier said than done."

"Not really."

"I want to know what they're after."

"If you already see that they're trouble, why would you spend one minute with them?"

The way he spoke made me realize I was indeed inviting them into my life. But now they were there, I couldn't stop wondering. Curiosity about other people's business is an addiction for me. I don't like admitting it. I don't like anything controlling me, but there it is, something does.

Maybe Vic and Rafe were just playing a sex game, but the

constant discussion of day trading made me think that was part of their game.

"Honestly. Stay away from them. Now, what did you find that belongs to me?"

"I didn't find it, actually. It came in the mail—a letter from the FBI. From their New York field office."

He was silent for several seconds. "Okay. I'll text you my address, and you can forward it."

"Does it have anything to do with Victoria and Rafe?"

"What makes you think that?"

"I mentioned it to Victoria. I asked her if she had a way to get in touch with you. It seemed like she wanted to get her hands on the letter. She was very interested in it."

"You didn't open it, did you?"

"No."

"Thanks for not letting her see it. I appreciate that."

"Is there something I should know about all this?"

"Why?"

"Should I be expecting the FBI to show up at my door?"

"No."

I waited for him to say more. Apparently he was doing the same.

After a moment, he cleared his throat. "Look. I think I'm free to say this…I'm working with the FBI on something…" He coughed harder. "Something regarding Rafe and Victoria —"

"What did—"

"That's all I'm going to say. That's all I *can* say, so don't start firing questions at me. They won't get answered. If you've had some…troubling interactions with them, I guess that's the best way to put it…if there's something you think might be of interest to law enforcement, I can pass on your name so they can get in touch with you."

My jaw froze. I felt as if my blood vessels had turned to solid strands of ice. The FBI? My name? No. Not ever.

"I can't tell you anything about it, but if you have any experiences with those two on a criminal level, an agent would be interested in talking to you."

"I don't."

"You said they were—"

"They haven't done anything criminal."

"Okay then. Please forward the letter. And if something happens, you have my number."

"Don't forget to send me your address."

"As soon as we hang up."

The call ended. A moment later, I received a text. I crossed out the address on the envelope and wrote the new one. Then, I deleted everything—the messages, the record of the phone call. I did keep the scrap of paper from Brian. I tucked it into the box with the roofie. I was not going anywhere near a guy who was involved with the Federal Bureau of Investigation.

I changed into workout clothes, took the letter to the lobby, and dropped it into the slot. I went for a run that lasted over an hour—up to Central Park and along the paths that wound in every direction. I didn't track the distance, and I didn't listen to music, just the throb of my heart and the hum of my thoughts.

38

I lied. Despite the ominous presence of the FBI, I still wanted to know what Nick had experienced with my neighbors. I'd managed to put it out of my head during my run, but when I was finished, it came back in a rush. Maybe Kent could help. Once he knew that I'd spoken to Nick, there was a chance he wouldn't feel as much need to protect Nick. It was possible I could get him talking more about what had happened. If not, I might figure out a way to speak with Nick without the hovering presence of law enforcement.

It must have been pretty serious if he had the FBI involved. What on earth had Rafe and Victoria done?

After my shower, I changed into high-heeled boots, leggings, and a dressy top and jacket. I threw on my winter coat and took the subway to The Moonlight Sonata.

It was an unusual time of day to be checking out a club of any kind. A lot of clubs wouldn't be open in the middle of the afternoon, but I'd checked their website and discovered they were open from eleven in the morning until two a.m., seven days a week.

I stood outside and studied the padded red door and those

heavy brass tacks. I grabbed the long iron handle and pulled. It was an effort to get it open. I kept my hand on the edge as I slipped inside the narrow opening I'd formed, feeling like Alice falling into another dimension.

The interior looked exactly like the website, so despite the website's 1990s feel in layout and color, their effort to present their image online was absolutely accurate. The room was large and dark. Three walls were lined with booths, and the center filled with tables nicely spaced. Four men sat in one of the booths. The rest of the tables were empty.

The bar occupied the wall at the rear, backlit shelves of alcohol reaching to the ceiling. Seated at the bar was an assortment of men with white, gray, and bald heads. An occasional woman dressed in bright colors broke up the monotony.

I approached the bar and ordered a martini. The bartender stared at me, obviously calculating my age, not for legal purposes, but relative to the other patrons. Still, he said nothing beyond asking what kind of vodka I preferred. I took a seat at the end of the bar. It was slightly curved, which allowed me to observe the others.

When my drink came, I took a sip and placed the glass in front of me. I wasn't sure what to do next. Everyone had glanced at me by now, several letting their gazes linger for longer than was reasonable, but it appeared that no one was curious enough to approach me and ask why I'd broken the age-barrier.

I took another sip of my drink and ate the first olive. This was getting me nowhere, and if I planned to drink martinis until someone spoke to me, that wouldn't work out well at all. I took a larger sip, then slid off the stool. Carrying my drink,

I walked around the others until I found a man seated between two empty stools.

"Mind if I sit here?"

He shrugged.

Not the welcome I'd hoped for. I settled on the stool and placed my glass on the bar. "Are you a regular here?"

He tugged on his earlobe, staring straight ahead at the rows of bottles. He had gray hair, cut short, and obviously kept trimmed on a regular basis. He wore a blue button-down shirt, although it was hard to tell for sure in the dim lighting. It might have been gray.

"Hookers are discouraged here," he said. "Didn't Stuart tell you that?"

"Is Stuart the bartender."

"Yes."

"I'm not a hooker."

"Then what are you here for?"

I lifted my glass and held it in front of me, far enough away to catch his peripheral vision.

He turned slowly. "This isn't a place where women your age tend to congregate."

I laughed. "Is there an age limit?"

He didn't smile.

"Am I bothering you?"

"It's a free country," he said. "But I'm not here to chit chat."

"Can I just ask a few quick questions?"

"Are you a reporter? Digging for dirt?"

"Nope. Just curious. Someone I know likes to come here, and I wasn't sure if it's a private club. The website didn't mention it."

"Why don't you ask the *someone* you know?"

"It's complicated."

"Sure it is."

"I noticed everyone seems older than I am. That's why I wondered if it was private, if it's expensive to join, or something."

"There's no membership. Most of us have been coming here for a long time. People your age don't find it to their liking. No electronic music. No fancy drink. Solid food, nothing exotic."

I nodded. "I can see that. I like plain, stick-to-your-ribs food."

"Good for you."

I took a sip of my drink.

"Do a lot of people that come here know each other?"

"Probably. I haven't asked."

"Maybe you know my friend."

"I already said, I don't come here to chit chat. Or pick up hookers."

"She's about my age. She has very short hair. She's thin and —"

"I've seen her around. Never talked to her. Did she do something to offend you? Or kill someone?"

"No." The conversation wasn't going anywhere useful. I needed to be more direct. "I think she meets people here for her business."

"Could be. Is she a hooker?"

"No. She's a...she trades...she's a day trader."

"Day trader?"

"She buys and sells stocks. Short term."

"Scammer."

"I think what she does is legal. And I don't think she—"

"I said I've never talked to her."

"Do you get people in here running scams?"

"Almost everyone's running a scam these days."

"Are they?"

He looked at me for the first time. His eyes were dark brown, steady and confident. "What do you want?"

"I just wanted to find out what my friend was doing here. Like you said, it doesn't seem like a place that's interesting to younger people."

"It's easier to bilk older people. We aren't as sharp as we were at one time. We're more sentimental, easily charmed. Most of us. But we try to look out for each other."

I nodded.

"Not that I'm saying your friend is out to get people. Just saying. Young women don't come in here, so if she does, it's probably because she wants something from someone, or something from a few different people. Maybe just looking for a sugar daddy. We do get that type in here. Hooker, sugar baby—is there a difference?" He snorted and picked up his drink.

The glass was filled with watery gold liquid and tiny ice cubes. I guessed it was whiskey and water. His hand shook slightly, and I wondered if it was his age or the possibility he'd been sitting in that spot for several hours.

"How long have you been coming here?" I asked.

"Forever."

"Are you here every weekend?"

"Every god damn day of the week."

"You must have some buddies here."

He shrugged.

It was clear the brief flow of information and opinions had stopped.

I ate the two remaining olives but left the last bit of liquid in the glass. There was nothing else I could find out here unless I figured out a way to follow Victoria inside and eavesdrop on whatever conversations she was having with the gentlemen at their club.

All I had was speculation. Although I suppose there were quite a few things I knew that were not happening there. Victoria wasn't meeting up with friends, and it was unlikely she was looking for a so-called sugar daddy. Despite Rafe's unconventional approach to relationships, it seemed unlikely she was looking for that sort of arrangement. But why the fancy outfit out of the past?

The man who hugged that bar seven days a week was right about one thing—she didn't go there to hang out. She wanted something from someone. I could have asked the bartender, but I didn't want my interest getting back to Victoria.

I needed to watch my back. I didn't think Victoria and Rafe could manage to manipulate me into something that would hurt me. I'm alert to that sort of thing—it's difficult to manipulate a manipulator. At the same time, I didn't want to be over-confident, arrogant and full of myself, thinking I was immune. Believing that Nick was stupid if they'd pulled him into something illegal without him being aware of what was happening. I'd made the mistake of being over-confident before. Skimming money from the candy bar fund-raising effort always came to mind.

What the hell had happened with Nick?

The martini had made me hungry. That, plus I hadn't eaten lunch. On the way home, I stopped at a Pho shop and ordered a large container of noodles and broth, veggies, and paper-thin beef. As I walked, the smell drove me insane, a thin aroma seeping out of the bag with every step, the steamy warmth seemingly intensified by the cold air around me.

At home, I opened the container. I didn't bother reheating it. The broth had cooled slightly, but not so much to undermine the flavor. I ate all the beef before starting on the noodles, glad to have something solid in my stomach, enjoying the comfort of the noodles once my stomach had stopped complaining.

When I was finished, I took a bottle of water and my cigarettes up to the roof. It was freezing cold, the sun going down in a milky sky, which for some reason made it feel colder. But I needed a cigarette. I didn't like putting it in those terms, but it was the truth. I needed the calming time with my thoughts, the aroma and the steady flowing in and out of the smoke.

I held the flame to the tip of the cigarette and inhaled. I'd positioned myself near the edge of the roof, the community ashtray beside me. I leaned on the half-wall and looked down at the street below.

As I inhaled for the third time, I saw two people emerge from my building—Victoria and Rafe.

They walked down the steps and stood by the curb. Victoria's arms were clutched around her middle, and she was looking at the ground. Rafe was talking and gesturing toward the street. Victoria moved away from him, and he grew more animated.

I stabbed out my cigarette and raced to the door. I hurried down the steps to the first floor and stood back from the doors, looking out. They were still there. They continued what was definitely starting to look like an argument. At one point, someone entered the building, but even as the door hovered partially open, I couldn't hear their voices.

Finally, they turned right and began walking. I shoved my hair inside my knit hat and went out, weaving among other pedestrians so there were always two or three people between them and me.

They walked eight blocks, turning onto Central Park West, then another ten blocks, and onto 74th Street, headed toward Columbus. They stopped across the street from a brownstone house. It looked almost out of place, charming and last-century, stark against the skyscrapers towering in the distance behind it. There was an edging of white along the bottom step from the snow that had lingered after the last time it had fallen.

Victoria stood several feet away from Rafe. She was hunched up again, clutching her body, her shoulders pulled up as she gazed at the house with a look of utter despair. Her back began to shake, and I realized she was sobbing.

Rafe took another step away from her. He was talking, waving his arms, looking at her. She kept her attention on the house. I moved closer, but not much, the street wasn't as crowded here, and all I had to shield me from their view was the line of cars parked along the curb. I couldn't hear a word he said.

After watching for several minutes, I sensed from Rafe's slowly fading gestures that his diatribe was coming to an end. I turned and walked quickly back toward Central Park, no better informed than when I'd gotten out of bed that morning.

39

As I waited for a traffic light on my walk back from following Victoria and Rafe, I pulled out my phone and sent a text to Kent.

Alex: *Dinner?*

He didn't reply. I arrived home, briefly considered knocking on his door, then turned toward my own apartment instead. I took off my coat and settled on the couch. I was staring at my phone, my mind traveling to the possibility that he wasn't interested, that he hadn't fallen hard, as Diana had suggested. That his minimalist life encompassed relationships as much as it did the furnishings and decor of his apartment.

My phone vibrated.

Kent: *Sure. I was going to text you. Should we go out?*

I smiled. My over-zealous agenda had clearly colored my thoughts regarding where he stood. I did have fun with him, and he was a creative and confident lover. There was nothing to not like, except maybe his proximity, which would make it difficult if things between us began to drift in the opposite direction as things often, usually did.

Another message arrived telling me he would stop by my

apartment, we'd get an Uber, and that he'd made reservations at a French restaurant. He hoped I liked snails. He wrote that —*snails*, not escargot. I wasn't sure whether to read that as playful or a revelation of his thoughts on the delicacy.

***

Seated across from him with a very small table between us, looking through the moving light of a candle that seemed to occupy nearly a third of the table, I waited for the server to uncork the wine. I was eager for a calming sip to slow my thoughts, bursting with questions about Nick and Victoria, Rafe, and the FBI.

We ordered our food. We sipped wine and talked about work.

The snails were delicious. Kent insisted it was only the garlic and butter I liked. If I'd had to eat them unadorned, I would find them disgusting. I didn't care. Each tiny curl of ocean-dwelling flesh had the perfect texture and buttery garlic flavor, dissolving throughout my mouth.

After the main course—veal in champagne sauce for both of us—was placed on the table, I turned the conversation to Arlinda. I told him about her penthouse and what it was like talking to her, feeling as if we'd crossed a barrier from client-photographer to something that felt like colleagues or friends, or something I couldn't quite define.

Kent suggested my job was an unusual one, that it might be hard to keep a professional relationship when everything about taking someone's photograph was so intimate. I agreed, just to be agreeable. Then I told him I'd asked her about day trading. The change in his expression was immediate.

"That was graceful," he said.

"Was it?"

"Moving from your client to our problematic neighbors so quickly—a perfect pirouette."

I speared a piece of veal and put it into my mouth. The sauce was incredible. I mourned that it would soon be gone.

"How did she react to you talking about your own issues when you're paid to focus on her?"

"It was casual. I just asked her what she thought about it."

"And what does she think?"

"That it isn't right for me because I don't have an innate interest in the business world."

He laughed. "Very perceptive."

"What, that she has insight into me?"

"I was being sarcastic. Isn't it obvious you need to be interested in those things if you're going to trade stocks?"

"I've always had the impression it wasn't much different from gambling, but it turns out it's a lot of work. And I'm a little confused about why Victoria is so eager for me to try it. At first, she made it sound like something you do in your spare time, that all you need are good instincts and an appetite for risk. Now she's—"

"I think I mentioned I'm not going to talk about them."

"You did." I sliced off another piece of veal. It was so tender, I could have cut it with my fork. "But I need to know what they want from me."

"No you don't."

I looked up at him. His tone was sharp, and it felt as if he was talking to someone who had a very different kind of relationship with him than I had. A wife, for example. He wasn't looking at me. I settled my fork on my plate and waited for him to lift his gaze. When he did, he didn't seem to be aware of how he'd sounded. I ate my piece of veal, chewing it slowly.

"It's simple, and you seem to want to make it complicated," he said. "Just stay away from them. Don't engage regarding their day trading. Simple. Finished."

"But I want to know what's going on."

"Why? It doesn't matter."

"I talked to Nick."

He raised his eyebrows slightly. "How did that happen?"

"I got his number from Brian."

He nodded. "Not very ethical, but okay. I'm surprised Brian did that."

"I had leverage."

"What kind of leverage?" He sounded nervous. I wanted to laugh, imagining he thought I might have slept with Brian to get the number.

"That letter from the FBI. I just told him I had something personal that belonged to Nick."

He nodded.

"Nick wouldn't tell me what the FBI was after, but he asked me whether Victoria and Rafe had involved me in anything criminal. He wanted to know if I was interested in talking to the FBI. Otherwise, he said he couldn't tell me anything."

The minute the words were out, I realized my mistake. I could have strung Kent along further, poked deeper if he thought Nick had told me something about my neighbors' crimes.

"So, I guess that's the end of that," he said.

"Why?"

"Have they involved you in something criminal?"

"Did Nick tell you they'd done anything illegal?"

"I told you everything I know."

"They never played these games with you?"

He shrugged.

I could see that they probably hadn't. He wasn't as easy to engage in conversation as I was, and he had a slightly intimidating appearance. It might have been that shaved head, along with the body of a man who lifted a lot of weights.

"I wonder what they did that was illegal? That involved Nick? Something so big that the FBI wants his help. It sounds crazy," I said.

"Are you this preoccupied with all your neighbors?"

"No."

"So, you're not asking everyone else about me, trying to find out what's going on in my life?"

I laughed. "You look so serious."

"I am."

I leaned on the table and touched the rim of my wine glass. I looked up at him with an inviting gaze. "I'm not checking into you."

"But you might."

I straightened and took a small forkful of lighter-than-air whipped potatoes. I licked the fork as if I was eating a popsicle. "You seem like someone who will tell me about yourself as we go along. And you're not doing anything illegal."

"That you know of."

"You're not trying to drag *me* into anything illegal." As I spoke, I thought about the illegal things I'd done. Kent would see those as far more threatening than anything Victoria and

Rafe might be up to. But I know what I'm doing. I'm careful, careful to the point of paranoia. Most of the time. Victoria and Rafe, especially Rafe, struck me as reckless.

"I just don't get your obsession. They can't *drag you into* something without you knowing."

"Obviously, they did something to Nick. Enough that the F-B-*I* is interested. That's not some petty crime."

He rubbed his hand across his face. "I really don't want to talk about this. It has nothing to do with me."

"You and Nick weren't close?"

"No."

"Do you stay in touch?"

"No. In fact, we didn't even say good-bye when he moved out. So I have no interest." He nudged his plate to the side.

The server scooted up to our table and picked up the plate. "Miss?" He looked at my nearly empty plate.

"Not yet." I smiled, and he backed away, looking concerned that he'd rushed me.

I ate the last piece of veal. I stabbed my fork into one of the three remaining straw-thin baby carrots and ate it, savoring each bite, regretting that the amazing food was almost gone.

"Do you want dessert?" Kent said.

"I was thinking about the cheesecake."

"Should we split a slice?"

I stared at him. I'd never heard a man suggest splitting a dessert. Usually, it was done reluctantly when a woman refused to order her own. Was he on a diet? Maybe he was hardcore about weight lifting and was worried about disturbing his balance of nutrients. But if that was the case, I didn't think he would be sharing a bottle of wine, having savored his own personal order of escargot, urging me to place a separate order for myself.

I told him I never shared dessert, and he looked thrilled. We didn't talk any more about Victoria and Rafe. It was clear that door was finally and firmly closed, so when we returned to our building, and he came to my apartment for a martini and sex, I didn't have any agenda other than enjoying his voice and his body.

40

Portland, Oregon

No matter how much time I spent gliding back and forth in the swing, gazing out my bedroom window, and waking from dreams to consider new options, I couldn't figure out a way that I was going to be able to explain the extra cash from my candy commission to my parents.

What I did decide was that the opportunity was too good to pass up. Tacking on a commission for my effort would be easy. It would be lucrative, and there was no way I'd be caught. On the very slight chance that someone who paid five dollars for a chocolate bar spoke to someone who had paid three, and they actually discussed price, I was confident they would see it as a contribution to a good cause—the church, and my development of job skills.

For the most part, I couldn't imagine that conversation ever happening. People get busy. They forget. People devour their delicious chocolate and move on to other things. I would figure out how to explain the cash once I had it in my hand, once I was ready to buy my car. And if I couldn't buy a car yet, I could save money for the future. Maybe that would be better.

I also decided that my bike was the best transportation. It was plausible that I needed it for candy sales, even in my own neighborhood. I reminded my mother I was trying to outsell my peers. I needed to move quickly from street to street.

She admired my initiative and tried to downplay what she saw as my lust for the cash prize. She liked that I wanted to help the church camp get their kitchen upgrade, and she liked that I was raising money for the church, period.

On Saturday mornings, when most people were home, I rode my bike furiously for a mile beyond our neighborhood. I wore shorts and cute tennies and a bright yellow T-shirt with a blue logo advertising our youth group. I put my hair in two French braids, which kept it neat while I pedaled through the breezy morning air. The hairstyle also added to my look of innocence and air of sweetness—a slightly childlike hairstyle for a high school girl. I went door-to-door with a huge smile on my face.

After two weeks and the sale of five hundred candy bars— a thousand dollars in my pocket—I was running out of nearby housing developments to approach. I took some of my earnings and bought an all-day bus ticket. The bus line kindly offered storage for bicycles, and I rode to the next town, holding my backpack on my lap and nibbling on a candy bar that I'd recorded as a sale, returning a few dollars of the money I'd earned.

A certain number of my customers wanted to write checks, which was a problem. They expected to make the checks out to the church. Several mentioned wanting to write the expense off on their tax return as a charitable contribution.

For those frugal customers, I offered to sell them extra candy, explaining I could then discount the bars to three dollars. I accepted their checks and ticked them off as a loss for my own income.

It was a bit of paperwork, trying to keep track of my different candy-buying customers, but I sat at my desk every Saturday evening and copied onto the forms the names and sales I'd jotted down in a small notebook while I was out selling.

The cash from those who were happy to pay more piled up in an empty shoebox at the back of my closet, buried inside a larger box that held my winter hats and scarves. I loved opening that box, loved touching the bills, arranging them in neat stacks, re-counting them every so often to make sure I was keeping accurate records.

When my stash hit three-thousand dollars, I was giddy, walking around the house with a huge grin on my face. My parents said it was nice to see me so happy. My mother asked if I had a crush on a boy. When I denied it, she looked at me sideways in a way that said—*I'll let you keep your privacy. I know what I know, and a boy put that smile on your lips.*

The window for selling candy would be closing in a few weeks, and I started to worry that I wasn't going to hit my personal goal, even though I'd soared past all the other kids in the youth group.

The woman coordinating the candy sales had made posters that were plastered all over the walls of our youth lounge—a room where we were encouraged to hang out before meetings started, lounging around on second-hand couches and beanbag chairs. Each poster had four thermometers on it, the names of the sellers printed in bold letters below. The red colored inside the outlines of the thermometers indicated the mercury rising past dollar figures listed along the side. Each week when we reported sales, the leader went around and colored in our thermometers to show those whose temperatures were rising the fastest.

My thermometer had been filled to the top after two weeks, so a second poster was made. This one was dedicated to me. It had a larger thermometer and a scale with greater increments. The second thermometer was already at the forty-percent mark.

On the last Saturday evening, after a very successful day, I came downstairs to get a snack. I wanted some cheese crackers to occupy me while I updated the form I would have to turn in the following morning with the cash and checks collected that week.

As I turned the corner from the foot of the stairs, I heard a female voice in our kitchen. It didn't belong to my mother. The woman's voice was shrill, and it sounded like she was lecturing my mother. I moved closer to the doorway, keeping out of sight. I made my way around to the space between the back door to the kitchen and the door to the basement where it was easy to stand in the corner and hear very clearly what was being said.

"You haven't dealt with her defiance. It's always been that way, and it's been clear for several years now that she was headed for trouble. It's much more difficult to stop the current as they get older. You ignored the warnings, and here you are."

"That's not fair," my mother said. "She has very strict rules."

It was clear they were talking about me. It annoyed me that

my mother thought she needed to explain her parenting to some other church lady. I recognized this woman's voice now. She had twin daughters who were Freshmen in high school. She kept them on a choke chain, even staying at the church during youth activities, waiting in our youth lounge because she couldn't bear the thought of leaving her girls alone with a bunch of other kids and an *inadequate* number of adults. I'd seen the twins at school, always together, looking terrified and standing too close to each other as if that gave them strength.

"Your *very strict rules* haven't taught her godly behavior, or paved the way for a humble, grateful heart. It's almost as if she has no conscience. Who even thinks of something like this?"

"She has a conscience. Don't say things like that. I said I'll talk to her. I'm not going to rush to a conclusion until I hear her side of the story."

"There is no other *side* to the story. My sister bought twenty-five candy bars, and she paid five dollars apiece. That's outrageous. Your daughter is stealing. And she's doing it by hiding under the church's blessing. That makes it a hundred times worse."

"I said I'd talk to her."

"And punish her, I would hope."

"You've made your feelings clear," my mother said. "Is there anything else?"

"The money needs to be returned."

"You're jumping ahead. You can't assume—"

"It's not about assuming. My sister *paid* five dollars for those candy bars. She commented that it was kind of a lot, but the girl who sold them to her—*Alexandra something or other*, she said—was so sweet and so enthusiastic. She told such a delightful story about her camp experience that my sister wanted to do all she could. She was taken advantage of. It's terrible. You should be devastated."

"I need to talk to her."

"Are you accusing my sister of lying?"

"No. I just need—"

"I expect you to let me know the outcome. I think you owe it to m...to my sister." A chair scraped on the floor.

I don't think my mother responded, but I couldn't be sure. I ducked out of the corner and hurried to the stairs. I climbed to the second floor quickly, trying not to run, which would make too much noise.

I shoved the forms and my notebook into my bottom desk drawer and sat on my bed with a novel. I knew that any minute, my mother would be coming into my room for a chat.

41

Reaching a dead end in finding out what my neighbors were up to, I turned my attention back to Stephanie.

It seemed as if I couldn't escape people wanting to mess with my head, and even though I usually liked the game of it all, I was starting to feel unsettled that quite a few people had the potential to de-rail my life in unforeseen ways.

The shortest path to Stephanie was through her daughter.

I sent Eileen a text and asked if she wanted to meet for a late lunch. It was raining, no snow expected until the evening. I didn't mind going out in the rain—good boots and a good coat do an excellent job of keeping me dry. Eileen felt differently.

Eileen: *No thanks. Too wet. Too cold.*

Alex: *I feel cooped up.*

Eileen: *Give me a call. Or go out and call me from the restaurant, I'll keep you virtual company.*

She followed this with a hysterically laughing emoji.

I put my phone down and thought about this. It was

Sunday. Most places would be packed, and eating lunch in a restaurant while juggling my phone didn't sound appealing. I wondered if she'd invite me to her apartment, but the presence of her mother would make that equally unappealing.

Alex: *Going for takeout. I'll call when I get back.*

Eileen: *Now I feel hungry. What are you getting?*

Alex: *Probably Indian.*

Eileen: *Even hungrier!*

Alex: *Hungry enough to get a few raindrops on your head?*

Eileen: *It's not a few raindrops. Have you looked out the window?*

I had. Water was coming down in icy sheets that were washing away a lot of the remaining snow from the last storm while turning other lingering strips of snow into ice sculptures outlining the roots of trees planted in their sidewalk openings.

Alex: *Ok. I'll call you. I'm bored. But food first.*

I dressed in a hooded jacket and jeans and knee-high boots, and still, I was wet when I reached the Indian place I liked best for their amazing tandoori chicken. I ordered an eggplant dish, naan, and, of course, tandoori chicken.

Back at home, I stripped off my jeans that had managed to get wet between the tops of my boots and the bottom of my jacket. I put on leggings, turned up the heat, and filled a plate with food. I took it to the couch, spreading a cloth napkin across my lap. A glass of sparkling water with lime sat on the table in front of me.

I rested my phone on top of two throw pillows, so it was closer to my face and made a video call to Eileen.

The first words out of her mouth were—"What are you eating?"

I told her what was on the menu and took a bite of naan

while she digested the image of my delicious food and went on about how jealous she was, how adventurous I was to go out in horrible weather, and how the turkey sandwich she was planning sounded dry and dull.

"Ask your mother to make you some homemade soup."

"She's not here. She had a thing after church today."

Eileen was an interesting person. She and I always found a lot to talk about. It rarely seemed as if there were five or six years difference in our ages. We both liked clothes. We both liked the artistry and power of makeup. We liked a lot of the same TV shows, and it was fun to talk about career plans with her, not that my career had had a lot of planning to it, or that I even had a career. So I suppose her obsession with modeling, her ambition to achieve something aside from simply earning a living, inspired me.

Even though she was now a relatively rich woman, it hadn't slowed her ambition at all. She still went out for photoshoots and commercial work five days a week and some weekends.

I was calling her to find out what her mother was up to, but it wasn't the only reason I talked to her. I viewed her as a friend. "I guess you're stuck with turkey. Unless you want to make your own soup."

"Takes too long."

"True."

I heard the sound of drawers opening and utensils moving about.

"Anything new in your life?" I asked.

"Not really. I have a shoot with a photographer I've wanted to work with for a long time, so that's kind of amazing."

"Nice."

"Things have picked up lately. It's kind of funny...ever

since I found out about all that money, I'm getting more interesting jobs, and better paying jobs. It's strange."

"The jujitsu of not caring," I said.

"That's what they say, but I've never experienced it. My brain has a hard time grasping it. How's your work?"

"Good. It's funny that you're going on a photoshoot and I'm doing them. But I don't think people are craving a chance to work with the unparalleled Alexandra Mallory."

She laughed. "It could happen. Just wait."

I took a sip of water and glanced away from the screen, so my next comment wasn't too intense. "Your mother shocked everyone with her new look last week."

"Shocked in a good way, I hope."

"Yes. Absolutely. She looks a lot younger. And very professional."

"I know. It's kind of cute. It was actually a lot of fun shopping with her."

"So it was your idea?"

"No. It was hers."

"Is it rude to ask if you used some of your windfall?" I knew it was rude, by almost any standard, but I needed to know. The answer would tell me how much Stephanie wanted to put into this unexplained transformation. If she'd spent her own money, it seemed like a huge warning to me that nothing was going to stop her in whatever she was pursuing.

Eileen laughed. "That's why I like you. Of course you know it's rude, but you ask anyway. You add that little caveat to try to soften it, but the question is the same."

I wasn't sure I'd tried very hard to soften it, but if she wanted to think that, I wouldn't argue.

"And yes," Eileen said, "I used some of my so-called

windfall. I wanted to help her. She's done so much for me. All my life. She sacrificed a lot when I was small, working long hours and taking care of me, making sure I got to do things other kids did like taking dance classes and wearing cute clothes even though she couldn't do things for herself. She deserves some pampering. I can tell she feels better about who she is. Please don't tell her I said that. Please. I shouldn't talk about her, but it made her so happy. And it made me happy. It felt like shopping with a friend."

"I won't tell. I'm glad she feels better. Is she hoping to meet someone, now that you're all grown up?"

She laughed. "I've been grown up for a while. I don't think it's about that. She just thought she needed to give a better impression."

The only other place where Stephanie needed a better impression was around Trystan and his team and our clients. She wouldn't be dressing like that, spending all that time putting on makeup, unless she had a very clear plan. Even though Eileen had paid, surely Stephanie felt uncomfortable letting her daughter treat her to a pricey makeover and an even pricier wardrobe without a very strong purpose to override that discomfort.

"I'm sure it will help her in her career, whatever her goals are," I said. "It never hurts to look good, does it?"

She laughed again. "Absolutely not. It's the reason my career exists at all—enticing women into believing they can look as good as an air-brushed photograph under flattering lights, with professional hair and makeup. But we'll all keep chasing that image, right?"

"Are you getting cynical about your own career?"

"I've always known that was true. Maybe now that I can

relax and I don't have to scramble as hard for a steady income, I see it more clearly. But I still think it's fun to make the most of how you look. For whatever reason, it feels good."

"It does," I said. "That was very generous of you."

"I don't see it that way. She earned every penny of it. And it's not like I don't have plenty to spare." She giggled. A moment later, I heard the creak of a door and the snap of a latch falling into place.

We talked for a while longer about a guy she was interested in. She'd met him on a photoshoot. He was in charge of the hotel setting where the photographs had been staged.

I hadn't learned why Stephanie was making such a dramatic change, but there was no doubt now that it was related to her dinner with Trystan.

42

The minute the apartment door swung open, Stephanie heard Eileen talking. Her voice was clear and slightly hyper. It carried through the small apartment. The words assaulted her ears, as shocking as if ice water had poured down on her head.

"She earned every penny of it. And it's not like I don't have plenty to spare." This was followed by an excited giggle.

The sound startled and upset her. She hadn't heard Eileen giggle like that since high school. Was something wrong with her? And what on earth was she talking about? Plenty to spare? Earned every penny?

Stephanie hadn't meant to eavesdrop. It was wrong. Not only in God's eyes, but it broke the trust of living in a shared apartment with your adult daughter. It made that daughter feel like a child again. Eileen would be incredibly upset if Stephanie asked her what those words meant, letting on that she'd been listening, but she needed to know. They frightened her.

Had Eileen been talking about her? Saying she'd earned the money Eileen spent on her new clothes? And what did that mean about money to spare? Since when? Everything about it bothered her, most of all the person listening on the other end—who was it?

Eileen was a private person. Just like her mother. Why was she talking about money at all?

As Stephanie turned to close the front door, she heard the sound of Eileen's bedroom door closing at the same time. So…Eileen must have heard her come in. It was fine that she wanted to keep her conversations private. It should be that way. Eileen had a right to her own life. But did she suspect what she'd said already had been overheard? If so, there might be a chance to ask a few questions without seeming too nosey.

Stephanie went into her bedroom and put her purse and computer bag on the small desk in the corner. She took off her coat and hat and tossed them on the bed. She rubbed her hands together, her fingertips numb with cold despite the gloves. She stripped off her church clothes, pulling on a new pair of jeans and a kitten-soft shirt. The clothes felt wonderful, like swaddling that seemed to smooth away the flaws in her body. Simply hanging around her apartment felt good because of the comfort and stylish look of the things her daughter had purchased for her. Except once again, that purchase had taken on the weight of guilt. She hadn't liked taking Eileen's money, and she had no idea how to make that feeling stop creeping in to torture her, stealing her enjoyment of the new clothes and her beautiful hair.

Seeing the stares of her friends at church, responding to the comments about her hair had been an ordeal. Although her senses had been alert to sniffing out judgment, she'd been aware of very little. People who spoke to her about the change seemed genuinely supportive. Their questions had been mild, not the sharp blades of accusation she'd expected. Still, after it was over, she was glad to escape the attention. It was nice to be noticed in a positive way, but her desire to stay out of the spotlight hadn't changed at all.

She made a cup of tea and a turkey sandwich. It surprised her to notice that the package of turkey had been depleted. It was both pleasing and unsettling that Eileen was so casual now about her weight that she would eat a decent-sized sandwich.

The sound of Eileen's voice continued seeping through the bedroom door until Stephanie's plate held nothing but crumbs and a curl of wilted lettuce. A moment later, Eileen entered the kitchen. "How was church?"

"Nice…" Her patterned response was to invite Eileen to join her some time, but she'd done it too often. The invitation would spoil the peace between them, transforming Stephanie back into the worrying, overbearing mother. But her overbearing nature wasn't gotten rid of so easily. The words came out before she could stop them. "You were on the phone a long time."

Eileen grimaced and went to the kettle. She refilled it and began gathering the things for a mug of tea. "What else can you do on a rainy Sunday afternoon? Do you want tea?"

Stephanie nodded. "If it's not too nosey, who were you talking to?"

"Alex."

"Oh."

"Don't be like that."

"I'm just worried. I've told you to watch out for her."

"I know how to choose friends, Mom. I've been doing it all

my life. Yes, I know there were a few bad choices—"

"Mmm, hmm."

"Okay. But I learned…and I know how to look out for myself. I'm almost twenty-seven!"

Stephanie felt several sharp replies pressing against her throat. She kept them inside, putting the mug to her lips instead.

"I'm sure I experience a different side of her than you do," Eileen said.

"There's only one side. She's a manipulator."

"I'm going to take my tea into my room if you keep talking like that."

Stephanie bristled. Why did Eileen think she was allowed to say whatever she pleased, but Stephanie had to watch every word? It made their relationship unequal in a new way. If she was supposed to restrain her motherly concerns, Eileen should also look at her own attitude.

"I couldn't help overhearing part of your conversation when I came home. I wasn't eavesdropping—your door was open."

"Just put it out of your mind. Whatever you heard, or think you heard."

Stephanie knew she had to choose. She wouldn't be given an opportunity to dissect everything Eileen had said. The money mattered more, and it might have the effect of revealing the rest anyway. "It made me uncomfortable to hear you talking about money. I already feel bad about all that you spent on me. I'm embarrassed if you're telling someone else about it."

"It's fine. Like I said, and you obviously already know, you earned it."

"I wasn't aware you have plenty of money to spare."

"I told you not to worry about it."

"What did you mean by that? Is she giving you money for some reason?"

"What?"

"Is Alexandra giving you money? Is that what you spent on —"

"Why would she do that?"

"I have no idea. She's manipulative. She's dangerous."

"Stop saying those things. Just because you can't get along, you don't need to poison my relationship with her."

"I wasn't aware you had a *relationship*."

"We're friends, which I don't have to explain to you."

Stephanie took a deep breath and held it for a moment. She needed to think this through. Getting into an argument would push Eileen right into Alexandra's arms. It was conventional wisdom among mothers—fighting against your child's friend—boy or girl—made that undesirable person more attractive to your child. It was some sort of perverse rebellion on the child's part, a desire to prove the parent wrong, a need to assert power over one's own life. Of course, that applied to young children and teenagers, but did the parent-child relationship ever change so significantly that those factors weren't still at work?

She needed to be careful. It would be awful to destroy her newfound closeness with her daughter. Eileen was everything to her, the only person in her life that she truly loved. She'd come so close to losing her before, through no fault of her own. If another breach formed between them, it would be Alexandra's fault, but Stephanie still had the power to maintain a bridge across the chasm.

The change in Eileen was driving Stephanie mad. Eileen was eating like a normal person, warmer to her mother, excited about life. She even seemed happier in her career, and Stephanie was pretty sure she was getting more calls to go out on photo shoots and television commercials. What was going on? It couldn't all be the result of Alexandra's influence. If anything, there should be some negative behavior that came from going out with that girl—drinking too much, and who knew what other kinds of risky, ungodly behavior.

It was confusing. A large part of her very much wanted to emulate Alex's confidence in her own life—Alex's lack of concern for how others perceived her and the firm belief that she deserved success—but at the same time, there was something deeply disturbing about that woman.

"Did you tell Alexandra you paid for my clothes?"

Eileen glared at her. "Stop treating me like I'm ten years old."

As if time itself were conspiring against her, the timer chimed to announce Eileen's tea was done steeping. She pulled out the bag, dropped it onto a plate, picked up her mug, and walked out of the room.

43

After following them to the brownstone, I didn't see Victoria or Rafe for three days. I started to wonder if they'd split up during the inaudible argument I'd witnessed. I couldn't recall ever going more than a day without seeing one of them.

They were so deliberate in their constant appearance outside of my apartment, I rarely returned home without encountering one or the other. If they missed me coming home, they knocked on my door.

On Wednesday evening, I was sitting near my living room window looking out, thinking about not much of anything. It was raining—a slow, steady drip that seemed more like water falling off the leaves of trees after a storm than water dripping down from the sky itself.

The sidewalk below my window looked to be deserted, although it was hard to tell because only the outer edge was in my line of sight.

Across the street, people were coming and going every ten minutes or so from the deli that was open until nine on Wednesdays. Most of them hadn't bothered with umbrellas, probably because of the odd nature of the rain, so they hunched and ran from Ubers or nearby buildings or the occasional taxi.

As it grew closer to nine, the foot traffic slowed. There was a rush of three people at five minutes before nine, and then the lights inside the deli went out.

I'd thought about texting Kent to see if he wanted to hang out, but I wasn't in the mood for a martini or sex, wine, or a cigarette. Not that there was any place to smoke with the constant drip that would make the roof garden miserable unless we huddled up near the door to the stairs.

As I considered the emptiness of my evening, a man ran across the street and pounded on the deli door. Of course the place remained dark, the door closed. A moment later, the man turned, and I saw it was Rafe. He began shouting at someone on my side of the street.

A moment later, he turned back toward the building, raising his arm and hitting the door with more force. It wasn't surprising that he thought they should open specially for him. He pressed his face against the glass, peering inside. Victoria came into view. She darted across the street. She was barefoot and wearing a flimsy dress. In that short time that it took her to cross the street, her dress began sticking to her back as if drops of rain were tacking it to her skin. She huddled under the narrow overhang.

Rafe turned to her, and they began shouting at each other. I got up and eased my window open, moving to the side so they wouldn't see me if they happened to look up, although they were so intensely focused on each other, I doubted that would happen.

This time, it was Victoria who had a lot to say. She was screaming at him, but even though I could hear her voice now, I couldn't make out the words. The splat of the raindrops, the distance, the occasional car passing by, and possibly the way voices carried between buildings made the words indistinct. She hardly seemed to take a breath as she cried out her complaint and rage. It had a pent-up quality, as if she'd reached the end of something that had been building for a long time.

I'd never heard them shouting in their apartment. I wasn't sure if that was due to the age of the building, that the walls were solid and well-made, or if they never shouted. Now I'd witnessed two fights in less than a week. Perhaps day trading wasn't working out as well as it had in the past. As Arlinda had noted, I didn't follow the business news enough to know if there had been any erratic movements in the stock market.

Rafe reached out and grabbed the front of Victoria's dress. The flimsy fabric tore and fell away from her body like tissue paper. She was naked underneath. She lurched away from him, tearing the dress further.

Suddenly, he was behind her. He grabbed her wrists and held them in one hand, forcing her body close to his, turning her toward the street. There wasn't that much traffic, but I sensed the cars that did go by were slowing, staring at the naked woman getting splashed by rain now as they'd moved out from the overhang.

Her face was contorted, and because they'd turned directly toward our building, I heard a whimpering sound coming from her. She squirmed, but he held tight. After a few minutes, she stopped fighting him. She seemed resigned to standing there all night, freezing and exposed.

I stood. I grabbed my coat and shoved my arms into the sleeves. I went into the bedroom and took another coat out of the closet and folded it over my arm. I picked up my keys and phone and went out. I hurried down the stairs, watching my feet, paying attention to the water that had collected on the steps from people coming and going.

When I reached the lobby, I increased my pace and pushed my way out the door.

Victoria and Rafe weren't anywhere in sight. I looked up and down the street. I crossed over and walked up to the next building. Where had they gone so quickly? Gathering my things hadn't taken that long, had it?

I continued along the street, letting the rain fall on my face, squinting to keep my eyes clear of water. At the corner, I turned in a circle, checking the cross street and looking back down West Fifty-first. Had they gotten into a cab? They wouldn't have had time to order an Uber during the few brief minutes when I was making my way down the stairs. It wasn't possible that I'd missed them. Unless they'd rushed across the street and up the stairs while I was in my bedroom. That scenario seemed unlikely in the amount of time that had passed.

I retraced my steps and walked to the other end of the street, peering into the alcoves of the buildings that had recessed entrances. No Victoria. No Rafe.

It made no sense that they'd gotten into a cab, or even run to the corner and disappeared in the darkness before I reached the street. She was mostly undressed. Where would they go? I returned to my building and pressed myself against the rough exterior under the narrow overhang.

I stood listening to the drip of water that sounded heavy and slightly thick, as if blood were falling from the sky and splattering on the pavement. The sound made me step away from my protective covering and look up, but of course, I saw nothing. No one leaned over the edge of the roof garden, bleeding onto the sidewalk below. The windows facing the street glowed with light behind closed blinds. From my own window, the light was brighter because my blinds were open.

I gave the street one last glance in each direction, then went inside. As I approached the last few steps to the second-floor landing, I walked more slowly, keeping my steps soft, almost soundless. I crept along the hallway and leaned against my neighbors' door. I pressed my ear against the wood and held my breath, listening.

The rooms beyond the door were silent. It didn't mean they weren't there, but I wouldn't find out anything about their raw, ugly fight by straining to hear through a door. I knocked softly. No one answered. I knocked a few more times and was greeted with the same deafening silence.

As I straightened, I glanced up at the ceiling. In the far corner of the narrow alcove between our two apartments, nestled in the corner like a cockroach that had grown the ability to fly, was a tiny camera. I was shocked for a moment, but it provided the answer to a nagging question—Victoria's curiosity months ago regarding surveillance cameras. At first, I'd thought her question was a ploy to crash my photography class. Then I thought she was planning to spy on Rafe. Now, it seemed they'd been spying on me. No wonder they always had a sense of when I was leaving or returning to my apartment.

I unlocked my door and went inside. Why was it so important to them that they know my routine? And did Brian know they'd installed that camera? He must, he was too attentive to every detail of the building's upkeep to have missed seeing it. Every time I wanted to vow I would stop thinking about Rafe and Victoria, stop trying to understand them, something new popped up, pushing me further into their convoluted world.

44

Since the evening when I'd photographed her in her home, Arlinda had had two private meetings with Trystan to go over the photographs and his analysis of the personality and aptitude tests. He'd given the rest of us an overview of their discussions, but of course, we didn't know the intimate, unvarnished details of every challenge Arlinda faced in her life. I wondered how much she'd shared those with Trystan.

A text from her in the middle of the afternoon on a Thursday surprised me by the sheer fact it had shown up. When I read it, I was even more surprised. She was inviting me to join her for a yoga class followed by tea and some *post-yoga sustenance* at an Indian restaurant near the studio.

I was quite sure Trystan would not think this was a good idea. In fact, I was sure Diana would also advise against it. Any contact with Arlinda after she was done with our services would mean nothing, but right now, it would distort whatever plan Trystan had laid out for her. It would disrupt the process. It would introduce confusion to our roles and damage her clarity.

I could have told her those things. At the same time, I was

aware that if she came away from her interaction with us feeling fully satisfied, no matter how that satisfaction came about, it would be good for Trystan in the end. It wasn't as if I was working to lure a client away from him. I was being unorthodox, crossing boundaries, and possibly undermining him and his process. But I was also certain that on one level, he would respect my disregard for the process in favor of his ultimate goal—providing Arlinda with what she needed to get *un-stuck*.

Arlinda and I arranged to meet in the lobby of the yoga studio, which was housed, ironically for me, in a brownstone. As I walked up the steps to the door with its beveled glass, I thought about Victoria and her adoration for the house she and Rafe owned. I wondered what the hold-up was in their moving out of their small apartment. I also wondered if any part of what Victoria had said about it was true.

Something about their body language as they'd stood across the street from that house spoke of longing, regret, and loss, not ownership. If the house belonged to them, wouldn't they have walked confidently up those steps as I was now?

It made no sense that they would lie about it. What did I care about where they lived or whether they could afford a multi-million dollar home? Were they trying to impress me? It seemed they wanted me to think they were more successful than they were, but what was the point of that? I suppose they hoped I would be enticed into day trading, expecting to emulate their success. But why did they care whether or not I became a day trader?

The scene in front of the brownstone and the more disturbing one outside the deli made me think that whatever weird game they'd been playing was starting to come apart.

I put those thoughts outside of my mind, looking forward to the controlled breathing and body movements of yoga that were designed to do just that—dissolve spinning thoughts. I vowed that Victoria wouldn't intrude while I angled my body into downward dog, and Rafe's mocking voice was not going to wind its way along my spine when I was twisted into a half lord of the fishes pose.

Inside the door, Arlinda leaned close and gave me a light, friendly hug, which I barely had time to return before she pulled away, not seeming to care whether or not I'd done my part.

The foyer was decorated with a few comfortable, armless chairs. A vase filled with white roses stood on an antique sideboard. They gave off an aroma of money, more small white buds than I could easily count, fresh and soft in the dead of winter.

The studio itself was a large room at the front of the building. An alcove lined with windows looked out into the branches of the trees planted at the edge of the curb. Sheer curtains hung over the windows, allowing the yoga participants to gaze at the natural beauty. The filmy fabric and the height of the first floor relative to the street, meant no passersby would be able to peer in at our slow, liquid movements as we worked our way from the centering positions through to the final corpse pose.

There were already six mats on the floor. Women were seated in the center of their mats, turned toward their neighbors, talking quietly. The teacher had set up a mat, a tiny fountain of trickling water on a low table, and a phone in a wireless speaker stand at the front of the room.

Arlinda and I pulled off our boots and put them in the small coat room that opened off the back of the class space. We hung our coats and returned to the studio. Arlinda handed me the turquoise mat she'd brought for me. We unrolled the mats, settled on the floor cross-legged, and waited for the class to begin. Arlinda said nothing in the way of small talk, and I followed her lead. I wondered suddenly at the point of inviting me to the class. Couldn't we have simply met for tea and *sustenance*?

On the surface, Yoga looks easy. It's not. Ninety minutes spent moving about in the confines of that six-foot mat can work up quite a sweat, depending on the teacher and the skill level of the students. Even if it doesn't go that far, the slow movement through various poses feels rigorous because muscles that often get ignored come into play, and the joints and tendons are being asked to work harder than usual.

The teacher started the soundtrack of bells and wood flutes. The arrangement was beautifully timed so that during pauses in the instrumental sounds, the fountain added its own background music. She spoke in a calm, low voice as she guided us through each pose. Her voice was soft but carried clearly throughout the room, making me wonder whether the space had perfect acoustics or she had a well-trained voice. Possibly both.

She walked around the room while she spoke, gently adjusting our bodies when the alignment wasn't quite as good as it could have been. She didn't push hard, didn't shame anyone who was so far from the required pose it was impossible to tell they were mirroring the others.

The ninety minutes flew by, and before I knew it, my body felt refreshed and strong, reminding me I needed to work yoga back into my life. Ten minutes every now and then was not the same thing. Moments later, we were sliding our arms into coats, feet into boots, and walking out to the steps leading to the sidewalk.

Arlinda said that despite the convenience, she preferred a taxi over an Uber. She didn't explain why, even when we were settled onto the hard bench of a back seat, careening along the six blocks that separated the Yoga studio from the Indian restaurant she'd chosen.

The place was packed, but they'd reserved a secluded booth near the back for Arlinda.

She opened her menu. "How hungry are you?"

"Not terribly."

She ordered garlic Naan, Oolong tea, and an assortment of dips for the Naan.

When the tea was poured and steaming in our small cups, she folded her hands and rested them on the edge of the table. "My instinct was right. I can't talk to Trystan about the changes in my life."

I'd known this since she first suggested it, and I think I'd known it since she'd thrown that glass of expensive red wine all over Cherry's white blouse. It had been a wordless statement meant to shock, an act of silent rage. It was meant to shut everyone up, meant to change the subject. In fact, it was meant to bring a sudden close to the evening. It had succeeded on every front.

I wondered if she'd ever apologized to Cherry. From what I'd observed of her, I guessed she'd simply handed over a check for the dry cleaning, possibly for a new blouse, and said nothing more about it.

She took a sip of her tea, recoiling slightly at the heat. "I know I'm putting you in an awkward position, but I knew from the moment you started photographing me that you see the world clearly, and that's what I need."

"Trystan is very insightful."

"You don't need to defend him."

"I'm not. It's the truth."

"I'm sure it is, but he's all about career growth—"

"Not entirely."

She smiled. She took a sip of tea. She turned and looked across the room, not appearing to search for anything in particular, just observing what was happening around us. Finally, she turned back. "This is deeply personal. So personal that I can't talk to my friends or colleagues."

"Trystan is very good at what he does," I said. "He has a lot of insight. And if you're worried that he won't keep your confidence, that would never happen. Never." The words coming out of my mouth surprised me a little. I didn't feel as if I was simply doing my job, saying what I was supposed to. I believed these things about him.

"But this isn't just about stagnation in my career, it's about my whole life. It's about who I am."

"Did you know that when you signed up with us?"

"No. I knew I was bored. I've been feeling empty, like I have no direction. I know I have control issues, which you saw with Cherry. I think the control issues come with having something that's your own, that you nurtured from an idea into something so big it sometimes looks completely unfamiliar, as if it has nothing to do with you."

"So, are you looking for our help with that? With not being so controlling?"

"Because it might damage what I've built? No. This is so

much bigger than feeling dead in my career. I think my desire to control everything is because I was trying to avoid looking inside, making my whole life about what was happening outside of me. And I've figured out the reason why."

"Then I suppose you didn't need us after all. Trystan will be disappointed."

"Not at all. In fact, it was talking to you that first night that made my eyes start to open."

"How is that?"

"When I told you that cooking was like sex."

I laughed. "That's random."

"It's not. I want to do something creative in my life. Building the company was what I loved. Now, it can take care of itself. It might not have my fingerprint on every single part of it, but it will continue to thrive."

"It sounds like you're saying—"

"Yes. I am. I want out. I want to pursue something with food. It makes me feel alive. But there's more than that. It wasn't just talking to you about it that opened my eyes."

The Naan and spreads arrived, and we both eased back from the intensity between us to taste the hummus, eggplant, and yogurt dips on soft, warm bread that indeed felt like sex itself.

"I know why I feel dead inside."

"Why is that?"

"When that guy knelt and proposed…"

I waited as she paused, staring at me, the tip of her tongue creeping out to touch her lip. She took a deep breath. "The reason I hated Cherry for bringing that up was because it was a huge turning point in my life. I knew I didn't love that man, but I regretted that I didn't understand what was really happening. I hate remembering it because I feel like I turned in the wrong direction after that. I met Russ, and we fell into a pattern, and now half my life has passed."

"Not half. Not technically."

She gave me a grim smile. "He's comfortable. I like him. But something…"

I wanted to tell her to stop tiptoeing around. She was very direct, and yet here she was talking about her love life as if she were a high school girl. I felt like I should offer a prompt of some kind, but I had no idea where she was headed.

"I talked to Serena about cooking. How I feel about it."

I scooped up eggplant dip with a piece of Naan, folded it to keep the dip contained, and put it into my mouth. Maybe she'd been waiting for my tongue to be incapacitated, maybe she'd finally worked her away around to it, for whatever reason, she spoke quickly, telling the story with an efficiency that made it impossible to react as I focused on chewing and swallowing my food gracefully.

"I feel very close to Serena. She's been beside me forever. She knows me inside and out. I realized, when I talked to her about this, that I'm in love with her. So I put my neck under the blade and told her. She feels the same." Arlinda's eyes filled with tears. "In that single moment, I felt like my life was starting over. Everything has meaning again. I'm ready to walk away from the Caruso Agency. Talking to her, I felt like I could do anything. I already told Russ, and he's in the process of moving out. I feel like I'm sixteen." She gave me a smile that indeed looked like that of a sixteen-year-old girl, full of life and hope.

I offered encouraging words, not really paying attention to what I was saying. All I could think was that it probably wasn't in the cards for me to ever experience feelings like the ones that were making her face look like it did right then. That thought should have made me sad, but instead, I simply felt calm and slightly detached. I was pleased for Arlinda and proud that I'd influenced her life. I was also curious what it would be like to be so overwhelmed by emotion that it transformed my face, but I doubted I would ever know.

45

When Trystan texted me and asked me to come to his office, I knew that I'd dodged his intrusive questions for longer than he liked. There was more to those questions and criticisms than a casual interest in my life. He wanted something, and for whatever reason, he hadn't been upfront about it.

This surprised me. Everything I knew about him so far was the complete opposite of hesitant and cautious. From the moment I first spoke to him, he'd given the impression he said exactly what he was thinking. He was a man who knew precisely what he wanted. At least that's how it was when he'd offered me a position working with him.

When it suited his goals, he'd had no qualms about changing my job description. He offered me a position as an innocuous customer satisfaction manager. I had accepted. Then, suddenly I was a photographer. I loved the change, but it hadn't come wrapped in hedging words and a delicate stepping around the issue.

I walked down the hallway and knocked on his door. This meeting was an unusually formal set-up. Most of our conversations were over food or drinks, in taxis on the way to visit clients, in elevators…It was clear he wanted an environment where nothing would interrupt us, and I would be unable to dodge his agenda. I would be sitting in a chair, facing him across a desk stripped of non-essentials, nothing cluttering the space between our two minds sparring with each other.

The good thing was that just as I wouldn't be able to avoid his interest, he would be forced to look me in the eye without the softening atmosphere of alcohol and explain why he was so incredibly concerned that I was closed off.

After I was settled, he gave me a welcoming smile. "How are things going?"

"Fine."

"We never closed the loop on that additional photography session with Arlinda. How was it?"

I was certain Arlinda was not the reason I was sitting there. "It was good."

"Any new insights?"

"We mostly talked about her house."

He nodded, devoid of curiosity about my vague response. "I want to finish our conversation about your attitude."

I laughed. It was probably not the best response, but it was genuine and immediate. "My *attitude*? You sound like my mother."

He ignored my laughter and my characterization of what he'd said. "My concern is that you can be very aloof, to the point of coldness. It comes across as judgmental, and that's not what we want to portray to our clients. It's also not good for our team dynamic."

He wasn't going to be diverted at all, that was clear. Mocking him regarding team spirit wouldn't help. "I haven't changed, so why is this suddenly an issue?"

"It's possible I didn't read you correctly when I interviewed you."

"I thought you were a pro at reading people."

"You defy the norms. I think you know that."

I crossed my legs and slid down slightly in my chair, trying to get more comfortable against the minimal padding and the metal frame that was all business—meant to provide a place to sit but not designed for a lengthy discussion about one's attitude. "I don't know what you want me to say."

"I want to understand why you close yourself off. You were almost hostile when we met with Jim Kohn."

I couldn't inform him that Jim Kohn was an unrepentant misogynist in every sense of the word. I needed my opinion about that man to remain my secret. Blabbing about the offensive, almost criminal flaws of someone you've killed is not the best way to keep others from thinking too much about something you want them to forget. Suddenly, they begin to ask themselves troubling questions. I didn't want Trystan to think about Jim Kohn's untimely death at all. "That was ages ago. There have been lots of others since him. I get along great with Arlinda. And with—"

"I brought up Jim because he was the one that struck me. And it was just after that I noticed the bad blood between you and Stephanie."

He hadn't noticed anything at all. Stephanie brought that bad blood to his attention by trying to get me in trouble, trying deliberately to damage his opinion of me. Maybe she'd succeeded. Maybe that's where all of this interest in my *coldness* was coming from. I'd assumed it was new, but it sounded as if he'd been brooding about it for a long time.

I gave him a crisp smile. "I can't change how I am. I'm not going to start talking about my personal life just to make other people feel comfortable."

"Sharing parts of our lives is the foundation of human interaction. Our entire business is based on being genuine, making connections with people. It starts inside these offices."

"I've made a very good connection with Arlinda. And I think I had some solid connection with Pete Torkenson. And Diana."

He sighed. He pushed his chair away from the desk and tipped his head back, staring at the ceiling.

I waited while he sorted out whatever it was he wanted to say next. It didn't seem like the conversation was going to have a very good outcome, and I was curious to see how far he would push this. Was he planning to fire me? Take away my plum job and give me something less interesting to do? But how would that work? I didn't think he would fire me right on the spot.

I needed to take control. I needed to do a bit of a sales job.

"I'm good at what I do," I said. "Our clients respond to me, and if any of them have complained, it's news to me. I get them to relax in front of the camera. I make them feel comfortable. And however I do that is what matters. I don't need to tell them my life story to make that happen. I think that's the important thing."

He sat up straight again and looked at me hard. "Is there something you're hiding?"

"I don't get why I need to tell everyone all about my life to be good at my job. What are you really trying to say?"

"You're intimidating to Stephanie."

"So this has nothing to do with our clients, it's all about Stephanie's hurt feelings?"

"It's more than that. She got me thinking about it. I want a harmonious group here. I want people on our team to feel connected to each other. There are only four of us. Conflict among us will bleed over to our clients. They can feel it. I want all of us to be our absolute best, at the very top of our game because the biggest part of what we have to offer is ourselves."

"Okay. I thought you were happy with my work. I'm confused about what you're trying to say. Just be blunt."

"Fair enough. I'm worried there's something I missed in you. I blame myself for that, and to be honest, it's made me question my own skills. But aside from that, I'm worried you're going to damage our reputation if you don't open up and show some vulnerability. We ask our clients to bare their souls to us. We can't be closed off. It causes imbalance and will make them feel overly exposed. There's a fine line between confidence and an arrogance that's off-putting. Especially in this field."

I closed my eyes, trying to think about what I should say next. He hadn't bought my self-promotion. I opened my eyes. "I can't be someone I'm not, Trystan. I like to keep my personal life private, and that's not going to change."

"Maybe I was wrong about focusing on your personal life. It's more about your general attitude. You tend to give off the impression you're never wrong, that you think you're superior. I thought if you shared more about your life, revealed your feelings and vulnerabilities, your confidence wouldn't come across as arrogance."

I couldn't see that this was going to go anywhere that was

satisfying to Trystan. He wanted me to be someone I was not. It was unsettling to not know what to say next, to not be able to calm whatever was disturbing him so much that he'd brought it up with me three times. He was overthinking everything. "We're close to having more clients than we can manage. I don't think my attitude is causing a problem with the growth of our client list, or our revenue."

"Yes. And because of our growth, I'd planned to make Stephanie a backup photographer. We're at the point where you're going to be overwhelmed with more work than you can manage. There are going to be inevitable scheduling conflicts. I'd planned to have you begin mentoring her, but your animosity toward her is obvious. Everyone feels it."

"*Everyone?*"

"Yes."

I wondered what Diana had said about me. Or, was he lying? Was Stephanie complaining about me behind my back, and Trystan assuming, without evidence, that Diana felt the same? Had a client complained? I couldn't think who would do that. Our clients surely had their flaws, but none of them struck me as the type who would be so timid they couldn't speak to my face if they had a problem with me. They were not people who allowed their opinions or conflicts to fester in some dark interior place.

I gave Trystan an ingratiating, slightly meek smile. "I can't change how I am. I'm not going to blab about my personal life because I just don't like doing that. But I can try to be nicer."

"This isn't about being nice. No one is asking you to tell your entire life story, to share the kind of intimate details that our clients include in their questionnaires. But it's not normal to be so secretive, to hide what you do on the weekends or after work. It's not normal to refuse to ever share a single shred of information about your hobbies, or to mention friends and family."

He would not like hearing about my hobby, I was certain of that. Still, it was clear to me now that I wasn't making enough of an effort to fit in. "It doesn't seem fair that I have to change my personality to be considered good at my job."

"That's not what I'm saying. Just be human. Genuine."

"I think I can do that. Is there anything else?"

He shook his head, the expression on his face making it look as if he was recovering from a bout with the stomach flu and finally felt he could move his body in normal ways without experiencing a tsunami of nausea.

I stood. "I might go out for Chinese food with my neighbor tonight," I said.

Trystan rolled his eyes.

"You asked about my weekend plans. My friends."

"I did, but please don't make an absurd game out of this. I know you're a professional. And you're a smart woman, just consider what I've said and work on being more open. You don't have to report your schedule to me."

I laughed. "I'll try to be more aware."

"That's all I'm asking."

If they wanted to hear stories, I could definitely come up with a few things, I would just have to keep them straight in my mind. Maybe I needed a journal.

46

Portland, Oregon

After Mrs. Palomar left our house, finished with ratting me out, and telling my mother how to raise me, my mother wasted no time. She may have sounded polite and protective of me when speaking to someone outside of our family, but I had only been sprawled on my bed for two or three minutes before the door opened, and she stepped into my room.

The first thought that passed through my head was one of appreciation. I'd expected she might enlist my father, and I'd imagined him raging into my room, full of righteous despair that all of his beliefs had been stomped on by his unrepentant, stubborn, hard-hearted daughter.

My mother settled herself near the foot of my bed and patted the space beside her, indicating I should move closer. "I have something important to discuss with you."

I hated that proprietary pat she gave when she wanted me to listen to a lecture, sitting on my bed as if it were a public bench. But it was better to save my energy for what was coming. Starting off with a refusal to respond like a dog reacting to a hand gesture wasn't going to help me.

As I settled beside her, she turned to face me. "I just spoke to Mrs. Palomar."

I waited, my face blank.

"Mrs. Palomar came by to talk to me about your candy sales."

So this was going to be one of those games where I was supposed to recognize the sin I'd committed, confess, and theoretically face less punishment because of my honesty. My mind spun, trying to decide the best way to react, trying to decide what aspect of my crime my mother was most upset about, what might get her to feel even a little bit of understanding for why I'd chosen the plan I had.

When I didn't respond quickly enough, she started talking again. "I think you know why she wanted to talk to me. Is there anything you need to tell me about all the candy you've sold?" Her eyes filled with tears, and I thought I heard a faint sob tear at her chest, which she stifled.

"I'm not sure."

"Don't make this worse by lying to me, even though every single thing you've done so far has been a lie. I'm so very disappointed." Now, the tears spilled out of her eyes.

So much for her suggestion to Mrs. Palomar that she wanted to hear my side of the story. She knew there was no side that was justifiable to herself, or to anyone else in the youth group, to anyone who had purchased candy, to my father, or to god himself.

"I'm not sure what I should say."

"How about not trying to calculate what will keep you out of trouble like this is some kind of game…" She sniffed and wiped at her eyes. "Try telling the truth. Tell me why it even entered your mind that it was okay to grab money right out of God's hand."

"It wasn't god's—"

"Have I raised a thief? A liar? You've always been a challenge to me, to your father and me, but I thought…"

She wasn't going to understand. She wasn't going to have one shred of concern for how unjust it was that my brothers got cars, and I had to earn money to purchase mine.

It was probably best to tell her what she wanted to hear and then accept whatever came after. It was coming no matter what. All I could hope for was that she'd learned enough about my father's style of punishment that she would devise a set of consequences without involving him. It wasn't even really the punishment I minded. It would be the non-stop flow of words and Bible verses that I'd be forced to listen to for weeks. It would be the extended prayers over dinner, recounting my failures to god, pleading for absolution, and the eternal rescue of my soul. It was exhausting.

"I don't think it's actually stealing because—"

"It's stealing." Her voice was commanding, a tone I wasn't used to from my mother. "We aren't going to argue about that."

"But just think about it. The money—"

"Don't talk to me with that attitude!"

I softened my voice as much as I could. "I'm sorry this happened."

"Sorry you were caught, or sorry for stealing?"

"The church is getting all the money they deserve and—"

"I don't want to hear your rationalizations. I want to know that you understand this is stealing—the lowest form of it I can imagine."

"But I didn't take money away from the youth group at all. They're actually getting more because I sold three times as much as anyone else."

"You lied, and you took money that didn't belong to you."

"I only lied about the price."

I felt her shoulders relax, as if she thought there was some kind of victory in my admission of a lie. That I was possibly feeling sorrowful for what I'd done. "You stole from people who want to support us."

"They knew what they were spending."

"It's still stealing."

"I don't see how. I really don't."

"Oh my." She covered her face with her hands. Her breath came out in short bursts, followed by sighs that seemed to come from a place deep in the endless realm of the human mind, that eternal space filled with thoughts and knowledge that no one can ever know the bottom of.

"They were happy to pay more money," I said.

"Because they thought it was for the youth group!"

"The church is getting everything they expect from every single candy bar."

Her hands fell away from her face. She turned toward me. "I don't know whether to be angry that you keep arguing with me or terrified for your soul because you honestly don't seem to realize what you did wrong."

"I know I lied, but everyone lies."

"That's not true."

"You lied. You told Mrs. Palomar you wanted to hear my side of the story."

She glared at me, suddenly aware that I'd known about this

before she came into my room. "I was being cautious. I didn't think she should be involved in our family business. I wasn't going to speak badly about my own daughter to someone outside of our family."

"It was still a lie. You didn't doubt she was telling the truth."

She looked away from me, staring at my bedroom window as if the force of her gaze, the desire to turn away from me, would shrink the darkness outside, allowing her to see into the leaves of the tree that held our swing, the branches reaching close to my bedroom window.

"I was only protecting you."

"I need to make money so I can buy a car. Besides, why should I be a slave for our church? That's what we are. We're working to make them money, and we don't get paid."

"There are prizes." Her body trembled as if she realized that wasn't the best answer because it sounded as if she might be agreeing with my point. She covered her tracks quickly. "But that doesn't matter. Not everything has to be about money. I shop and cook meals for our family without getting a paycheck. I do it out of love."

"And you don't think you're a slave?"

"That's a terrible thing to say. Slavery is a serious issue that none of us has experienced. What makes thoughts like that even come into your head? Sometimes I think the devil has truly gotten his claws into your heart."

I shifted away from her. She put her hand on my knee, gently squeezing my leg as if to apologize for what she'd said, but without actually retracting her words. She wanted to be sure I was afraid of my dark nature. At the same time, she wanted me to know she loved me.

Both of us were quiet for several minutes.

"Whether you acknowledge your sins or not, you stole money from those people. You told them lies about the church and where the money was going. You—"

"But I didn't—"

"Don't interrupt me." Her voice was much louder than usual. I closed my mouth and vowed I would listen until she finished. It was better to listen quietly to her angst-filled lecture than to risk my father over-hearing. She clearly wanted to keep this from him, or he would have been standing in front of me, his voice raised to full volume, the wrath of god pouring out of his lips and bouncing off my skull.

"You need to return the money. I'm not going to tell your father because it would break his heart, and his poor heart has enough cracks in it already." She sighed. "You're going to contact every single person who purchased candy from you. You'll visit them and tell them what you did. You'll return the money and ask if there's any work you can do to help them out, to show that you deeply regret how you hurt them, how you damaged the reputation of our church."

"I didn't hurt them. I—"

"This isn't a discussion."

I wondered how she planned to make sure I contacted every single person.

"I want you to show me where you've hidden the money."

I remained silent, my back straight, my eyes fixed on the dresser across from us. I could see the tops of our heads reflected in the bottom edge of the mirror that hung on the wall above the dresser.

"I'll tear apart every piece of this room, so if you don't want that, show me where it is."

I went to the closet and took out the box filled with the cash for my car. I handed it to her.

Without looking inside, she settled the box on her lap. "Now, give me your list of customers."

I sighed. "I didn't charge all of them five dollars. Not if they wrote checks."

"Then show me the list of those you defrauded."

"I didn't—"

"The list. I want it now."

I went to my desk and got the list.

After she took it from me, she stood. "I'll be driving you to each house. I'll wait in the car while you return the money and tell them what you've done. So don't sit there thinking you'll come up with a different scam to get out of this."

When she left the room, she had the box of cash and the list. I wondered where she would hide it, but I was certain it was someplace that I'd never discover, someplace my father never went.

I laid on my bed and stared at the ceiling. I closed my eyes and imagined having my own car, but the image felt blurry and very much like a dream instead of something that might happen soon. The fuzzy shape of my car was dissolving behind my eyes.

47

New York

Since Eileen refused to see the deep and dangerous flaws in Alexandra's character, Stephanie had decided to take matters into her own hands. In order to find out how big a hold Alexandra had on her daughter, Stephanie would need to get that information directly from Alexandra.

She'd prepared carefully for this. Every day that week, after she finished eating her sandwich, she'd gone to an alley two blocks from the office. Like a rat hunched in the shadows, she pulled a pack of cigarettes and a lighter out of her purse. With a trembling hand, she flicked the lighter, usually requiring several rough pushes with her thumb before the flame burst out. She touched the tongue of fire to the tip of the cancer stick, as she preferred to call it, and then placed the cigarette between her lips. She then coughed until she felt as if her lungs and eyeballs were bleeding.

After several days of this, the coughing lessened, which both relieved and frightened her.

It was difficult to reconcile the glamorous image that

Alexandra projected when she casually held a cigarette between her fingers with the coughing, the stench of the smoke, the ashy, sour aftertaste, and the knowledge that each breath was introducing another microscopic amount of deadly chemicals into her body.

Part of her wanted to mirror that image she held in her mind of Alexandra sitting on the steps of her apartment building, looking so confident and relaxed. Another part of her felt like a fool for taking up something so obviously damaging to her health. She was behaving like an ignorant teenager.

What was she trying to prove?

She wasn't sure, but she did feel somewhat calmer knowing it was only for a short time. She was not planning on becoming a smoker. She just wanted to have a bit of fun— project a dangerous, uncaring attitude, maybe even to Trystan at some point. But right now, she simply wanted to get close enough to Alexandra to carry on a conversation that would go deeper and be less contentious than their usual encounters. She was certain that smoking was the key to this.

By Friday afternoon, she was ready. Alexandra had come out of Trystan's office after nearly half an hour in there. When she passed by Stephanie's door, her face wore the same confident expression as always, but there was something more aggressive in the movement of her body, a tension that said she wasn't happy with whatever had been discussed.

Alex went into her office and emerged a moment later wearing her coat and scarf, carrying that large leather messenger bag with its buckled straps that she used instead of a normal purse. No matter what color her outfit was, she carried that scuffed, dark brown bag.

Stephanie grabbed her own coat, waited for three minutes after the outer office door closed behind Alex, and then went into the hallway. She pressed the elevator button.

When she reached the lobby, she looked across the expanse in time to see Alex pushing open the glass door and stepping outside where she immediately stiffened her shoulders against the cold.

Stephanie hurried after her. She followed for three blocks until Alex stepped into a small garden that consisted of a single bench, a few shrubs, and a table meant for setting down cups of coffee. The table was covered with bird droppings.

From two buildings away, Stephanie watched her take out her cigarettes and light one. After Alex had taken a few puffs, Stephanie jaywalked across the street. As a thank you, she received a long, loud honk from a taxi. She jumped, startled and scared at the sound. The taxi was quite a distance away, and the honk had been completely unwarranted.

When she turned back, Alex was laughing.

Stephanie stepped onto the curb and approached Alex. "Mind if I join you?"

Alex waved her cigarette in the air. The smoke drifted across the space in front of Stephanie. Her eyes watered, but she didn't cough. "Why?"

Stephanie pulled out her pack of cigarettes and lit one, knowing she looked awkward, fumbling, and decidedly unsophisticated.

"Since when are you a smoker?"

"Stress does strange things to you," Stephanie said. She'd prepared this response, expecting to be questioned about her sudden change of habit.

Alex inhaled and blew out a stream of smoke. "Why are you stressed?"

Stephanie shrugged. "Maybe life is all about stress."

"Could be," Alex said.

"I worry about my daughter. I've told you that before."

"You have," Alex said.

This was harder than she'd expected. It wasn't so easy to turn a conversation in the direction you wanted. Especially with someone who seemed to enjoy giving vague, short responses when most people would be more open. Most normal people, she reminded herself. "I guess you and Eileen have gotten pretty friendly."

Alex shrugged.

"You're a little old for her." Stephanie was annoyed that she'd blurted this out. She needed to be more careful. She needed to get information, not push Alex into an even more hostile mood than she was all on her own.

"Is there an age limit on friendship?"

Stephanie laughed. "No. It just surprises me."

"We have a lot in common."

Stephanie nodded. She placed the cigarette between her lips and inhaled. Suddenly, she saw the appeal in giving your attention to a cigarette. Maybe that's why Alex was often slow to reveal what she was thinking. The act of smoking interrupted the normal flow of speech. And it helped her to sort out her thoughts, to slow down. In all her prayers begging God to help her get better control of her tongue, she'd never had a clear-cut response from Him, and now, it turned out doing something she'd always considered ungodly was helping her to do just that. She sighed.

"What's wrong?" Alex said.

"Nothing."

"A lot on your mind?"

"Yes. I really do not want to talk about my daughter behind her back, but I have to tell you, she seems a lot…" She took another drag on the cigarette. She needed to be careful here. She was not going to betray Eileen. At the same time, in order to find out what was going on, she needed to give something on her side. "She's a little…hyper since she started hanging out with you."

Alex laughed. "Have you been keeping track?"

"I don't have to. Mothers are intimately in tune with their daughter's moods and feelings. We sense when there's trouble, and we notice the slightest change. When you're a mother, you'll understand. It's difficult to explain to someone who hasn't experienced it."

"I'll never be a mother."

Stephanie gasped softly. She'd never heard a woman make that proclamation, and with such a firm tone, a tone of absolute certainty. But she was not getting drawn into that. She needed to know what Alex wanted with her daughter. "What made you want to be friends with Eileen?"

"I already told you, we have a lot in common."

"Like what?" She hoped the next remark was not going to announce that Stephanie herself was the common thread that drew them together.

"You're awfully curious, for not wanting to talk behind your daughter's back. Are you trying to find out about things in her life she might not want you to know?"

"Such as?"

Alex laughed. "What do you want, Stephanie? You came out here and pretended to take up smoking for a reason. Are you worried about the money?"

"Money? What does that mean?"

Alex smiled. "Eileen hasn't talked to you about money?"

Stephanie shook her head. How did Alex always manage to get the upper hand? No matter how well-prepared Stephanie thought she was, no matter how she tried to be clever, to stay one step ahead, to consider in advance what she should say, Alex won the battle that played out in every single conversation.

Alex put the cigarette to her lips, she carefully drew the smoke into her mouth, easing it back out into the cold air in what seemed like a single loop. "You know—that email you sent me. You mentioned that Eileen was up to no good because she craved money. She would bleed me dry, or some crazy nonsense like that."

Stephanie felt her face grow warm. She had no doubt her cheeks were flushed, and that Alex was fully aware of her discomfort. She regretted that email. At the time, she'd been so upset, so frightened for Eileen, so determined to stop these two from becoming friendly. It was maddening. What did Alex *want* with a woman only a few years out of college? They had nothing in common in terms of their careers. She worried the only thing that drew them together, aside from complaining about her, was drinking. Maybe that was why Eileen had gained weight. Too much alcohol. Although that wasn't right, Stephanie had seen for herself that Eileen was eating normal meals again. She sighed. She was tired of smoking. It tasted nasty, and she didn't feel at all sophisticated. She felt like a homeless woman, hunched against the cold, addicted to an ugly, disgusting habit because she didn't know what to do with her hands or the empty hours that filled her days. "I regret writing that email," she said.

"I'm glad to hear that." Alex laughed. "It sounded a little nuts."

Alex didn't bother to soften her opinion with more pleasing words. She never did. And in this case, Stephanie couldn't argue. She felt even more humiliated. It *had* sounded nuts. She barely remembered what she'd written, and she didn't want to. "Eileen has a lot of modeling friends. So it's nice that she's able to make time for you once in a while."

Alex looked at her, that impassive expression that dominated her face most of the time. She wasn't bothered by what Stephanie had said, and she didn't make the effort to defend herself against the obvious insult. In fact, she didn't even seem insulted.

Probably because she knew she'd won. Again.

But Stephanie had learned one thing. It was likely that Alex had befriended Eileen simply because she could, for the sole purpose of upsetting Stephanie. And there was that bit about the money. What did that even mean?

48

Watching Stephanie try to smoke a cigarette had been the most entertaining thing I'd witnessed in a while. After she left, I took out another cigarette and lit it. This wasn't good for me. I knew that even as the flame grabbed the tip. A moment later, my body let me know it with a sudden rough cough.

A man passing by the tiny pseudo park looked at me and smiled as if he was happy to see me coughing my lung out of my mouth.

I couldn't be annoyed with him. Not really. He was right to gloat. My smoking was increasing, and my running and lifting weights had decreased during winter in New York. Yoga, aside from the class with Arlinda, had disappeared almost entirely off my weekly schedule. Running in Central Park was fantastic, but getting there was less enjoyable as I dodged people walking to appointments and sauntering to restaurants. The snow and cold kept me inside more often than they should have. It was almost impossible to run in the snow, but I shouldn't have been such a whiner about the cold. Once I started moving, I was fine.

The smoking needed to be addressed, and thinking about Stephanie intruding on my smoke breaks was a big motivator. It had been useful to have her approach me. I'd learned something I wanted to know—that she had no idea Eileen had come into four million dollars.

It wasn't surprising she didn't know about the inheritance, but it was surprising that Stephanie hadn't questioned where all the money for her obviously expensive makeover had come from. Maybe she thought Eileen's modeling career was far more successful than it was. Or maybe she was more naïve than I realized, completely unaware of what things cost. Still, it seemed to me it would have been impossible to stand in a department store and try on clothes without seeing the price tags, even if she didn't know what her new hair and makeup had cost her daughter.

It didn't matter that those few minutes watching her try to pretend she was enjoying a cigarette had been productive. The thought of standing in my little park, accompanied by Stephanie, was horrifying.

If she planned on making it a regular thing, it would ruin smoking for me. I didn't like her. I didn't trust her. And I did not want to be bonding with her, no matter how much it meant to Trystan. I'd managed to skirt around his comment about mentoring a woman for whom I had absolutely no respect, but I was sure that easy dodging was temporary.

Maybe there were enough forces coming together in my life to drive me to finally quit what the majority of the human race viewed as a dirty, disgusting, deadly habit. I knew I had to do it someday. I knew I was constantly risking something I didn't want to lose—feeling strong and healthy. I would have to give it serious thought. Later. For now, I took a drag on my cigarette and blew the smoke out slowly into the cold air, returning my thoughts to the immediate problem.

While Stephanie was talking, my mind had gnawed below the surface, recalling my conversation with Trystan. I didn't like the outcome at all. I felt like I'd caved and agreed to be someone else just to give him and Stephanie the feel-goods. His request was ridiculous.

I'd known since I was a child that it was important to paint smiles and polite comments and feigned interest over some aspects of my personality in order to fit into the world. After I committed murder the first time, I knew I couldn't let people see that it was easy for me to kill. I couldn't let them see that I lacked certain emotions they took for granted, emotions that ruled their lives and their choices. They wouldn't understand, and they would shun me for it. People hate things they don't understand in others. Hate with highly intense emotion, in fact, emotion strong enough to drive them to kill. It's rather ironic.

But there was a limit to that covering up of who I am. Sometimes it's just too much work, and sometimes it accomplishes nothing. There are also those people who I find monumentally unpleasant. I'm not going to kill every single person I find disagreeable, but I'm also not able to easily become the chameleon I should be for them. It's not just that it's too much work, I simply don't want to.

Stephanie was one of those people. First of all, she was too much like my father. And while I had to work to find a balance of power with my father because my very existence depended on him taking care of me when I was a child, I needed nothing from Stephanie.

I didn't want to hear her religious rules, and I didn't find her interesting enough to keep my attention.

Now, Trystan wanted me to make nice with her. He wanted me to stop intimidating her. He wanted me to be open and genuine with her. It was amusing to me because Stephanie herself was not genuine. She used her religion as some kind of outer covering, a suit of armor that she thought would keep her safe as she battled her way through the world, trying to beat everyone into agreeing with her. I had no idea who she really was inside. All she cared about was getting others to follow her rules. Her life appeared to consist of nothing but rules.

If Trystan thought about it from a different perspective, he would probably find himself feeling unbearably sad for her.

Maybe I should quit while I was ahead. Literally. He knew I was an asset, and he would find me hard to replace. It would be difficult to find someone who could make his clients relax into their own selves in front of the camera. And that replacement certainly was not Stephanie Cook. Someone could mentor and train her for years, and she still wouldn't have the genuineness to enable her to perform that function.

Didn't he realize that? And if he didn't, and he thought it was so critical for me to become someone else, wouldn't it be better to resign so that I had the satisfaction of keeping the upper hand? I imagined he would argue with me, that he might tell me I was taking things the wrong way. But in the end, he seemed to think the success of his business depended on this. If I didn't comply, he believed it would spoil our allure. I put out my cigarette in the concrete container filled with damp, slightly grimy sand.

I walked back to the office, keeping my pace brisk, my thoughts focused on a single point. It was close to four o'clock, and the shadows across the sidewalk were deep and thick, the air so cold I saw my breath as if I were still exhaling cigarette smoke.

Inside our offices it was stuffy. I dropped my coat on the guest chair in my office because I anticipated leaving soon.

Trystan's door was open, and he looked up as I raised my fist to knock on the doorframe.

"Hi, Alexandra. What's up?" He leaned back.

I stepped inside and closed the door. I didn't acknowledge the gesture he made toward the guest chair. "Would you like me to resign?"

He sat up suddenly. "Of course not. If you think that, you completely misinterpreted what I said."

I ticked off the points on my fingers, holding my hand where he could see it. "Talk about my personal life. Don't intimidate Stephanie. Mentor Stephanie so she can become a photographer. Is there anything I misinterpreted in all of that?"

"Please sit down."

"This is a quick conversation. I just need you to explain what I misinterpreted."

"Please don't be difficult."

"I'm not being difficult. I won't have hard feelings if you think this isn't working out. I've had some time to think, and although I might be able to talk more about what's happening in my life outside of work, I'm not going to do that with Stephanie. I get along quite well with Diana, and we do talk about things unrelated to work, so this is all about Stephanie. And you."

"Please don't take offense. I'm not criticizing you. I want to know you better. You're a smart and interesting person."

"Thank you."

"You've been an asset to this venture."

"I believe the client list has grown faster since I joined."

"It has."

"So clearly, our clients don't have an issue with me. And the things you want from me aren't going to change my interactions with them. Not significantly."

"I like the camaraderie. I've been clear about that."

"You have."

"Why is it such a problem for you? I'm not asking a lot. We just want to know you better, to feel more of a team connection."

He was asking more than he knew. It was absolutely too much. It was out of line, and I was pretty sure that in a big company, it would be considered some form of harassment. "Like I told you before, I can't be someone I'm not."

"You said you would try."

"I will. I'll try to be nicer to Stephanie, but we're not ever going to be friends, and I'm not ever going to tell her much about my life, and I don't think mentoring her is a good idea. She's not a fan of me either. You know that, right?"

He looked defeated. He sighed. "I hope you won't resign."

"I don't want to, I just want to make sure we understand each other."

"I don't understand you at all, Alex. But I do understand your point, and I'm not asking you to be someone else."

I smiled. I took a step back.

He tried to form a smile. "Have a good evening."

"Absolutely."

I wasn't entirely sure where we'd left things, but pleased that I would get to continue studying people and pushing them outside of their comfort zones through a camera lens.

As I stepped into the hallway, I caught a glimpse of Stephanie. She disappeared quickly into her office. Before I passed by her office, the door closed without its telltale click. I felt her presence there, waiting for me to go away.

49

My weekend was quiet. Victoria and Rafe appeared to have vanished. I knew they were not busy fixing up their brownstone because something had definitely gone sideways with it. They were no longer taking possession of the house Victoria craved with the desire of someone longing for more romance in her life, if they had ever owned the house at all.

On Saturday morning, I went for a three-mile run through the park. I extended that to four miles on Sunday. I didn't smoke at all. I got together with Kent, and we spent most of Saturday afternoon in bed, then ordered Chinese food for dinner. This meant the information about my personal life that I'd provided to Trystan was true, the Chinese food just happened on a different day than the one I'd mentioned to him.

On Sunday evening, Trystan sent a group text message telling Diana, Stephanie, and me that we would have a quick meeting on Monday at nine to close off our work with Arlinda Caruso. He sent a follow-up message just to me, saying that Arlinda had let him know I was free to update our team on why she no longer needed our services. She'd told him about her insight, but said I was free to provide whatever additional details seemed important for our work.

At five minutes after nine, we were seated in our conference room—Trystan at the head of the table, Diana at the opposite end, and Stephanie and I facing each other across the shorter space, staring each other down like the combatants we were.

As I studied Stephanie's nervous movements, the absence of the large cross struck me again. Had Eileen told her to stop featuring it at the center of every outfit she wore, letting her know it failed as a fashion statement? I also wondered how many cigarettes Stephanie had smoked over the weekend, or if she was already finished with that experiment now that she knew she wouldn't get any information about her daughter out of me.

In the center of the conference table was a cardboard tray holding four coffee drinks labeled with our names. I had to admire Trystan for knowing what each of us liked and bringing in something fancy instead of asking us to rely on our usual home-brewed coffee. Beside the coffee carrier was a plate from the break room with four croissants arranged like a pinwheel.

I took a croissant, napkin, and the cup with my name scrawled on the side. The others followed my lead.

"This probably won't take long," Trystan said. "As I mentioned in my message, Arlinda says she's gotten what she signed on for and more. She won't be working with us going forward. You can archive her files."

"That's odd," Diana said. "She only met with you twice, didn't she?"

He nodded.

"What's going on?" Diana said. "Did she feel she wasn't ready? Did she ask for a refund?"

"No. She's very pleased with us. In fact, she's recommended our services to several friends."

"Nice." Diana nibbled at her croissant, then put it on her napkin. "But what is there to recommend? She didn't finish the process."

"She had a conversation with Alex. She told me that Alex would be able to let us know the details of the realizations she's experienced."

Stephanie glared at me. I turned my gaze away from her, looking at Trystan for a cue that he was ready for me to speak, sipping my latte at the same time. The drink was hot and creamy and perfectly made, the coffee strong. I took another sip, letting it melt across my tongue.

"Are you going to tell us the big secret?" Stephanie said.

I pried the lid off my cup, took a long, steaming swallow, and began telling them about my evening with Arlinda and the radical change she'd implemented in her life without any help from us. Well, maybe some help—from me—but I did my best to downplay that. Although I deserved credit, I didn't need more pointers from Trystan about my arrogance.

"She realized after her temper over something that was said at her dinner party that she'd missed a crossroads in her life quite a few years ago."

I told them the story of the workplace proposal and her misunderstanding of what it meant.

"After she started working with us, she realized her boredom and feelings of emptiness were not entirely related to her career."

I told them about Serena, about cooking, and that Arlinda

had never explored where her attraction lay. I looked at Diana. "I have to show you some photographs I took after she told me. The change in her face was incredible. It seemed as if I was looking at a different person. We talked about how she'd taken so many risks with her agency, but not a single one in her personal life."

When I finished speaking, the room was silent.

I heard a few slurps of coffee, and then Diana spoke. "Good for her. She—"

"I'm disappointed, of course," said Trystan. "But it's good that she resolved her feelings."

Diana gave him a condescending, possibly forgiving look at the interruption, which he didn't apologize for or even seem to be aware of.

He continued—"I'm concerned that when she recommends us, she may give a slightly distorted impression of what we do."

"We'll just need to be more precise about setting expectations when we receive new inquiries," Diana said. "It shouldn't be a problem."

Trystan looked at Stephanie. "Would you work on that Stephanie? Modifying the information we give people when they first call? And you need to work on updating the slide deck we use to outline the details of what we offer."

She stared at him.

He gave her a hopeful smile, waiting for a response.

Stephanie blinked slowly, her carefully made-up eyelids moving like luxurious curtains across her eyes. She continued staring. Her gaze turned in my direction, a quick, angry glance like the slash of a knife. She forced her attention back to Trystan.

"Stephanie?" Trystan's voice was louder, as if he believed she hadn't heard him, that her mind had drifted elsewhere.

She looked at me again, giving me a look of pure hatred.

"I think you'll find that challenging and interesting," Trystan said.

It was almost pathetic, listening to him trying to get her attention. He was trying so hard to please this woman. I didn't get it.

At first, I'd thought he felt sorry for her, but now I really wasn't sure. He was so worried about her being happy, about her feeling comfortable and fitting in, about her career in general.

Why didn't she get some self-respect and figure out her own career? I couldn't understand why he felt it was his job to make her feel valuable.

If she didn't like her job, that was on her. She'd known what it was when he hired her. Didn't she?

"Stephanie." Now he no longer sounded so placating. "Did you hear me? Is that something you can start working on? We should get it done sooner rather than later. I'd like to see some drafts by the end of the day tomorrow, unless you have a lot of other things on your plate."

"I have nothing on my *plate*." Her voice came out in a hiss. "You…"

We all waited for what was coming next, for whatever was causing those blank stares that flickered with rage then went dead every few seconds.

It was slightly shocking to witness her refusal to speak for nearly five minutes, while her boss floundered around as if he needed to soothe her before she flew into a murderous rage.

The silence lingered, but she didn't finish whatever it was she planned to say. She stared at him, and he returned the stare.

I'd never seen him at a loss for words.

50

After the meeting ended in silence, we all retreated to our offices. The silence swelled around us, all of our doors closed, everyone sinking below the surface of their own thoughts.

I wasn't quite sure what had happened. Stephanie was seething about something, but did Trystan know what that was? The looks between them, the looks she shot at me, were absurd in their failure to communicate. Why didn't they just say what they were thinking? If they couldn't do that, why not keep their thoughts off their faces? It accomplished nothing, and I didn't like that I felt dragged into a passive-aggressive guessing game.

My curiosity was intense, but after a while, I managed to let it slide out of my mind. If their drama continued, I'd find out the details eventually. Turning it over in my head turned me into a hamster on her wheel.

Sitting in front of the computer was the last thing I wanted to be doing, but I had no photography appointments for the next three days. Our other active clients were all in different phases of the working sessions with Trystan, their photography complete, Diana's assessments fully catalogued. In the days after that, I had three appointments most days for nearly two weeks, which was the crush of activity Trystan was concerned about.

The lack of activity led to a considerable amount of overthinking. The problem was, everywhere my thoughts wandered, they encountered a brick wall.

I felt like going out for a smoke, but I didn't want Stephanie to show up and crash my party. I felt like going for a run to soothe my nerves, but that wasn't doable in the middle of the workday.

I still hadn't talked to Trystan about the fact that I was wasting my time spending hours in the office and should be given more control over my schedule. Working from early morning into the evening, and spending weekend time taking photographs would be fine. I could manage the workload if I had more freedom. Every time I was around him, there was something else going on and my plan to make the request tumbled out of my mind.

For the rest of the morning, I ran on that hamster wheel after all. Finally, it was close to lunchtime. I pulled up electronic copies of the menus from a few nearby restaurants. As I studied the offerings, I was overcome with boredom for the familiar food. Maybe I needed to go farther away from the office, treat myself to something nice.

Without a warning knock, my office door swung open so hard it slammed into the doorstopper. The stopper batted it back toward Stephanie, who stood there looking as if she wanted to kill me. Literally.

She walked toward my desk and stopped beside my chair. She looked down at me. "You're poison."

"Excuse me?"

"You have no morals, and you're going to destroy everything that Trystan built here."

I glanced toward the open door. Was she talking to me, or was she putting on a performance? Her voice was louder than normal, and I couldn't tell if she wanted Trystan and Diana to overhear or if she was so upset, she wasn't paying attention to how the sound of her voice might be carrying past their closed doors.

Noticing my attention on the open door, she lowered her voice, but only slightly. "I don't care who hears me."

"Those are harsh words," I said. "I don't think—"

"How dare you? How dare you steal my idea."

"Your idea?"

"Don't play dumb." She folded her arms.

"I don't know what you're talking about."

"Yes you do."

I shrugged. I turned back to my computer and closed the restaurant menus. I opened a browser window and started to type.

She splayed her hand across the center of my screen, leaning over me to reach it. She was now at an awkward angle that made the danger of her falling onto my lap considerable. "Don't you dare ignore me. Trystan asked me to give insights into our clients. I did that for Arlinda Caruso, and you stole my insight."

I pushed my chair away from the desk and away from her hovering body. "Calm down. I didn't steal anything."

She straightened. Her face was red, the dark red of her skin bleeding through carefully applied makeup.

For half a second, I thought she might slap me. I braced

myself for the assault, but she backed away. I glanced toward the door, wondering if her angry tone had brought Trystan or Diana out of their offices. The doorway was empty. Maybe they'd overheard, but didn't want to know.

"I'm sick of you," she said.

I gave her a warm smile. "That's pretty obvious."

"You're a snake."

"Hiss."

The color of her skin grew darker, almost burgundy. I thought her head might explode. She backed toward the doorway and slammed the door closed. In a less well-constructed building without such solid walls, it might have made them shudder, but I doubted there was enough reverberation for the others to hear.

"What do you want, Stephanie?"

"I want you to tell Trystan you stole my idea. I was the one who said Arlinda needed risk in her life. You sat there this morning and barfed that out like you thought of it. All you did was take pictures and try to make yourself her friend so she wouldn't want to deal with Trystan. You undermined his role."

"Everything she told me came from her own insights. I had nothing to do with it."

"Don't give me that. I saw that smug look on your face. It's still there."

"I think you're projecting."

"You need to tell him."

"There's nothing to tell him. I didn't take credit for anything."

"Except totally changing her life. When it was my idea."

"It's her life. It has nothing to do with you. Or me. Or any of us."

"Bullshit."

I laughed. "Are you allowed to say that?"

"Shut up."

"I'll ask you the same question again—what do you want?"

"I want you to tell him what you did. He clearly forgot that it was my idea. But you know it was. I could see it in your eyes the whole time you were talking."

"I have nothing to tell him."

She moved closer to me again, as if she thought her proximity would intimidate me. It felt like she wanted me to be afraid of her. I wondered if she really believed she could frighten me, if she could frighten anyone. "If you don't tell him, I will. And it won't go well for you."

"Feel free."

She glared at me. Her face lost all of the color it had generated over the past several minutes as she thought through how that might play out and realized that it would make her look foolish and do nothing at all to me.

She kicked the leg of my chair. "What's wrong with you? Why are you like this?"

"I don't know what *this* is."

"You don't care who you hurt. You don't care what anyone thinks about you."

"Why should I care what anyone thinks? It's impossible to know that."

She stared at me, confused. "Because that's what people do. That's how human beings are."

I grabbed my mouse and locked my computer screen. Once I was out of the building, I would search for a restaurant on my phone. I sort of wanted someone to have lunch with, but asking Diana at this point would prevent me from making a quick escape from Stephanie's drama.

I stood and pushed my chair close to my desk.

"You're not leaving until we finish talking."

"I don't have anything to talk about." I grabbed my things off the coat rack and went to the door.

She moved quickly, placing her body so it was blocking the handle.

"I'm going to lunch. I don't think there's anything else to say."

"I'm not moving until you admit you stole my idea. Trystan gave me the responsibility of providing insight at the beginning, and you just grabbed that and pretended it was yours. It's not fair, and I'm not letting you get away with it."

"You're imagining things."

"I'm not."

"Arlinda came to her own conclusions. I just happened to be there."

"You're going to ruin all his work, taking credit for what other people do."

I sighed. "Get out of the way."

"After you apologize."

I grabbed her arm and pulled her away from the door. She resisted, but I was stronger. I also didn't care if she hurt herself trying to stand her ground. Finally, she stumbled toward me, and I reached for the door handle. I pressed down and yanked open the door.

"You aren't leaving."

"I'm done."

"Fine. Then I'm going to—"

"Do whatever you want. I'm hungry." I slipped out the door and left it open. I hurried through our reception area, putting on my coat as I went. Once I was in the elevator, I leaned my head against the wall and closed my eyes.

Something had to change between us, but I was at a complete loss regarding how to make that happen.

51

Stephanie's eyes filled with tears. Her lips and hands trembled uncontrollably. Alex had shoved her aside as if she were acting out the shoving aside of Stephanie's career. Why was this happening? God had abandoned her. The new clothes and beautiful hair hadn't helped at all.

Trystan had treated her like a piece of nothing during that meeting. He was completely oblivious to what Alexandra was doing. It was clear he'd forgotten about Stephanie's presentation when they first started working with Arlinda, and that meant the insight she'd offered hadn't stayed with him for more than a few minutes.

She'd never felt this hopeless and unwanted. Not in a long time. Not since she was abandoned by the man who had promised to love and cherish her before he went and did the exact opposite, tearing her heart into shreds.

She had no idea what she was doing wrong, and she felt like a fool—a stupid, pathetic fool—for believing an expensive blouse and designer shoes and streaks of color in her hair were going to change her life.

God had abandoned her because she'd abandoned *Him*.

Now, she had no idea where to turn or what to do. If she talked to her church friends, they would tell her she was following the ways of the unbelieving world—paying too much attention to her outward appearance, worshipping her own self. They would tell her she should be humble. She should be grateful for a stable, well-paying job, for a kind boss, for a successful daughter. They would tell her to look for ways to be kind to Alexandra, to serve her.

They would tell her to pray. To have faith.

She'd done every single one of those things.

Well, maybe not the part about being grateful for her job. But there was nothing wrong with wanting a better job. It was normal to want interesting and satisfying work. Most of her friends had that. It wasn't fair. There was absolutely nothing ungodly about wanting a job that had been promised to you!

She left Alex's office and returned to her own, closing the door and leaning against it. She stared at the window across the room, the faint image of her handprint still visible from when she thought she'd received divine guidance on how to manage this impossible situation.

What a joke.

She wasn't managing it at all, and she had no guidance whatsoever. She was utterly lost, stumbling around in the dark with no clear thoughts in her own mind, and deafening silence from Heaven.

She dragged herself to her chair and flopped down. She covered her face with her hands, careful even in her despair not to press too hard, to avoid smearing her makeup. She couldn't even cry, because that would leave her face dark and muddy and ugly. Her stomach rumbled. Maybe she should have followed Alex to lunch. But what was the point?

Talking to that woman was impossible. Stephanie had never experienced anything like it. Words fell out of Alexandra's mouth like they were deliberately crafted to confuse and frustrate. Alex lied without even blinking or averting her eyes. Half the things she said were so rude it made Stephanie gasp.

What kind of people had raised someone like that?

She lowered her hands from her face but kept her eyes closed. She had to think. She had to calm down. Maybe she should go to one of the cathedrals and pray. She'd done it before. The doors to her own church weren't open during the day like the doors to the Catholic churches. Those churches always invited you in with candles and the awe created by soaring ceilings and stained glass. There were usually only a few people scattered about, all of them careful not to intrude on the private conversations others were having with God.

It was okay to pray in a church like that. Even if their teachings were different, they were still closely related. And the buildings were magnificent. They made you feel like God was there after all.

She sighed, folding her hands as if already in prayer, knowing she wouldn't go. She didn't feel like praying. She needed to *do* something.

Scooting closer to her computer, she opened a browser and tapped around a news site. She wasn't really paying attention. The stream of information that was far away from her everyday life helped to numb the fury inside her, allowing her to think while slowing her thoughts so they didn't race in mad, angry, wounded circles.

After a while, it came to her. It came out of nowhere, as these impulses often did. This time, she had no inclination to attribute it to God or any other form of heavenly guidance. It was just an idea. A thought. It couldn't be worse than any of her other ideas that had failed spectacularly.

She needed to see what could be learned at Alexandra's apartment. Alex was so secretive about where she lived. Why was that? She was secretive about her life in general. For all Stephanie knew, Alex was married but didn't wear a ring. She might be living with a man or even another woman. She might be living with an elderly parent or a sibling or in a small commune.

There was no reason that knowing about Alexandra's living situation would do anything at all to help Stephanie with her job, but she would take this one step at a time. Knowledge was power, and she needed to get power over that woman one way or another. If she didn't, her whole life might crumble around her. Alex could get her fired, running to Trystan with her lies and taking credit for Stephanie's work. Worse, far, far worse, she was in a position to destroy Stephanie's relationship with her daughter.

It was risky. Alex might arrive home unexpectedly. But she had to find out whatever she could about who else lived in the building and who, if anyone, shared the apartment itself.

She opened the PowerPoint file that held Trystan's presentation for new clients. She would dig into the changes he wanted and try to get something worked out for him quickly. There was a certain amount of energy pulsing through her now that she had a plan. She would put that energy to good use and then leave early. Alex usually stayed in the office until five-thirty, often a bit later, unless she had a photography session.

Three hours later, she stood in front of Alex's apartment

building. The sun was going down. It would be dark before Alex arrived. Now that she was here, she wasn't sure what she could do. The obvious next step was to wait for someone coming or going to allow her inside.

If she had the kind of chutzpah that Alex possessed, she could easily walk boldly up to a stranger and give them a convincing story of why she belonged in the building. But she wasn't used to casually telling lies like Alex did, and she wasn't used to approaching people she didn't know as if they would be thrilled by the intrusion, eager to listen, and sympathetic to whatever story she made up.

She shoved her hands into her pockets and hunched her shoulders, trying to stay warm. It didn't work. Her hands felt better with the extra layer of fabric, but hunching her shoulders did nothing aside from making her neck and back ache. Still, it seemed as if relaxing them would allow the cold to access more parts of her body.

As she clenched her muscles and shivered and tried to think of what she could do, a man hurried up to the building, entered the code, and pulled open the door. Stephanie moved toward him.

"Excuse me."

He turned and gave her a friendly, almost leering smile. "Hi."

"I was here earlier today visiting a friend, and I lost my necklace. I just wanted to look around the lobby, if that's okay? I know I was wearing it when I left her apartment." The words tumbled out of her mouth like satin ribbon. Was it really this easy to lie?

He raised his eyebrows, causing them to disappear beneath the edge of his knitted hat. "That sucks."

"I know." Her eyes grew watery, stinging from the cold.

He looked sympathetic. "Was it worth a lot?"

"Yes." She nodded gratefully. "It's 24-karat gold. A chain with a cross."

"Shit. That's serious. I hope no one swiped it. They'll have the wrath of god on them." He laughed.

She wasn't sure if she should laugh or not. Was he mocking God? Or was he serious, understanding that the value was more than the quality of the gold? "I hope not." She smiled.

He stepped to the side, opening the door wider so she could enter. She went inside, relaxing into the warmth of the lobby.

"I'll help you look," he said.

"No, that's okay. I just appreciate that you let me in."

"I insist." He walked toward the corner closest to the door and looked behind the potted plant that stood there.

She went to the opposite corner. How would she be rid of him? She now realized she had no idea what floor Alex lived on. This had been a ridiculous plan. She felt the time moving too fast, an increasing tension that if Alex showed up early, it would be very bad. "I don't see it. I guess it's gone... somewhere on the street."

"That would be terrible," he said. "By the way, I'm Rafe."

"Sharon," she mumbled. What had she been thinking? What she wanted to know was whether Eileen had a secret plan to move in with Alex. She wanted to find out if any of her things were already here. But of course, that was impossible. She'd had a vague idea of talking to the building manager, but standing here made her see how ridiculous that was.

"I'm really sorry about your necklace," he said.

"It's okay."

"It's not. It really is not. It sounds like it might be sentimental, not just valuable."

A wave of guilt struck her chest, thinking about her beautiful cross lying in her jewelry box at home. Her only hope, at this point, was to see what this very friendly guy might have to say. "This is a nice building."

"It's alright."

"It's not huge, with too many people. I hate that."

"Yeah. It's good."

"Are people friendly?"

He shrugged. "Some are, some aren't."

"What floor do you live on?"

"Second."

"Do you have a roommate?"

He grinned. "You're very curious."

"It's just such a charming building."

"Thinking of moving in?"

"Are there any vacancies?"

"I don't think so. I live with my girlfriend. There are a few one-bedroom units—two on my floor, and I think two or three on the third, but I don't know about the others."

She nodded. This was going nowhere. She wasn't about to ask directly about Alex. If this guy knew Alex, Stephanie wouldn't be able to lie her way out of that. She sighed. "Well. I guess I'll get going. Nice talking to you."

"Yup. Hope you find it."

She shrugged and gave him a smile that she hoped said things didn't always work out the way you wanted, but that was okay. It was not how she felt, but she felt better for trying. If she really wanted to know Eileen's plans, she should ask her own daughter. She just had to get herself into a state where she wouldn't blurt out vicious comments about Alexandra in the process, rebuilding the wall between them that had only recently started to come down.

52

Portland, Oregon

For one of only a few times in my life, my punishment was delivered by my mother. As far as I ever knew, my father never heard anything about what I'd done to raise money for a car.

It took three long, boring days for my mother to drive me around to every single house where I'd made an unauthorized commission on candy sales. I handed the cash to each person, ticking their names off my list as we went. Most of them were so shocked, they just shook their heads when I made the required offer to do work around their house or yard. Then the door closed slowly and firmly in my face. They didn't deliver lectures. They seemed mostly anxious to minimize their contact with me.

My mother's eyes filled with tears each time I told her about a customer's refusal to offer me work that would *atone* for my immoral behavior.

"They probably don't trust you inside their homes." She sniffed loudly. "This breaks my heart. Do you see what you've lost? You squandered your name for filthy cash. A damaged reputation is almost impossible to repair."

I had no doubt my reputation was damaged, but I also was aware that most of the people who purchased candy from me didn't want me in their homes because they didn't know me, not because I was a thief, as my mother kept reminding me.

During our slow drives up and down the blocks where I'd ridden my bike just a few days or weeks earlier, we argued about whether or not theft was an accurate description of what I'd done.

"They were happy to pay the higher price," I said.

"I wish you would stop saying that. They weren't *happy*, they just didn't know any better."

"It's sort of like a tip," I said.

"It's not at all like a tip. A tip is something you give willingly."

"Well, I don't see why all of us should have to sell candy, and we don't get anything out of it. It's not right. It's probably illegal."

"It's called volunteer work. And you get a nice camp experience."

"The youth group leaders want us to go to camp more than we want to go. So they can make sure we learn everything they're excited to teach."

"That's a terrible attitude." She pulled the car to the curb in front of a two-story house with a fence around the entire front yard. "We'll finish this conversation when you're done here."

There were four houses on this side of the street where I'd sold candy. She would wait in the car in front of the first while I made my way up the block.

I knocked on the door. It was opened by a guy about my age. A guy I'd seen at school but who was into sports and not someone I'd ever talked to. "Hi. Is your mom home?"

He shook his head. "What's up?"

I glanced back toward the car where my mother had slid down in the seat so she could observe me through the passenger side window. She hadn't given me instructions about what to do when the person I'd *sinned against* wasn't home. I really did not want to come back.

I held out the twenty dollars. "Your mother bought candy bars from me. I was selling them for a church fundraiser."

He looked at the two tens in my hand. "What's that for?"

I hesitated. Would my mother know what I said to him? Of course not. "I charged her the wrong price."

"Okay." He took the bills.

When I didn't immediately turn to go, he looked up from the cash in his hand. "What else?"

"Nothing."

He frowned. "Okay, well, thanks." He started to close the door.

"Tell her thanks for buying the candy."

"Sure thing." The door closed.

I knocked again.

He opened the door right away. "What?"

"I've seen you around school," I said.

"Yeah, me too."

"What's your name?"

"Brady."

I introduced myself. "We should hang out sometime."

He looked startled. "I guess. I don't usually hang out with church-y people."

"I'm not very church-y." I smiled and leaned on the porch railing and told him why I'd really given his mom the twenty bucks.

When I was finished, he laughed. "I'll look for you at lunch some time."

"And tell your mom the whole story, okay? I'm in trouble, and I'm supposed to tell the whole story."

He laughed again. "Sure. Whatever. See you at school." The door closed more slowly this time.

I walked down the path, smiling at the thought of going to school the following week, at the thought that I was almost done with this exhausting waste of time.

When all the money had been returned, and I'd called Mrs. Palomar to tell her I'd cheated her sister and had now returned the money I owed her, my punishment was complete. At least that's what my mother said. But it wasn't really.

The following weekend she told me she wanted to take me out to lunch at my favorite Mexican restaurant. When we were seated across from each other, a bowl of freshly made tortilla chips, a dish of salsa, and another of guacamole between us, I was expecting the final blow. I scooped up guacamole on a chip, dipped it in the salsa, and took a large bite.

"I understand you feel it's unjust that you weren't given a car when you got your license."

I stared at her. It wasn't that I *felt* it was unjust, it *was* unjust.

"Every child is different, and we've tried to raise all of you with consideration for what each of you needed most, based on your personalities, your temperaments, your weaknesses."

I saw it coming like a car barreling down a hill right at me, but I remained silent, filling myself with chips, adding more and more hot salsa while she talked.

"Your father and I have been concerned about how self-absorbed you are. And of course, concerned that you haven't submitted yourself to God. A car is a privilege. Do you understand that?"

I nodded.

"It's not something you're owed. And in your case, we think it would be better if you didn't have that kind of freedom at this point in your life. You're still under our care for a few more years, and we won't give up on you."

That last part sounded harsh. It made me wonder if they had considered giving up on me.

I gave her a meek smile. My mother was kind to me. She didn't try to push me into conforming to her world with the same brute force my father used. And she didn't seem to get so excited when she punished me, didn't get the almost gloating look of power that often consumed my father.

It was best not to say too much and just enjoy the Mexican food. I might not have a car, but that didn't mean I couldn't get out of the house. I thought about Brady and wondered if he had a car yet.

53

Two days after Stephanie went off on me regarding the *theft* of her *insight* into Arlinda's life, which was no insight at all, and had nothing to do with what Arlinda had discovered about herself, Trystan asked to see me.

As I passed by Stephanie's office, her wide-open door gave me a clear view of her for a split second. She looked directly at me, smiling with a triumphant look in her eyes that told me things were about to escalate, and not in my favor.

I was pretty sure she'd overheard me asking Trystan whether he wanted me to resign. I'd wondered why she hadn't brought it up to me. Now I knew. She'd figured out a way to use that information, persuading Trystan to undermine his own decision. Again. I couldn't understand why he was so indecisive. It wasn't like him, and I wasn't going to leave his office without doing my best to get an answer to that question.

"I've thought a lot about our discussion last week," he said.

"So have I."

Not at all curious about my thoughts, he plowed ahead. "Everything else aside, our organization is growing. We can't let the photography become a bottleneck to giving our clients an efficient process. It wouldn't take much to overwhelm your schedule."

I placed my hands on top of each other, studying my fingernails. They'd grown quite long and were painted black. Some rough edges were starting to show. I really needed a new manicure. A nail trim was in order, and I was ready for a change in color—something less dramatic. Taupe, maybe.

"Are you listening to me?"

I looked up. "Yes."

"I don't think you are."

"My schedule might become overwhelming."

"And…?"

I looked up at the ceiling, trying to recall whether I'd had a sense of him speaking after that. "The company is growing, and—"

"You're not taking this seriously."

"Because I already know what you're going to tell me. So just say it."

"Well, I'd like to have a conversation about it. I'm not giving orders, I'm not—"

"I think you are. Stephanie keeps complaining, and for whatever reason, you're more worried about her job satisfaction than mine."

"Did she tell you about our conversation?"

"She didn't have to," I said.

"What does that mean?"

"It's pretty clear that you've changed your mind. You want her to be the backup photographer. All that about my schedule getting too crowded was paving the way."

"And what are your thoughts on that?"

"You already know. She and I don't get along."

His voice became hard—"The two of you are acting like children."

I tried to digest this. He wasn't wrong. But sometimes what looks childish on the outside is actually quite serious if you bother to dig below the surface. Even children, when they have screaming, crying fights, when they're pretending to play at running a shop, or making up strategic games for spying on their siblings and friends, are deadly serious. They're fighting for their power. They're stubborn about getting what's right for them and for their position in the world, even when that world is make-believe.

The way Trystan looked at me, and the way he spoke about the trouble between Stephanie and me, suggested we were being petty. I think if he were with a group of men, he would have called it a catfight, even though he wasn't the type to categorize women with that kind of degrading language. But he might. Even enlightened men can be dismissive sometimes.

"I'm not acting like a child. I'm trying to deal with a woman who runs to you with complaints and made-up stories, who tries to undermine me, writing me ridiculous, threatening emails, and whines because I happen to have become friends with her daughter."

"I didn't know you were friendly with Eileen."

"Why would you? It's not important, and it has nothing to do with my job or anything we do here."

"Does Stephanie feel like you're involved in her life in a way she didn't anticipate and maybe feels threatened by?"

I stared at him. If he wanted to consider Stephanie and me childish, he needed to take a look in the mirror. Or maybe childish was the wrong term. He saw us as childish and was acting like a parent who wants to force their children into playing nice.

"Could that be causing some of the trouble?" he said.

I changed my belligerent stare to a look of utter disdain. He didn't seem to pick up on it. "Eileen and I started talking, and we clicked. She's an adult. I'm an adult. Stephanie, apparently, is not."

"Okay. We're getting off track here," he said. "Since you've figured out that I want Stephanie to be your backup. I need you to work with her to get her up to speed. I think a little mentoring about effective interaction with our clients would be helpful."

"You're making a mistake."

"I know what I'm doing. This is important."

"Why do you placate her? I don't get it."

"This has nothing to do with placating. I need another photographer. Please don't argue with me."

"She won't do as good a job as I do."

"Probably not. We'll work it out to be sure the key images are done by you, as well as the most critical events."

"Aren't all of them critical?"

He leaned forward, pressing his fingertips on the desk. "I need another photographer, Alex. I'm asking you to mentor her."

"It sounds like you're *telling* me."

"Okay, then. Yes, I'm telling you."

"Why not hire someone who can work on-call? Someone who can interact better with the caliber of people who come to you for coaching?"

"She's fine with our clients."

"Chatting over the phone, sure. I think there are things you don't know."

He gave me a steady look and said nothing. After a moment, he turned toward his computer. "Work out a schedule for how long you think it will take. Send it to me with the steps you plan to follow, as well as a start date."

I stood. "It almost seems like she has something on you."

He laughed. "Don't be ridiculous."

"Why are you so worried about her feelings? Why do you keep flipping back and forth on this?"

He didn't look up. "Have a good evening."

I walked out of the office without wishing him the same. When I passed Stephanie's office, the door was closed.

On the subway, I tried to think about what had happened. I didn't understand why he was willing to risk the animosity between Stephanie and me escalating. I wasn't going to change, and he understood that. Stephanie couldn't handle my bluntness. She couldn't handle my lack of concern for what people think of me. She didn't like me, and there were deep-rooted reasons for that. A full-blown battle seemed far worse for his consulting than a slight backlog in photography.

I wasn't even sure what a mentor was supposed to do in this situation. It was a lot more than just showing her how to frame a shot, which I was pretty sure every person on the planet knew how to do to some extent. She would never be able to get our clients out of their own heads, their own internal monolog like I could. The skills I possessed couldn't be taught.

In fact, it was likely she would cause our clients to become more self-conscious. Her extreme self-consciousness, and what sometimes looked like self-hatred, would spill all over them, splashing across their clothing, staining them more permanently than a glass of red wine.

Trystan would see that soon enough.

I pictured trying to show Stephanie how to put herself in the background, making herself unnoticed when taking video, imagined explaining how to chat with clients. Then I thought more about the concept of mentoring.

If he wanted her to do even a halfway decent job, I would have to figure out a way to help her to mirror some of my personality traits. And that didn't mean smoking. I smiled, recalling her clumsy effort to smoke. From the corner of my eye, I saw the woman beside me giving me a strange, slightly frightened look. It wasn't normal to see someone on the subway smiling without some obvious stimulus. Still, I left the smile on my face and let my imagination run wild—I could guide Stephanie into all kinds of new experiences. Maybe I should mentor her as a killer. She certainly had those vengeful instincts, trying to frighten me with her images of dark angels.

I laughed out loud. The woman beside me stood and moved to the back of the car, positioning herself so she could keep her eye on me.

54

I stepped out of my apartment door, ready for a run. It was early Saturday morning. We were in the midst of a short burst of Spring weather—those February days that whispered Spring had arrived were always unsettling—everyone knew it had not, but we felt it anyway.

I wore a long-sleeved T-shirt, hoodie, and leggings. I hadn't smoked all week, and it felt surprisingly good. My body felt cleaner, more connected to the clear sky and the soft air. I wondered how long it would last, but it sure was making me more excited to go for a run.

When I turned from locking my door, Rafe was leaning on the stairwell railing. He stepped away from it, blocking my way. "I need to talk to you."

"I'm going for a run."

"This will only take a minute."

"Not now." I stepped around him, but he moved again, standing with his feet spread and arms crossed. "Get out of my way."

"Don't be so bitchy."

I gave him a decidedly bitchy look.

"We get that you don't want to invest twenty-five thousand to get started day trading, so we want to make some investments for you. All we need is five grand, and we can get you a very nice return. Once you see what can be done, your fear—"

"No thanks."

"It's not an offer that you get to choose. If you don't agree, Victoria will let Brian know about your little secret."

"I don't have any little secrets." His words made my bones freeze, but I was sure he knew nothing about me, no matter what he thought. It was a bluff. He was a gambler after all.

"You've been smoking in your apartment, and that's cause for eviction."

I laughed. "You're threatening me? That's quite an investment opportunity."

"It's not a threat."

"Then what is it?"

"We've tried to help you. We feel sorry for you. It's hard to watch someone's stubbornness and fear keep them from benefiting from our expertise."

I laughed. "Get out of the way. I'm done with this."

"You'll be evicted without any chance to fight it. The lease says—"

"There's nothing to tell him. I've never smoked in my apartment."

"Vic has a good relationship with Brian." He gave me a leering grin to emphasize his words.

"So you're going to lie about me to force me to give you money that you'll *invest* for my benefit? What kind of weird, twisted deal is that?"

"Brian will believe anything Vic says. You can bet on it."

He was right. Brian probably would believe Victoria, and he already distrusted me. He was a guy who allowed my neighbors, for whatever reason, to install a surveillance camera aimed right at my front door.

I wondered how long it had been there. I still couldn't understand why I'd never noticed it. I suppose I wasn't in the habit of looking at the ceiling.

Did Rafe hope he had footage of me smoking in the hallway? Was that why it had been installed—in the hope of discovering some leverage with which to extort money for their day trading venture, which was clearly facing a downturn?

It made my head ache, trying to understand what they were after. I almost wanted to tell Nick I would talk to the FBI. But the risk was enormous. Making that kind of commitment then backing out was much too dangerous.

It was best to never talk to anyone in any kind of law enforcement on the one in one hundred million chance that I might be asked intrusive questions about all parts of my life. On the chance I might invite someone checking into me.

"I never smoked in my apartment, so you can tell him whatever you want. All he has to do is walk around the place and take a few deep breaths. He can crawl around and sniff the carpet if he wants."

"Smokers are so clueless," Rafe said.

"How is that?"

"You reek. Don't you know that?"

I said nothing. I knew there was a lingering odor, but I never smoked in enclosed places, and I really didn't smoke that often.

"You think the smell isn't there, but that's because you've adapted to it. A non-smoker can smell it anywhere. In fact, I'm surprised Brian didn't say anything when he was in your apartment a few weeks ago."

He was backing me into a corner. He was probably right that the scent lingered on my coats and scarves. It might be in my hair. It might have filtered down through the pillowcases into my pillow, bits of it clinging to my comforter. "You can't force someone to invest money. And why would you want to?"

"You don't get that *either*, do you." He smirked. "You think you're so smart, but you're not so hot and clever as you think."

I went to the railing and started stretching my calf muscles. I would wait for him to run out of steam so I could get on my way. I didn't want to piss him off until I figured out how to keep them from filling Brian's ears with lies. I looked down at my foot, my leg pushed forward as far as it would go, feeling the lovely pull in that muscle all the way down to my Achilles. "What are you talking about?" I said.

"We already made a huge investment in you, and you aren't just going to walk away from it. That's not how things work."

I began stretching my other foot. "I still don't know what you're talking about."

"I'm talking about you playing dumb. All the meals at our apartment, the drinks, the dinners out, the—"

"I provided alcohol half the time. We're on a completely even footing with money. Not that I owe you anything. Those were social occasions, not business expenses."

"Vic spent time teaching you the ins and outs. She showed you some of our trade secrets. You observed some of our algorithms in action."

I laughed, a genuine laugh at the idea of Victoria giving me trade secrets, at the idea of them even possessing *trade secrets*. "You're out of your mind."

"I'm not. And you owe us."

I moved around him. He grabbed the hood of my sweatshirt. I wrenched to the side, conscious of the stairs descending before me, glad that I was wearing running shoes and not the slick-soled boots I often wore to work or in the evening. "Let go of me."

Surprisingly, he did. "So, I need that bit of cash before trading starts on Monday."

"I'm not giving you any money." I jogged down a few steps, then started moving faster. I didn't look up, which would have thrown me off balance.

"Where are you going?"

I shouted back up, my voice echoing so loudly in the stairwell, I wondered if Kent might hear me. "For that run I mentioned." I moved faster, stepping onto the landing where the stairs turned.

Suddenly, he was right behind me. He grabbed my hood again, and this time he didn't let go, pulling so hard the zipper dug into my throat. I knew I could get him off of me easily, but with the stairs before us, it didn't seem like the best move.

"You aren't going to get away with this," he said.

I thought about the FBI. Was it worth it? Would it scare him enough? Did I want to give away that piece of knowledge for free? It was better to hold back, to wait and see how things evolved. The best thing might be to go to Brian first, get him on my side, draw him into my view of things. I could even suggest I was afraid of Rafe.

I relaxed, and the hood sagged against the back of my neck. The zipper eased away from my throat, but I still felt the dig of its sharp teeth on the tender skin. "I need to think."

"About what?"

"You caught me off guard. I had no idea you were so…"

"What?"

I shrugged. He let go of the hood and moved so he was facing me.

I gave him a frightened, tremulous smile. "You scared me just now." I paused for a deep breath. "I never thought about the things Victoria said. I don't remember any secrets, though."

"Our investment in you is substantial."

"Well, let me think."

"There's nothing to think about. You don't have a choice."

"It's a lot of money. I'm not sure—"

"Don't give me that line of bullshit. You have plenty. And you don't need time to think. You can think while you take money out of your account."

He backed away from me.

I nodded. I said nothing, allowing him to interpret the nod however he chose. I ran down the rest of the stairs and out the doors, not stopping until I was two blocks from the apartment. When I paused, I took a photograph of where the zipper had caught the skin of my throat. Then I walked quickly toward the park, trying to figure out what I was going to do.

55

The minute I got back from my run, I dug Nick's info out of my nightstand drawer and sent him a text message telling him I needed to talk.

He replied, asking what had changed. I said I needed to talk to him, that I didn't want to put my thoughts into a text message where they might be seen at some point. I wasn't sure by whom or how on earth this might happen, but a phone call was better. Unless he recorded me, it would be my word against his. I didn't think he had any reason to record me. I thought it was likely the words he used and the quality of his voice—stiff and false, or relaxed—would tell me if he was doing something like that.

We connected late in the afternoon. I was stretched out on my couch, an iced latte on the floor within arm's reach, and a dish of salted cashews beside the drink. I was prepared for a lengthy call, if that's what it turned into.

The first words out of his mouth were—"What's up? Did Rafe…"

I waited, hardly breathing, hoping to learn more about what they'd done to him, but after stopping himself, he remained in control and didn't succumb to finishing the thought.

"What were you going to say?"

"You have to tell me," he said. "I can't talk about it."

I sighed. "They're trying to blackmail me, I guess that's the best way to describe it. Although it's not really blackmail—threaten is a better word. Rafe threatened to get me evicted if I don't give them five thousand dollars to invest for me."

"Good."

"Good?"

"I mean, I think the FBI would love to have you on their —"

"No. I told you no."

"Then why did you contact me again?"

"You said if they did something criminal, I should let you know."

"I said if you're willing to work with the FBI."

"Why can't you tell me exactly what they're looking into?"

"Because it's sensitive. The agent would have to brief you."

His casual use of the word *brief*, an official-sounding word, made my stomach clench. "I can't do that. I don't have time, but I'd just like to understand what they're up to."

"Don't give Rafe, or Victoria, any money, and you'll be fine."

"Did you give them money?"

He was silent, not wanting to tell me yet again that he couldn't share any details. I was sure his silence also proved he'd given them money to invest. Why else would he be involved with the FBI? Surely he knew I could figure out parts of it. His secretiveness seemed a little ridiculous. I supposed he was just following their rules. I could see that, but still… "That's great you're helping them," I said.

"Uh-huh."

"But still, I need to know what's going on."

"Is that why you called? To beat me up on a question I already answered?"

"I need to know what they want. And since you had a very bad experience with them, it almost seems…it seems selfish to not give me some insight."

"The only insight you need is not to give them any money. Stay away from them."

"Yes, but now they're threatening something that could get me evicted."

"The offer still stands. The FBI would very much like to talk to you."

"I just can't."

"Why not?"

"It's complicated," I said.

"Do you have a more involved relationship with them? Are you already hooked in or something? Tell me what's going on."

I muted my phone and ate several cashews. I sipped my latte then un-muted as he asked for the third time what was going on. "I assume you did give them money," I said. "And I'm guessing you didn't get the incredible profit they guaranteed or you wouldn't be talking to the FBI. But I don't see how that's a crime. If you gave them money willingly."

He was silent. Suggesting he wasn't very bright to hand over a large amount of cash to people like that wasn't going to shame him into telling me what had happened.

His simple suggestion was correct. Kent had said the same thing. It wasn't complicated. All I needed to do was walk away from them. Why was I pushing so hard for information that really had nothing to do with me? Maybe because it seemed easier to pry it out of Nick. The way things were headed, I could lose my apartment. I could try to get Brian on my side before they painted me in a bad light, but Brian was more difficult to manage than Nick. Nick was a stone wall in front of me, but Brian was a thick, sucking swamp.

"I don't understand why it's a secret. Maybe I would talk to the FBI if I knew what they were trying to do. Not knowing anything makes it feel too risky."

He laughed with a snorting sound. "Why would it be risky to talk to the FBI?"

"I have a demanding job. I can't afford to give all these hours to something like this."

"Well, thanks to those two, I don't have a job anymore. I had to quit because I couldn't afford to stay in New York. I'm back in Minnesota, living with my parents. And just so you know, guaranteeing returns on an investment is considered fraud."

"So how much did you give them?"

"I told you, enough that I couldn't afford to stay in New York. Couldn't afford to rent an apartment anywhere right now."

"You seem like a smart guy. They must have been very clever."

He blew air out in short puffs. I could picture him starting to hyperventilate, even though I'd never seen him, had no idea what he looked like. In the sound of his breath, I felt him shift toward my side.

It sometimes astounded me how flattery, even a mild but genuine compliment, brought a person onto your side of the fence. Maybe he was finally wondering whether telling me a few things would truly jeopardize an investigation by the FBI. What did it matter? I was nobody, disinclined to talk to any officials, and certainly not likely to tip off Rafe and Victoria.

Sensing he was ready to relax his principles, I moved in to close the sale, or maybe, for the kill. "I'm just not sure what to do. If you tell me what happened, maybe it will change my mind."

"About what?"

"About talking to the FBI."

"They asked me not to reveal any details. They insisted, actually. If it ever got back to Rafe and Victoria…it might really damage whatever they're doing to catch them in the act."

"In the act of what? Are they in trouble with the SEC? Or for blackmail or…what?"

"Rafe Goddard is being investigated for fraud."

"How are they planning to catch him at it?"

"I definitely can't tell you that, because I don't know any details."

I popped a cashew into my mouth and sucked off the salt. I chewed quickly and washed it down with coffee. "It must have been terrible, having to move out of New York. I love it here. And this is a nice apartment, if you prefer charm over ultra-modern touches."

He laughed. "Yeah. I liked it. Until they moved in."

"Sometimes, she almost assaults me when I come out of my apartment," I said. "And they've installed a surveillance camera outside my door, in that space between the two apartments."

"Interesting. That could be good information. I'll pass it on."

I held my breath for a moment. Nick had my cell number. It would be easy for the FBI to find me, wanting to know more about the camera. Had I made a terrible mistake getting in touch with him, revealing too much? All because I just *had* to know what was going on? Why couldn't I leave it alone? "For all I know, the manager put it there," I said. "You should tell them to check with him."

"I think they'll just be glad to be aware it exists."

Now, as if my own risky revelation had punctured a hole in his reserve, the story began to trickle out.

"I was beyond stupid. Victoria flirted with me all the time. Really aggressively, and right in front of Rafe."

"I know how that is. It's been the same, with him."

"Eventually, we hooked up. That very same night she tells Rafe about it. He comes pounding his fist on my door. After that, it got weird. He never really did anything, but he stalked me, made me feel like he was biding his time until he found a way to get me somewhere isolated and beat the shit out of me. Or worse."

I thought about the night I'd kissed Rafe. It was clear I hadn't fit into their plan as smoothly as Nick had.

"First, they wanted to teach me how to trade. When I balked at the up-front deposit that's required to open an account, they came to me with this plan to invest money for me. They would make me an awesome pile of cash."

"They've been trying to get me to make trades since I moved in. They're relentless."

"Even now, I'm not sure why I agreed. They have a way of putting themselves into every part of your life, and I felt like they owned me or something. I don't know. I half-believed them. They were so sure about it. And they made me feel like I was part of their relationship in some weird, fucked-up way that I can't explain. So I gave them five thousand bucks."

"Same as he asked me."

"Right away, they lost half of the five grand. So they showed me all these charts and gave me all this stuff to read about how they could make it all back and give me a higher than average rate of return. If I gave just a little more, they could set me up nicely. They said getting out at a loss was the behavior of a coward and not the way people make money in the market. I gave them a thousand. Within a few weeks, they handed me a check for over seven grand. And they asked me to sign an agreement."

"Wow. I assumed they've been lying about all of that."

"Yeah. Well, you must be smarter than I am. Or more careful. Or less greedy."

I laughed, and he joined me.

"So I gave it all back to them, and another two thousand. In a few weeks, they gave me about fifteen hundred bucks, and then I was hooked. So I gave them twenty-thousand more."

I gasped softly, and it wasn't put on. I was shocked, but a small part of me whispered that it could have happened to me. Seeing that they really did have a knack, getting that much cash in such a short time—he was right. He wasn't stupid, he was just eager to take big steps forward, to accelerate his life. I saw the attraction.

"So yeah. And when it all disappeared, I decided to get in touch with the FBI. Victoria told me they used to live in LA, and Chicago before that, so I figured I wasn't the first greedy moron."

I half-understood how it had happened to him, but I also thought about how clumsy they were as they kept trying to snag me in their web. Maybe not everyone is as suspicious as I am. And I wouldn't have felt guilty sleeping with Rafe, so I definitely hadn't fit properly into their profile.

Nick, from a quiet, easy-going family in Minnesota, had been easier to manipulate.

We talked a bit longer, and I said I would think about whether I could make time to work with the FBI. But as soon as I hung up, I knew I would tell Trystan my phone had been stolen, and I needed a new one, along with a new number. I would also need to find a new apartment. Soon.

56

On Sunday morning, I knocked on Victoria and Rafe's door. It was only six, but I hadn't seen Victoria since the night Rafe had torn her dress off. I hadn't told Nick about that or the scene across the street from the brownstone or her hanging out at The Moonlight Sonata. I'd learned a lot from him, but I still had questions he couldn't answer. If Victoria would talk to me, genuinely talk rather than playing games, I was leaning toward guessing her answers would tell me their stunts were instigated by Rafe.

Something about her furtive behavior when she'd gone to that bar in shoes not meant for a cold New York winter, suggested she was following orders, doing something to please him no matter how miserable it made her. Especially seeing the delicate straps and narrow-heels of those sandals on the feet of a woman who wore Ugg boots nearly every time I saw her.

Her behavior, when I'd observed unnoticed, was that of a woman who saw her life slipping out of her control. I'd been far too subtle when I said Rafe didn't appreciate her. Now, I would be blunt.

She was holding a mug of coffee as she opened the door. She was already showered, dressed, and made up, but looking like she would prefer to go back to sleep for another hour or two.

"What's up?" She slurped her coffee.

"I'm going out for breakfast. Want to come?"

She turned to look at the room behind her. The computer screens were dark, the blinds still closed. The bedroom door was also closed. She turned back. "I'm not sure, I—"

"Have you eaten? I'm starving."

"Not yet. I was going to make…" She sighed. "We usually have waffles on Sundays."

"Is Rafe up?"

"No, but he'll be pissed if we go without him."

"We can bring something back."

"I'm not sure." Again, she glanced over her shoulder. "I could ask him." She slurped her coffee.

"Come on. We'll be back before he wakes up. You could still make him waffles."

"He won't like it."

"Won't like missing breakfast, or won't like you going somewhere without permission?"

She laughed.

It was a strange response. "Should I report him for human trafficking?"

Her expression changed suddenly to one of shock. She looked ready to cry.

I leaned against the doorframe. "So you're not allowed to go anywhere without him? You have to be here to mix the batter the moment he opens his eyes?"

"No." Her hand trembled as she lifted the mug to her

mouth. "It's not like that."

"Then come with me."

"What time is it anyway?"

"A little after six."

She turned away from the door. She moved out of my view into the kitchen and returned a moment later without the coffee mug. She grabbed a jacket, hat, and scarf off the arm of the couch, adding her purse to the stack of things in her arms.

In the hallway, I glanced up at the unobtrusive camera, but she didn't notice me doing it.

She grudgingly agreed to walk three blocks to a diner that opened for breakfast at five on weekdays, six on the weekends.

We settled into a booth in the back corner, spreading out our things on the wide, turquoise Naugahyde benches.

We both ordered bacon, eggs, hash browns, and toast. She ordered orange juice instead of coffee.

Settling back, she looked out the window at the empty street beside us.

"What have you been up to?" I said.

"Same old..." She sighed.

"Me too."

She didn't acknowledge my comment or ask anything about what I'd been doing.

"You seem down," I said.

"I didn't sleep much."

"It's more than that." We only had an hour. I couldn't waste time being diplomatic and careful about delicately moving the conversation to her recent fights with Rafe. "I think something bad is going on in your life."

"You don't know anything about me."

"I know more than you think."

Her head jerked toward me, and she stared at me with jittering eyeballs, her lips partially opened, showing me gritted teeth. "I thought you just wanted to have breakfast. Why are you harassing me?"

"I saw you and Rafe in the rain. When he tore your dress."

She stared at me.

"What happened?"

"It was an accident."

It definitely was not an accident. I waited for her to say more, possibly backtracking on her lie. "I saw you out at night in summer clothes, freezing and walking to a club that—"

"Are you following me?"

"Just once or twice."

"That's creepy."

I shrugged. "I was curious."

"Where I go is none of your fucking business."

"Do you know that Rafe kissed me? That he tried to have sex with me?"

"You better not be saying what I think you are."

"I'm not saying he assaulted me, but do you really want to be with a guy who's going around kissing other women, trying to—"

"It's not a problem."

"Most people would absolutely think it's a problem."

"He and I understand each other."

"That's what he said, although, in his version, you were the understanding one, not him. I don't really see him as an understanding guy."

Our food arrived. Victoria grabbed her knife and fork as if

they were defensive weapons. She stabbed the egg and yolk spilled out. She dragged her knife across the white, added some hash browns to the mix, and shoved it into her mouth as if she felt she needed to plug it.

"It's pretty clear you're not very happy, and Rafe is a little shit."

"Don't say that." She drank her orange juice, putting the glass down firmly.

"Why do you go to The Moonlight Sonata? It sounds like hookers hang out there to meet older guys. Men with money."

She put down her fork. She took her napkin and blew her nose. When she took it away from her face, her eyes were red. The rather astute server appeared with a handful of additional napkins. Victoria gave her a watery smile, and I thanked her.

She blew her nose again. "Why are you doing this?"

"Because I think you need some help."

"I'm fine. We're fine."

"What happened with the brownstone? I thought it was your dream house, that you were ready to move in?"

She burst into tears. She pushed the plate away, leaving the perfectly cooked bacon, now soaking in egg yolk, to get cold and soft and unappealing.

"You can trust me."

"With what?"

"With whatever's going on."

"Nothing is going on."

"I don't like it when men treat women like shit, and all I can see is Rafe doing exactly that to you."

"He doesn't."

"Then why were you shouting at him across the street from

the house that's supposed to be yours? Why did he rip your dress off? And why are you crying now? Something's wrong."

"There's nothing wrong."

"Do you want to live your life scared and crying all the time?"

"No."

"Then tell me."

"I can't leave him. If that's what you're thinking."

"Why not?"

"We work together."

"So? You can work just as well by yourself."

"He needs me."

"I'm sure he does. But do you need him?"

"I love him."

"Is he your pimp?"

"God, no." She laughed, then began crying again. "I mean, it's not what you're thinking."

"Why do you go to that club if you're not looking for old guys with money?"

"We just find men who might want to invest, to make money day trading."

"If day trading works so great, why do you need all these *investors*?"

"The investing is Rafe's thing, I'm not up to speed on all the details."

"Do you love him, really? Or is he a bad habit?"

"We've been together since I was fifteen."

"Fifteen is pretty young."

"I can't imagine my life without him."

"Are you sure? Who's better at trading stocks? You or him?"

She looked away. In a soft voice, half mumbling, she spoke. "Things haven't been good. Maybe for a while. I don't like what we're doing, but...he..."

I drank my coffee while she continued to stare out the window. I ate a slice of bacon, chewing slowly. "Does he know how to manage a trading account at all?"

Her body shook with a sudden onslaught of sobs, like something coming from nature, a storm that had been brewing for a long time. The server passed by. She looked at me with alarm. I gave her a grim smile and nodded my head to suggest she should move on quickly.

"Okay," Victoria said, trying to draw oxygen and speak at the same time, her voice soggy with tears. "You're right. He messes it up. Every single time. We had the money for the brownstone. We even made an offer. I honestly thought it was ours. I worked years to build up our savings, and he took crazy, huge risks that were more like bets on a roulette wheel than investments. He lost everything, and our offer, my offer, on the house blew up."

I made a comforting sound, not wanting to talk too soon, blocking what might be coming next.

"He wants me to have sex with people we meet who he thinks might be good targets for investing with us. Every single time, I believe him, that this time it will be different and we'll actually help other people make money. But it never works out. We lose their money, our money. As much as I work on it, I can barely make back enough to keep us going." Finally, she turned toward me. "So yeah, I knew he tried to have sex with you. Mostly it's been men, almost always men, and that's my *job*. That's why I go to The Moonlight Sonata. To convince guys who are lonely...maybe their wives are dead or they got dumped…that they owe it to their grandchildren to not have such conservative investments. I tell them the main points of Rafe's story about how to get some growth."

I took a sip of coffee seconds before the server darted up to refill my mug, pouring the dark liquid in a thin, perfect stream without a drop spilled on the table. "Why don't you leave him?"

"I can't do that. What would he do without me? He'd probably be homeless. It would break his heart. And mine."

"It wouldn't be your fault if he was homeless, or your problem."

"I can't do that to him."

"You aren't doing anything. You'd be taking care of yourself." I knew I had to risk more. If I were vague enough, it would be okay. "What if someone reports you to the police? You'd be in so much trouble."

"Reports me for what?"

"For whatever it's called that he's doing. I'm sure it's not legal."

"He has agreements for people to sign. It's all above-board. Maybe not having sex with them…but even that, we're consenting adults. That's what he says."

"He could destroy your life. If he hasn't already."

Suddenly her face cleared of her despair. "Love is supposed to be until death do you part."

"That's if you're married."

"Rafe said it's like we already are. And we are going to get married. Soon. I'm not sure when, but we are. Probably this year."

"So if he didn't teach you day trading, how did you learn it?"

"I taught myself. Took some online classes. I like math. I'm good with numbers…" She picked up her glass and drank the rest of the orange juice.

It made no sense to me that someone could be so smart with numbers and so naïve and even stupid about relationships. But I suppose everyone has different kinds of intelligence. That's what the psychologists and self-help books say.

I finished eating while she watched. We walked back to the apartment building without talking.

57

Church had been uninspiring that morning, and Stephanie knew exactly why that was. She was miles away from God and what He wanted her to be doing. She knew this, but trying to figure out what that was had become too confusing and absolutely exhausting.

She'd found herself going to bed every night at eight-thirty, half-sleeping through ferocious dreams that made her wake in the morning still tired. The routine of cleaning her face and removing eye makeup every night, just to put it all back on again in the morning, was demoralizing. No one really noticed because no one took the time to even look at her face, much less make eye contact.

When she gently wiped her eyes at night, it felt like all she'd done was smear money across a cotton pad and throw it in the trash among loose hairs and dental floss and dirty tissues.

After an uninspired lunch of a turkey sandwich, eaten alone at the table because Eileen had gone out somewhere, she went to the small desk in the corner of her bedroom. She needed to pay bills. She'd been so tired every evening it had seemed like too much work. But payments were due. She was never late, and she couldn't let the task slip another day, even though it felt slightly ungodly to be thinking about money, to be doing that kind of work on a Sunday. It wasn't that she had to adhere to Old Testament laws, and she wasn't even sure if that was a law, but it felt wrong, somehow.

She settled into the chair, feeling chic in her thick, well-made leggings and a silk tunic. It was ridiculous to sit around the house all by herself, wearing clothes that cost what these had, but she did feel good. She couldn't deny that she felt elegant and comfortable at the same time. Anyone could come to the door, and she would be eager to answer it. Still, she knew that over time, the fabric would grow tired and weak, and she would have ruined something without it ever serving a real purpose. She could have paid bills wearing a T-shirt and pants from a discount store.

The computer took forever to boot up. While it did, she sat with her eyes closed, trying to pray. Nothing came. Her mind was empty, just as it had been during the morning service. Maybe that meant her soul was equally vacant.

As she worked her way through the utility bills, adding money to her MetroCard, paying the cable bill, she looked at her checking account balance. It was lower than it should be.

The numbers danced in front of her eyes. What was wrong? It was nothing dramatic, nothing that suggested her account had been compromised. Just...too low.

After several minutes of staring at the discordant number, it came to her. Eileen hadn't written the check for her share of the rent and their expenses this month. Usually, she was right on time, the check sitting on the kitchen table the morning of the first. Today was the tenth, and Eileen hadn't written a check or mentioned anything about it.

Stephanie pushed the chair away from the desk. The answer was obvious—all those clothes, the very things covering her body, keeping her comfortable right now, the soft sway of her hair on her neck, had cost Eileen an enormous amount of money she didn't really have in her account.

Using credit cards during their shopping spree was normal. It was simpler. It was what everyone did. And Eileen had assured her there was no problem, she would have no problem paying the total when the statements came. Clearly, she did not. The credit card bills must have overwhelmed her this month.

Her eyes filled with tears. What had she done? All in her pursuit of vanity—useless, empty vanity, which of course was what vanity was at its heart. Emptiness. She'd wasted money, spit in God's face, and put her daughter in debt, setting a terrible example as a servant of God and as a mother. There wasn't enough in Stephanie's savings account to pay Eileen back. Tapping into her retirement savings meant an early withdrawal penalty.

Tears began to spill out of her eyes. She stood and went to the bed. She let herself fall onto the pillowy comforter.

She woke at the creak of the front door opening. She got up and scurried across the room, closing her bedroom door softly. She needed time to think before she spoke to Eileen. It would be a difficult conversation, and she didn't want to cry in the middle of it. Appearing composed and in charge was important—admitting her own guilt in what had happened while also being strong. Eileen would need her help to cope with what must be devastating debt.

In front of the mirror, she used a cotton-tipped swab to

brush away smudged eyeliner and mascara. She patted her skin with a towel, trying to wake it up, to get the blood flowing. When her face looked decent, she bent over and touched her toes, holding the pose for half a minute to invigorate her muscles.

It was just past three. She'd slept for nearly two hours, a ridiculous amount of time when she considered all the sleep she'd gotten during the week. What was wrong with her? She pushed the thought aside. Right now, Eileen was what mattered.

She half expected to see her daughter watching TV in the living room, but the screen was dark. She knocked on Eileen's door.

"I'm doing yoga," Eileen's voice was muffled. "I missed my class."

It was an obvious lie. She probably couldn't afford the fee that was collected at the start of each class. It was possible she'd had to cancel her gym membership.

"I'm making tea," Stephanie said. "Do you want some?"

"Give me fifteen minutes, okay?"

"Sure." She hoped her voice sounded casual, reassuring. In her own ears, it sounded weak and frightened.

When Eileen was finished with her yoga, they sat on the living room couch, mugs of peppermint tea steaming on the table in front of them. "I wanted to talk to you about something," Stephanie said.

Eileen laughed. "Don't sound so serious."

"It is serious. Very serious."

Eileen stretched out her legs, propping her heels on the coffee table. "So, what's the problem?"

"I want to understand how bad your financial situation is

thanks to my foolish, childish over-indulgence."

"What?" Eileen leaned forward to pick up her mug. She settled back and crossed her ankles.

"I want to know how bad your debt is."

"I don't have any debt. What made you think that?"

Outside, a cloud moved in front of the sun, and the room grew dark. "You didn't give me your check for expenses this month. I feel terrible that I just now realized how bad things must be."

"Oh. Sorry about that. I'm not sure why I forgot."

"Don't lie to me."

Eileen laughed. "Lie? Why would I lie?"

"Because you don't want me to feel bad about all the money you wasted on me."

"It wasn't a waste. Not at all. I wanted to do it, and I told you that. Several times."

"You need to be honest. We can work this out together."

Eileen turned to face her. "Work what out? I don't know what you're talking about."

"When I noticed you hadn't written the check, I realized what I'd done." Her vision grew blurry as tears washed across her eyes. She blinked. "I'm so sorry. I was so stupid to get caught up in my appearance. I'm not twenty years old. I need to accept—"

"Stop talking. You aren't making any sense. I said, I forgot. I think I had an early call on the first, and then it slipped my mind. I'll do it as soon as we finish our tea."

"I haven't worn some of the clothes, so we could return those. And I could lend you some money so you can at least pay off some of the cards and then you won't have to deal with as much interest and—"

"I don't owe anything on my credit cards. Why do you assume that?"

"Because you didn't—"

"I forgot. Okay? You sound crazy. The last thing I'm worried about right now is credit card debt." She laughed. "I have the opposite..." Eileen put the mug to her lips and sipped her tea.

"What were you going to say?"

"Nothing."

"Yes you were."

"Never mind."

Eileen placed the mug on the coaster and stood. She went into her room. She returned several minutes later, holding a check. She held it out to Stephanie. "Here."

Stephanie looked at the slip of paper. It was five hundred dollars more than the usual amount. "This is too much."

"I'm proving to you I don't have any debt. Stop thinking about what your clothes cost. It matters how you feel, and you look great. You need to relax and *enjoy* feeling good. In fact, I think you're due for another manicure."

"If you're not in debt, where did you get all this money?"

"Things are going well."

"What changed so suddenly?"

"Better paying gigs," Eileen said.

"What were you going to say earlier?"

"It's nothing. I'm going to go catch up on a few shows."

"I'm worried about you."

Eileen picked up her mug. She moved closer and placed her hand on Stephanie's shoulder. "There is absolutely nothing to worry about. I'm doing great." She smiled, then disappeared into her bedroom.

Stephanie felt something clawing at her stomach. Eileen was keeping something from her. Eileen forgot how well her mother knew every subtle gesture and expression that flitted across her face. She acted as if she had a lot of money, but there hadn't been any remarkable changes in her schedule or the kind of modeling jobs she was called for. She talked about them often enough. There had been a handful of better opportunities, but nothing to explain the money she seemed to be tossing around as if scattering seed for the birds.

What was she hiding?

Stephanie wasn't sure how she would find out, or how long it would take, but she would definitely find out. The timing of Eileen's sudden abandon with money seemed like it might be tied to her relationship with Alexandra. The thought sent a wave of nausea through Stephanie's stomach.

58

Victoria hadn't told me anything I hadn't guessed the essence of. Obviously, I hadn't known the details, but it had become clear over time that Rafe was using her. I'd come to see that the skill in the stock market belonged solely to her. He'd repeatedly shown who he was.

I was tired of him, and her, to be honest, but a lot of her tiresomeness was the direct result of his domination. She'd been a kid when they got together. It wasn't surprising she thought she loved him. He was familiar. Familiarity, feels like love to some people. They can't imagine a life without that face and those hands and the sound of that voice. Contemplating the loss of those physical realities, the grief of losing those familiar pieces of their lives, feels like love.

She might not appreciate seeing her decades-long boyfriend removed permanently from her life. Not right away, but she would later. And I didn't think *later* was too far away. She just needed a chance to experience a different kind of life. Once she had a chance to be an adult without his perverted influence, once she had a chance to enjoy life without his presence and his demands, I was certain she would know something good had happened to her.

It might appear arrogant to presume I knew what was best for Victoria's life, or anyone's for that matter. But it was clear when Rafe tore her dress, aside from all the other things he'd done to her, including pimping her out, no matter what she wanted to call it, he was starting down the one-way path to physical abuse. Perhaps he'd already reached the end of that path, and she hadn't told me.

Of course, there was also an element of self-preservation in my decision. It was him or me. If I'd wanted to put my mind to it, I would have figured out a way around him, but I didn't want to. This guy was not an asset to the human race.

However, killing him was going to be tricky.

I wasn't sure he would be willing to meet in a hotel, which had become my preferred location for luring people to another plane of reality, whatever that might be. The anonymity of the room and the ease of coming and going without attracting too much notice made a large hotel ideal. Hotels are designed for crime—the entire concept can be easily adapted for selling illicit goods, kidnapping, even murder. I'm sure there are other things I haven't thought of.

I lay awake for hours trying to think of possible scenarios for getting Rafe where I needed him, playing out each one step-by-step to see which felt the least risky.

At about two-thirty in the morning, I finally saw it was quite simple after all. Rafe was primed to blackmail me into *investing* money with him. All I had to do was tell him I didn't feel comfortable going into his apartment to give him money with Victoria there. I felt guilty for kissing him and more…I couldn't stand knowing she was going to help me make a lot of money after I'd betrayed her. Even in my own apartment,

I would know she was close by, wondering what was happening between her boyfriend and me. Of course, he would tell her I'd given them the stake they asked for, but I wouldn't be aware of when that happened. I would explain how I needed that distance.

The story was flimsy, worse than flimsy, but simple.

I wasn't sure if he'd believe the guilt aspect, knowing what he did about me. But I'd decided the promise of sex in a hotel room, far from his beloved and cherished fiancé and business partner, would be too enticing for him to give my story any deep consideration.

I set about making my usual preparations. I bought plastic bags and rope, cleaning products and latex gloves, duct tape, silk scarves, and a new pair of scissors. Purchasing new scissors and rope and a roll of duct tape every time I did this was wasteful, but it's one of many ways I've kept myself pure. Nothing could secretly pick up stray hairs or dead skin from living inside my apartment, being used for other purposes, then carrying my DNA into a hotel room that contained nothing from my body.

I also bought new bottles of vodka and vermouth, a jar of olives, stir sticks, and cheap martini glasses.

The hotel I chose was near a subway stop fifteen blocks from where we lived. It was another risk in my plan because he would surely question why we had to meet quite that far from home. Did Victoria's aura extend for miles, casting a pall of guilt over me from fifteen blocks away? Still, it was all about distraction. And anonymity.

This was the other thing making me think I was cautious enough in spite of a barely believable story—not only was Rafe vulnerable to seduction, he was even more eager to get his hands on my money. They were in a bad situation, and I was sure his head was already moving on to the next step when he would extract even more cash from my gullible, craving hands.

After the basic supplies were packed in a new suitcase, I moved on to the more interesting, and honestly, satisfying part of every killing.

For some reason that I couldn't identify, I felt this situation called for a slightly larger investment. Instead of buying a cheap wig, I went to a specialty shop. The blonde, long wavy hair I chose was outrageously expensive, but it looked like living hair. It was silky and nicely cut and contained highlights that were as good as what you might get on natural hair in a salon.

The rest of my outfit consisted of a black suit that featured a cute fitted jacket and flat shoes with sharply pointed toes. I wanted to look like I had money while also looking like one of those women who was hard to peg—*Is she a stay-at-home mom or a fashion designer, an artist or a pharmaceutical rep? Is she someone almost famous who we don't quite recognize, or a poser?*

I put my new clothes and the wig in a garment bag and sent a text message to Rafe.

When I suggested the hotel, providing the name, he wrote back immediately—

Sure. Whatever floats your boat. This was followed by a grinning—leering?—emoji.

I'd over-thought everything. But over-thinking has always worked out well for me, so I didn't regret it.

59

I took the subway to the hotel the day before I planned to meet Rafe. As in the past, arriving early helped the clerks at the desk to see me as an entirely different person because they hadn't seen both aspects of me coming and going on the same day. The gap in time meant they didn't take too much notice of how my body moved when I walked or the sound of my voice if I happened to speak to them a second time. By the time I passed through the lobby for the final time the following evening, a blonde in a black suit, they would have forgotten all about the woman who paid cash and handed them a New Jersey driver's license. It was a document that cost a fortune due to the last-minute search for an already existing license with an age and facial shape close enough to mine. The woman in the license photo wore glasses with thick black frames, dictating the appearance I presented at the lobby desk—red-framed glasses and no make-up. My hair was tucked under a black wool hat that covered most of my forehead.

After checking in, I carried the garment bag over my shoulder, pulling my suitcase behind me, as I walked briskly to the bank of four elevators.

Inside the room, I put away my things, shoving the suitcase onto the shelf in the closet and piling up blankets and pillows to conceal it. I arranged the alcohol and olives with the ice bucket beside the glasses, so I was ready to mix the martinis without wasting time. I'd bought a steel water bottle to use as a makeshift shaker.

Rafe had agreed to meet me at a bar around the corner from the hotel.

The following day, I arrived at the bar before him. I looked more or less like myself, although I wore very heavy black eye makeup and had my hair tied back in a knot, slicked and tight across my skull.

When he saw me, he gave me a strange look but said nothing about my face and hair. This was probably because he was completely focused on the neckline of my dress. It descended in a sharp V to the bottom of my breastbone in front, and slightly lower in the back.

A martini sat on the small table in front of me.

He pulled out the chair across from me but didn't sit down. "I thought we were going to the hotel?"

"Don't you want a drink?"

"We can have drinks in the room. Did you bring cash or a check?"

"A check."

"I thought I told you cash was better."

I shrugged.

He sighed.

"Are you going to sit down?"

He plunked himself onto the chair. The cocktail waitress appeared a moment later, and he ordered a gin martini. I suggested vodka was better. He rolled his eyes, but he changed his order.

While he waited for his drink, I slowly ate my olives, watching him watch me. He remained uncharacteristically silent as I nibbled my way through two of the three giant olives.

When his olive-less drink arrived, we toasted the thrill of making money—my words, not his. He took a long swallow. I took a very tiny sip and then began running my finger around the rim of the glass, talking about how I'd changed my mind regarding his plan to earn money for me.

"The more I've thought about it, the more excited I am about this investment," I said.

He grinned.

"So many people make millions in the market, why shouldn't I be one of them? And it's absolutely terrific that you and Victoria are doing it for me, since you have experience. If I tried to do it myself like you first suggested, it would take me forever to get up to speed."

"You're right." He took a few more sips of his drink. "You look fuckin' awesome."

I smiled. "Thank you."

"Kind of dressed up."

"I love getting dressed up. It feels good. And it makes me...I don't know..." I shifted to the side and crossed my legs so he could see my stiletto heels.

He grinned, an eager look that made his eyes glaze slightly. His pupils expanded with desire, even in the overly bright light of a bar that was more about looking for someone to hook up with than offering atmosphere and intimacy.

When his glass was nearly empty and mine still almost full,

he pushed his chair away from the table. "Are you gonna drink that or what?"

"I have a little bit of a headache."

"Don't start that shit."

I laughed. "I think I just need some water. Should we head out?"

He stood and walked to the bar. A few minutes later, he returned, shoving the receipt into his front pocket. "All taken care of."

"Thank you."

"You didn't drink it," he said.

"But the olives were awesome."

"If you say so."

We walked to the hotel and took the elevator to the tenth floor.

"Seems kind of insane to spend all this money on a hotel when your apartment is four feet from mine."

I said nothing. We stepped out of the elevator, and I directed him toward the room.

Inside, I opened a bottle of water, and sent him out to fill the ice bucket. When he returned, my water was half gone, and I declared my headache cured.

I started mixing martinis while he took off his shoes and flopped on the bed. I tossed the remote to him and suggested he look for something interesting. As he got caught up in a basketball game, I turned my back to him and added the roofie to the shaker so it was well-dissolved. He was involved enough with the TV that he didn't notice I was mixing our drinks separately.

I kicked off my shoes and settled beside him on the bed. I handed him his drink, and we each took a sip. He put his hand on my leg and slid it up beneath the hem of my dress.

"Hey, what's the rush? We have all night." I laughed softly.

"I've waited a long time for this."

"Well, you can wait another fifteen minutes while you enjoy the fabulous drink I made."

"I already slammed the other one. I'm not sure—"

While he spoke, I dipped my finger in his drink and put it to his lips, letting him suck off the vodka and an infinitesimal amount of the roofie.

He took several deep swallows of his drink. I put my glass on the nightstand and slid off the bed.

"Where are you going?"

I reached into my purse and pulled out a red scarf. "Won't this be fun?"

He laughed, although his laugh had a nervous edge to it.

I trailed the scarf across his face. I took his drink and put it on the nightstand, pulled off his shirt, and returned the drink to his hand. While he swallowed it in quick, eager gulps, I let the scarf dance across his chest and stomach.

When the glass was empty, I told him I needed to use the bathroom. I stayed in there for twenty minutes. At the five minute mark, he called out for me. After ten minutes, I heard him trying to call out again, followed by a loud thud. I assumed he'd tried to get out of bed.

I found him passed out on the floor beside the bed. A surge of irritation passed through me. I preferred to have him leave the world while lying on the bed. It took me a good ten minutes to hoist him back into position and tie his wrists with the first scarf. I removed the rest of his clothes while he moaned and mumbled. I pulled the receipt from the bar out of his pocket and put it in my bag. Then I tied his ankles with a second red scarf, knotted several times.

When he was in a good position, definitely sliding into a deep state of unconsciousness, I got to work pulling a plastic bag over his head and securing it around his neck with duct tape.

I returned to the bathroom and waited for twenty minutes.

After I was sure he was gone, I removed the plastic bag and tape, tying the third scarf around his neck to suggest erotic asphyxiation. I cleaned the room, washed the glasses, and put all the drink ingredients in my suitcase. I changed into my black suit, scrubbed the makeup off my face, and applied lighter tinted moisturizer and a bit of mascara. I cleaned the bathroom thoroughly. I put on the wig and my leather gloves before I did a final wipe down of doorknobs and faucet and table.

When I walked through the lobby, no one even glanced at me, and I sort of regretted the money spent on the well-constructed wig.

60

After they discovered and identified Rafe's body, then contacted Victoria, I didn't see her for two weeks. During the first few days, I left her alone. I half-expected her to pound on my door or greet me on the landing as she had in the past, but she made herself invisible. Finally, I knocked on her door. There was no answer. Every day after that, I continued knocking with the same result. I sent her text messages that went unanswered.

The police came by and talked to Brian, Kent, and me. I assumed they talked to everyone in the building and that they spent considerable time with Victoria.

I was holding my breath, wondering if the FBI would show up, wondering if they even knew Rafe was dead. Occasionally, the silence from those nameless, faceless investigators weighed like an iron plate on my chest. I felt confident I could talk my way out of almost anything, and I was supremely confident there was no physical evidence to tie me to the body in the hotel room, but it was on my mind throughout the day and whispered to me from my dreams.

I didn't hear from Nick, which gave me a sense of security,

but I couldn't decide whether it was false.

Was it possible, if they weren't too far into the investigation, that they'd dropped it when they received notice of his death? But wouldn't they still be pursuing Victoria? She was complicit if nothing else, and from Nick's perspective, she was an equal perpetrator. It would be the same for the FBI. Perhaps I hadn't heard from them because they were still setting a trap and needed to modify it now that they only had a single prey.

The police asked me basic questions along the lines of how many months I'd known Rafe, what our relationship was like, and whether I knew of any enemies or illicit activities he might be involved with. I smiled and looked scared and nervous to be talking to police officers. I said no to every question. All I knew about him was that he liked sports and loved New York City and liked to tell stories about it.

The risks I'd taken to be rid of Rafe were not insignificant, and it made me question my compulsion to be rid of people who deserve to die. Still, it was a risk I relished. I liked the thrill of carrying out my plans, I liked the satisfaction of knowing I'd made someone's life better.

After days of persistent knocking, Victoria finally answered the door. Her face was smooth and untroubled. There was no obvious red around her eyes or blotched skin that suggested unrelenting grief. I wondered if she'd been in shock all this time and hadn't grieved at all. I wondered if she felt nothing. And I wondered for a moment if she felt guilty because she was secretly relieved to be rid of him.

"Hi." She didn't pull the door wider to invite me inside. The room behind her looked the same, although from what I could see, one of the computer screens was no longer there.

"How are things?"

She shrugged. "Weird."

"Are you working?"

She nodded.

"Do you want to come over for a drink? Or go out and grab something to eat?"

"Not really."

As we studied each other, trying to figure out where the other fit into our life, my eyes were drawn to the spot where the surveillance camera was attached. The camera was gone. So either Brian had been involved with its installation or Victoria had stepped out of her apartment after all.

"What are your plans?" I said.

"Plans?"

I tried to gauge her state of mind, her feelings toward the things she'd done, all, according to her, at the instigation of Rafe. She didn't have an over-active conscience as far as I'd observed. She wasn't broken up by her loss, and she seemed to lack interest in speculating about what had happened to him.

Not that I was her best friend, a companion to whom she was prone to pouring out her heart, but she had told me quite a lot about herself. Was that all part of the game, or had her attempt at friendship been genuine?

All of these questions led to the big question—If the FBI contacted her, what would she do?

"I was wondering if you're planning to move."

"I've thought about it."

My next step was a slight betrayal of Nick, but how did I know he wouldn't just as easily betray me? And I had to make the safest bet, the one most likely to keep me from becoming a person of interest as they like to say.

"I can't tell you much, but I heard the FBI was looking into Rafe. You might want to get out of here, hide as much of your life as you can."

She stared at me. "The FBI?"

I nodded.

"How do you know that? What do you mean? Why were they—"

"That's all I can tell you."

"Well, shit." She let the door fall open and took a step back. "What do I do?"

"I don't know what they know. But maybe you can make yourself disappear?"

"From the F. B. I? How would I do that?"

"Shut down your trading accounts? I'm really not sure. I don't know if you can hide from them if they have your social or any other details on you."

She closed her eyes. A moment later, they flashed open. "One of the men I met at The Moonlight Sonata...he's a defense attorney. Or he was. He's retired, but still..."

"That's way smarter than my ideas, which won't work if they already know who you are."

She lunged at me and wrapped her arms around me in a smothering hug. I patted her back. When she pulled away, her face was lit with energy, and I could see her eyes bright with plans.

We talked for a few minutes longer, and then she thanked me.

That afternoon, I sat in front of my window sipping a cup of tea, thinking about nothing much. Just after four o'clock, I saw her emerge from our lobby in her fifties' style dress and her strappy sandals. She was pulling a suitcase and had a large purse slung over her shoulder.

A few minutes later, a cab pulled to the curb, and she climbed inside. I never saw her again.

61

On Sunday morning, I took an Uber to a park and nature preserve on Long Island. It was a ridiculously long ride for a run—over an hour—but I needed to get outside of the city. I needed to breathe deeply and run for a long time without passing the same scenery multiple times. In the preserve, I was able to run on trails where the towering buildings of Manhattan didn't loom so large as they did when I ran in Central Park.

The birds seemed louder here, or more prevalent. Maybe it was just that I was used to pigeons, and here there were a lot of songbirds. I breathed in lungfuls of seemingly fresh air. When I was finished, walking around to cool off, I saw two teenage girls seated on an iron bench.

They sat with their legs sprawled in front of them. They wore jeans and hoodies and lots of makeup. The makeup was expertly applied and seemed to contradict their slightly shabby clothes. They were smoking. They laughed and talked, frequently pausing to look at their phones. They would take a puff without moving their eyes away from their screens. Bits of ash floated off the tips of their cigarettes and landed on those shiny screens. Sometimes they brushed the ashes off, sometimes not.

I paused the brisk steps of my cool-down walk and stared at them. I had a brief, jarring glimpse of my younger self, although without the ubiquitous access to a smartphone. In the next moment, they looked like figures out of a dystopian future—more connected to each other through the digital network than the human one. Something about their mindless smoking made me wonder whether smoking was really as calming and reflective as I'd always told myself.

Had I been deceiving myself because I liked the old-time glamour of it? Smoking was a habit that was only glamorous in the two-dimensional world of black and white film, without the smell that lingered indefinitely, turning to a thick, dank odor. It was a world without the coughing and shortness of breath that was surely creeping up on me.

Smoking might look cool and seductive when a younger woman does it, but not so much as she ages. Stephanie was proof of that. Not that I would ever in a thousand years be anything like Stephanie, but she did show me, on a daily basis, what life might look like when I was fifteen years older.

Why had Stephanie decided to take it up? Did she have a subconscious desire to be like me, even though she would be horrified at that thought? Or she simply thought smoking was a way to connect? I really had no idea, but watching those girls, feeling my body stretched and challenged and strengthened from my run, I felt the desire for a cigarette shrink to a tiny dark spot inside of me. Almost like a dark spot growing on a human lung.

When I got home, I tossed my cigarettes and lighter in the trash. I would miss it for sure, but with Spring not too far away, with yoga classes offered all over the city, I was confident I could get past that.

***

A month after Rafe died, the FBI did come calling. Their questions were even simpler than those I'd experienced from the police, and I realized as they spoke to me that I wouldn't have to ditch my phone or my apartment after all. Not yet.

All they wanted to know was the nature of my relationship with Rafe Goddard and Victoria Ryan. They wanted to know what I knew about their day trading business. I explained that they were very excited about it, and that was it. I said they talked about how they loved it but never gave me any details. They wanted to know if Rafe or Victoria ever tried to coerce me into giving them money. They wanted to know if I was aware of anything they'd done to violate the law. I said no.

I was only familiar with one person who had violated the law. So far, the FBI and the New York City police knew nothing about her.

A Note To Readers

Thanks for reading. I hope you liked reading about Alexandra as much as I enjoy writing her stories. I'm passionate about fiction that explores the shadows of suburban life and the dark corners of the human mind. To me, the human psyche is, as they say in Star Trek — the final frontier — a place we'll never fully understand. I'm fascinated by characters who are damaged, neurotic, and obsessed.

I love to stay in touch with readers. Visit me at my website: CathrynGrant.com

To find out when the next Alexandra Mallory novel is available you can sign up for my new book mailing list here: CathrynGrant.com/contact.

As a thank you for signing up, you'll receive a free Alexandra short story — Death Valley.